MW00464807

COME SHELL OR HIGH WATER

Molly MacRae

COME SHELL OR HIGH WATER

Kensington Publishing Corp.
www.kensingtonbooks.com

KENSINGTON BOOKS are published by

Kensington Publishing Corp.
900 Third Avenue
New York, NY 10022

All Kensington titles, imprints and distributed lines are available at special quantity discounts for bulk purchases for sales promotion, premiums, fundraising, educational or institutional use. Special book excerpts or customized printings can also be created to fit specific needs. For details, write or phone the office of the Kensington Special Sales Manager: Kensington Publishing Corp., 900 Third Ave., New York, NY, 10022. Attn. Special Sales Department. Phone: 1-800-221-2647.

KENSINGTON and the KENSINGTON COZIES teapot logo Reg. US Pat. & TM Off.

Library of Congress Control Number: 2024932265

ISBN: 978-1-4967-4427-2

First Kensington Hardcover Edition: July 2024

ISBN: 978-1-4967-4429-6 (ebook)

10 9 8 7 6 5 4 3 2 1

Printed in the United States of America

*For my boys, Mike, Gordon, and Ross,
and our wonderful times on Ocracoke.*

Acknowledgments

How do you spend time in a place you love that, for various reasons, is too far away? I do it by gathering a bunch of imaginary people and going there with them in a book.

My family and I have no special claim to Ocracoke Island, but Ocracoke claimed our hearts from our first visit in 1979. Mike and I were lucky enough to take our boys there every summer for quite a few years after that, often with Pat Crowley and her family. As our lives and the world got busier, the visits became less frequent. I'm luckier than the rest, though, because I spend my writing days believing I *am* there.

Many thanks to John Scognamiglio and Kensington Books for letting me visit Ocracoke through the Haunted Shell Shop mysteries, and to copy editor extraordinaire Jeffery Robert Lindholm. Thank you to my agent, Cynthia Manson, for seeing what fun a pirate ghost could be. Maureen, our intrepid heroine, gets her name from Maureen Kerwin, my friend for sixty-seven years. Thanks, Pat Crowley, for letting me turn you into a national park ranger. Nancy Lawson, thank you for lending us the vacation rental booklet that started our island adventures all those years ago.

Special thanks to the Isleib sisters—Martha, a former Ocracoke teacher who answered a hurricane of questions for me, and Roberta, who put us in touch.

There are many fine books written about life on Ocracoke. I particularly recommend *Ocracokers*, by Alton Ballance; *Ocracoke: Its History and People*, by David Shears; *Digging Up Uncle Evans*, by Philip Howard; *Howard Street Hauntings and Other Ocracoke Stories*, by Philip Howard; and *A Blessed Life:*

Growing Up on Ocracoke Island, by Della Gaskill. To read more about the real-life piratical Lloyd brothers (minus their fictional younger brother, Emrys) read *Treasure Island: The Untold Story,* by John Amrhein, Jr.

Electra is not on the National Hurricane Center's list of names for hurricanes past or present. Hurricane Electra, in this book, is my invention.

I've tried to get the geography of Ocracoke right and to capture the flavor of life on the island, past and present. I hope my version lives up to the real place. If not, the mistakes are mine. The real Ocracoke shines.

Chapter 1

On the tail of a hurricane, half-drowned in the chaos of whirlwind, deluge, thunder, and lightning, I washed up on Ocracoke Island.

Okay, it wasn't that dramatic. Hurricane Electra *had* blown through that week in mid-September but, as Atlantic hurricanes go, Electra was medium to mild. And I *had* arrived on Ocracoke, but I hadn't washed ashore. I know a ranger in the U.S. Park Service, and she took me over in her boat, that afternoon, when she went to survey damage to the national park campground. I was half-drowned, but half-drowned by my assumptions, not the storm.

"Love the pink life jacket, Maureen," Patricia had said over the gurgling engine noise of her boat before we set out from Hatteras Landing for the crossing to Ocracoke. Patricia Crowley and I have known each other since college, thirty-plus years. We don't see each other often, but she always looks unruffled and in control when she's in uniform. "The pink looks good with your white knuckles. We haven't left the dock yet, though, so you might want to give your grip a rest."

My hands, both of them glued to the edge of whatever you call the dashboard thing on a Park Service boat, looked fine to me. "This cabin's kind of small—"

"It's a pilot house."

"—and we're standing shoulder to shoulder in it," I pointed out, "so if I get seasick, I'll step outside."

"No, you won't."

"Okay."

Patricia also *sounds* unruffled and in control when she's in uniform. Despite her calm, my knuckles and I did not relax. That's why, by the time Patricia eased the boat away from the dock, my knuckles looked like bleached bones. I stopped looking at them and concentrated on not whimpering. Or being sick.

"It's getting kind of rough," I said in a conversational whimper.

"This is the smooth part. Wait'll we hit the waves in the inlet."

"Maybe we should turn back?"

"Nope."

"Okay."

"I'm doing you an unauthorized favor by taking you along," Patricia said. Shouted, because the engine was making more noise. "Remember that, in case anyone has occasion to ask, because it isn't regulation, but we'll get around that by not saying anything or, if pressed, by saying that a lot of what happens before, during, and after a hurricane isn't regulation."

"I really appreciate this."

"Good. You should. And I'll appreciate it if you return the favor by not falling overboard and by hoping we don't founder."

"Founder?"

"Sink." She patted me on my drawn shoulders, and I thought about screaming *"Don't take your hands off the steering wheel,"* but I didn't want to distract her, in case it wasn't called a steering wheel. It didn't strike me as the best time for nautical vocabulary lessons.

On the other hand, the best time to go shelling on the sandy ribbon of barrier islands off the coast of North Carolina is after a big blow like Electra. And because I'm a former malacologist (a biologist who studies mollusks, although freshwater mussels and not seashells, in my case), I could *sort* of make a case for being there. But confusion, disruptions, and mopping up follow even a mild hurricane. There was danger in the surging waves, and evacuated tourists hadn't been given the all-clear yet to return and finish their idyllic beach vacations along the Outer Banks.

Also, there's that *former* thing. I was a working malacologist, but those jobs, like some of the rarer freshwater mussels, are hard to find. I'm all about shells, though. I've been collecting them, and folklore, fables, and myths about them, for most of my life. I've had minor success publishing picture book retellings of the stories I've collected. I get occasional storytelling gigs, too. More than occasional, really. It still surprises me that I can call myself a professional storyteller. My late husband called me his fabulous fabulist.

So, yes, I arrived on the tail of the hurricane. I blew in to see what else had washed ashore. And I did cling to my assumptions because that's how assumptions work. If I go to the trouble of making them, I figure I might as well believe in them. That's why I thought I could be clever and careful enough to comb the deserted beaches for shells and not get into trouble. And it's why I believed that my other reason for making the trip to the picturesque town at the southern tip of Ocracoke Island wasn't totally mad, either.

"How can you study animals that live in the water and still be so uncomfortable around boats?" Patricia asked by way of unnecessary chat after sideswiping a particularly angry-looking wave the color of gunmetal. Or a hungry shark.

"Wading," I answered succinctly. "Small streams and rivers. Is that a fin over there?"

"Where?"

I didn't point because I didn't want her taking her eyes off our briny, white-capped "road." I would have been happier with my own eyes closed, but two of us watching for whatever might lurch out of the sea at us was a higher priority. "And I'm not uncomfortable around all boats. Only boats that might founder. Near sharks."

We didn't founder, but it was a slow, rough, and rolling ride from Hatteras to the ferry landing at the north end of Ocracoke. Patricia knows her boat, though, and she knows the waters of the inlets between the Outer Banks islands as well as anyone can with the constantly shifting shoals of sand in the channels. The landing was as far as we'd go. No point in courting trouble by continuing south to the village docks by water. Besides, Patricia keeps her park service truck at the ferry landing when she's off-island.

After we tied up, we transferred my backpack and duffel to the back of the truck. We took Highway 12—the only way— down the center of the island, watching for the inevitable post-hurricane drifts of sand on this road, just as we'd watched for them in the water. The island is so narrow in places that you can easily see the ocean to your left and Pamlico Sound to your right as you head south. It's a wonder the storm surge from Electra hadn't cut right through the island, creating a new inlet, as happened on Hatteras Island after hurricanes Irene in 2011 and Isabel in 2003. But there's something about fragile Ocracoke that's kept it in one piece. There's something about the families who've lived there for generations, too. They aren't fragile at all. Many of them stay put when hurricanes come howling, riding out the wind and the flooding, then resolutely cleaning up and getting back to business after the hurricanes move on. I, who travel white-knuckled in stout Park Service boats, am not sure I'd ever have the nerve to ride out a hurricane.

Patricia was kind and took me all the way south to Ocracoke

Village, driving several miles past the entrance to the camp-ground. I asked her to put me down at the edge of the village, though, so I could walk the rest of the way.

"The wind's kicking up again," Patricia said, "and we're probably in for more rain. You know where you're going?"

"And I know who's going with me."

"What?"

"Sorry. A line from a song and an old movie reference. One of Jeff's favorites." She looked at me. I looked away. It's been a year and change, but I can't get used to the pain, sorrow, or pity in people's eyes when I mention my late husband. I haven't gotten used to him being gone, either.

"You were kind of quiet the last half of the trip," Patricia said. "Were you terrified?"

"Oh, gosh no." I'm not often accused of being too quiet. I smiled to show there were no hard feelings for a trip that fell just short of terrifying.

"I didn't even get a corny joke out of you. I think I shouldn't have brought you. That trip scared the giggle out of you." Concern put a crease between her steady brown eyes.

"No joke? Is that what's bothering you?" She knows I collect jokes and folklore about any kind of shell and the seven seas in general. "Okay, here's one, and let it not be said that I don't have the perfect joke or story for any occasion. What lies at the bottom of the ocean and twitches?"

"Not a clue," she said.

"A nervous wreck."

She laughed and started the truck. "Stay safe," she called with a wave.

Stay safe. Easy for the ranger in the vehicle with rubber tires to say. I stood in the middle of the two-lane highway and watched that vehicle getting smaller and smaller. The rain started again as I walked the familiar mile or so into town. And then the lightning.

Chapter 2

"Is it safe to touch her?" an anxious voice asked.

"Perfectly," another voice said. "I turned the generator off as soon as I saw the lamp cord and the water on the floor. But I can't find a pulse." A woman's voice? Cool and calm, like Patricia. But not Patricia. And too cool and calm for someone who wasn't feeling a pulse. Why wasn't she upset? I knew I would be. *Most* people would be, right? A hard pulse is a good thing to find.

"Let me try." The anxious voice again. It sounded like a creaky old man, and I realized that a cooler hand had taken my wrist. Wait a second. *My* wrist?

"Anything?" the woman's voice asked, not sounding urgent enough.

"Hmm," the creaky voice said. Creaky's cool fingertips moved over my wrist, searching, pressing. "Could be a flutter. Might not be anything—"

"Try harder," I shouted, trying to show these two how to panic properly. Or thought I shouted. I couldn't tell. Didn't know if I'd said anything at all because I couldn't hear myself over that loopy person mumbling about seashells. Selling seashells by the seashore.

"Ah, there we go," Creaky said. "Pulse and poetics. She's back in the land of the living." He kept hold of my hand. "And there's both mysteries solved, too. Who she is, and why she's in Allen's shop. She's the one he was expecting."

"Do you think so?" Cool Woman asked, turning into Skeptical Woman faster than I seemed to be processing things. "If she's here for Allen, then where is he? And when did she get here? And how?"

"You're asking too many questions, Glady, and not the right ones," Creaky said. "Of immediate importance is, Will she be okay? What do you think?"

"That we should call Dr. Allred."

"Allred evacuated with the tourists. Where's his sense of community? What kind of a doctor defects because of a *downpour*?"

"He isn't an O'cocker," Glady said. "He's only lived here nine or ten years."

"Five."

"Are you sure? It seems like he's been telling me he knows more about living on the island than I do for decades."

"Glady, you were a nurse."

"A long time ago in a galaxy far away. Say, do you remember that '72 Galaxy I used to drive?"

"Glady, focus. Will she be okay?"

"I loved the color of that car, and you're the one who needs to focus, you old fool. I was a nurse for six months fifty years ago, and if you remember, I'm the one who couldn't find her pulse. The car was the green of a mermaid's tail."

I tried to tell them I'd be fine as soon as I could open my eyes and get up off the floor. That I didn't need a doctor, no matter where he was, how long he'd lived here, or what he drove. As for fishy mermaid tails . . . I'd seen *something* in the water, but . . . Maybe these two knew about it and I should raise my hand to ask. But they kept talking over me, as though I wasn't there. Or wasn't all there. This whole situation was confusing. I tried to lie quietly and think.

"*Gladys.*" Anxiety had crept back into Creaky's voice.

"It's all right, Burt," Glady said. "I'm not ignoring you or disagreeing with you. I'm giving her time to come around naturally, which she seems to be doing. She's breathing evenly, and she's stopped babbling. But if you really want to know what I think, I think she looks like a drowned rat."

She called me a drowned rat. That wasn't nice. But it sounded funny if you said it over and over. Drowned rat, drownedrat, drowned, drowning. *Drowning.* I did show them how to panic, then, and struggled against the cool hand holding my wrist, fought to the surface of—what? Waves? Where was I? I coughed and sputtered and tried to breathe.

"She wants to sit up," Creaky . . . Anxious Voice—*Burt*—said. "Help her, Glady. You can get down there. My back and knees won't let me."

I felt an arm move behind my shoulders. I gulped for air as though I'd surfaced in the ocean, and I grabbed at that arm as though I might slip beneath the waves again. The arm held me closer, pulling me into an embrace with damp wool.

"Shh, now, shh," Glady said. "The wind's dying. Rain, too. Shh. We saw the light on over here and thought Allen had come home."

Kind voices, even if they didn't like the doctor. The damp wool didn't matter. Eyes still shut, I wanted to drift off on this damp woolly life raft smelling of lanolin and ozone. I was warm and dry and—*ozone?* I remembered a flash, a jolt—lightning? My eyes popped open.

A nut-brown man leaned toward me, peering into my face. Old as a wrinkled walnut. A bearded walnut. With an effort and a grimace, he straightened, then smiled.

"Welcome back," he said. The creaky voice I'd heard was his.

"Back?" I sounded like a croaker myself. I pulled away from the arm and the comforting wool. Sat up straighter and looked around. Table legs, cupboard doors. A table lamp, its shade awry and cracked, tipped onto the floor not far from my bare feet. When had I ended up on the floor? In a shop? And where were my shoes and socks? A battery lantern stood on the table near the door, where the lamp had been when—

"Welcome back and welcome home," the woman's voice cut into my confused inventory of my surroundings. "We're the Weavers. I'm Glady. Sometimes Gladys. Always glad to meet a friend of Allen's."

Gladys, Glady, owner of the woman's voice, also belonged to the supportive arm and the damp wool. The one who hadn't sounded worried about feeling no pulse in my wrist. Gladys sounded like a name from my grandmother's generation. This one looked more like halfway between my mother and me. Late sixties, tops. She held her hand out, and I shook it.

"Maureen," I croaked. "Maureen Nash."

"Pleased to meet you. Any idea what happened?" Glady asked. She didn't wait for an answer. "Allen's been expecting you, and look who else has."

I looked around for the third voice I'd heard. Third voice? When had I heard that? Heard *him*. Definitely a man. Allen? I knew that name. Allen Withrow. I didn't see anyone but a brindled tabby checking me out with sleepy eyes. I blinked my eyes slowly, and it came over and headbutted my hand.

"This is Bonny," Glady said. "Named after Anne Bonny, pirate queen."

"Hi, Bonny." I rubbed her between the ears. "Is Allen here?"

"Did you see him?" Burt asked.

"I don't know. Does he have an accent?"

"Not a real Ocracoke brogue," Burt said.

"He lived off-island for too long," Glady said. "Left his 'hoi toide' accent there when he came back."

"Where you left yours?" Burt sniped.

Glady might have left her Ocracoke accent somewhere, but the sniff she gave Burt hadn't lost a single grace note of derision.

"He doesn't have a British accent?" I asked.

"Who?" Burt asked. "Allen? What gave you that idea?"

Hearing him, I thought. Hearing someone, anyway. But not Allen? So someone else. Someone younger than Burt. Maybe that guy standing in the doorway. Humming that song about what you do with a drunken sailor. Except—I blinked a few times to clear my befuddled brains and eyes, and there was no one standing in the doorway. But the humming . . . It definitely came from somewhere near the open door.

"None of this seems normal," Burt said.

No kidding, I thought. He sounded anxious again. I felt more than anxious. Not sharks and foundering-boat anxious, but what was going on? What the heck had happened? But did I want to drag myself to my feet and go peering into dark corners for the drunken sailor hummer? No, I did not. I wanted to stay snuggled up to Glady's damp sweater. Wake up somewhere warm and dry and familiar.

"Glady," Burt said. "Stop petting her head like you've found a stray kitten. She didn't answer my question. She's stopped talking. What if she's going into shock? Shock will drop someone as big as an ox, and she's no bigger than . . . no bigger than you were before you let yourself go."

Glady and her bosom bristled. "It takes one to know one, Burt. And I haven't let myself go. I let myself *grow*."

"The point *is*," Burt said, "shock *kills*. We can't afford to have her drop dead on us."

"*Dead.*" That word came out of me. More forcefully than I meant it to. Possibly with more certainty. It got their attention. "I saw him. Dead."

Glady clutched me to her wool bosom as though I were a string of pearls. "Who's dead?"

Chapter 3

Who was dead and how did I know? I remembered getting out of Patricia's truck. Grabbing my stuff out of the back. I'd put the backpack on. Slung the duffel and life jacket over opposite shoulders. Waved goodbye. Jogged into town, the backpack bumping my spine. I'd felt like a military recruit doing a fully loaded training exercise. My hopes? That the duffel was waterproof as advertised and that I wouldn't need the life jacket anytime soon—like in the next puddle.

The place I'd rented would be down the next road to the left and around a few bends, not far from the Ocracoke Light—a charming lighthouse that's photogenic in any weather. I hadn't stopped to take a picture. The rain slashed as I rounded the corner. At the *crash-bash* of thunder, I gritted my teeth. At the honk from a vehicle that had come up behind me, I jumped sideways into a puddle. Up to my ankles. What a friendly place, I thought, after swearing. I waved a hand over my shoulder and kept jogging. The vehicle came alongside and slowed. I wiped the swear-snarl from my face, took my eyes off the puddles, and glanced over. Patricia.

She lowered her window. "Get in. You've proved your point. You're invincible."

"I'm not—"

"I'm getting wet. You're getting in." The window rose.

The truck's bed now sloshed with a shallow pond, so I crowded duffel, backpack, life jacket, and myself into the passenger seat. "You're bossy," I said by way of thanking Patricia.

"I'm a leader," she said. "Where are you staying?"

I told her. She nodded and said she knew the place. "Cute. About big enough to swing all that crap you're hauling."

"It isn't that much stuff."

"Exactly."

We followed the road, turned another corner, then pulled into the short drive of a squat, square house. As if on cue, the rain stopped. The clouds didn't part to let a shaft of sunlight bathe the house, but a crow settled on the roof over the front door and polished its bill on the edge of the gutter. I like crows, so I took that as a good sign.

"If a crow is on the thatch, death soon lifts the latch," Patricia said.

"Is that your way of saying have a nice vacation?"

"Sharing information about local wildlife."

I eyed the crow as it drank from the gutter, then hopped in for a bath. "So is death and thatch a local superstition?"

"Nope. No thatch for roofs around here. No need to worry, either. That's not your door. You're in the yard." She pointed to a smaller square building not big enough to be called a house but with more flair and possibly more room than a garden shed. "See? Cute as a bug's ear and about as big."

"I love it already, and the crow can visit anytime it wants."

"That's the spirit," Patricia said. "Unlike that malarky about death lifting a latch, if you feed a crow from your front door, it's good luck. You can trust me on that because I'm a park ranger."

"Almost as wise as Smokey Bear."

"Wiser. See ya."

I'd schlepped my things down a gravel path lined with bleached clamshells and up a step to the front porch. If the house wasn't much bigger than a garden shed, the porch wasn't much smaller than a bathmat. The door unlocked to the entry code I'd been sent. I turned to wave to Patricia. Too late. Rather than turn around and go back, the pickup's taillights disappeared as they continued down the road.

Shouldering the door open, I'd surveyed a compact, ship-shape space. Like a jigsaw puzzle, all the basics and a few extras had been shimmied into place. Tiny complete kitchen to my right with two windows, like square portholes, one over the sink on the back wall, one over a two-person table on the front. A fence post topped with a small platform strewn with bird-seed stood outside the window over the sink. To my left, the living room with a love seat, bookcase, flat-screen TV, photographs of seashells on the walls, and two more square windows, one of these on the back wall and the other on the side wall. Clean and homey, my temporary quarters smelled of lavender.

Directly in front of me, in the middle of all this and making an eccentric room divider, ladderlike stairs rose to a loft over the living room. I shucked my baggage and climbed up to the bedroom—a somewhat dangerous bedroom without much headroom under the slanting ceiling. I'd have to literally crawl into the bed, which was a mattress on the floor made up with white linens and a flowery garden of a patchwork quilt. A low bureau stood against one knee-high wall. At the foot of the bed, there was enough room for my pack, duffel, and life jacket, so they'd be out from underfoot down below.

The only other thing I'd need . . . Where, in heaven's name, had they squeezed in the bathroom? Now needing it desperately, I'd discovered it hidden behind a discreet door in a corner of the living room. It had precisely enough space for a toilet, sink, and postage-stamp-size shower.

The whole place was adorable. Patricia was right, too. Not enough room to swing the little bit of stuff I'd brought with me. Not enough room to swing a dead man, either. I hadn't been looking for a dead man, but I'd been looking for something, hadn't I? So what *had* I been looking for when I found *him*?

Chapter 4

"For Pete's sake, Glady, give her room," Burt said. "If shock doesn't kill her, you will. You're going to suffocate her. Don't say anything else about dead bodies, either. This one probably leapt out of whatever brain fog or waking nightmare she's been through, and now you're adding to the hysteria."

Glady still had me in her clutches, but she loosened them to give Burt a piece of her mind. "The point, Burt, as you like to say—"

"Point." I pulled away from Glady and pointed a finger at her, then swiveled it to Burt. Swiveling made my head spin, so I raised another finger to cover both of them at once. Unsteady fingers that stabbed at them a few times more than pointed. *Stabbed. No! No more stabbing!* I tucked shaking fingers and hands into my armpits. "There's a place. A point." *But no stabbing. Don't think or talk about it. Don't talk? That's not my way. Talk.* "Walk. I walked there."

"Springer's Point?" Burt asked. "One of my favorite places. Have you heard the stories about Blackbeard's last battle off the point? *Gruesome.* Have you ever been here for our Pirate Jamboree? End of October? If not, you are in for a treat— complete with a parade of golf carts decorated like pirate ships. I have a spare eyepatch. Want to borrow it?"

I put my hands on the top of my head. Gingerly. "Sorry. It's coming back to me slowly."

"Stop badgering her with your inane questions," Glady said. "Hon, what kind of knucklehead idea was it to go traipsing down to the point without shoes?"

These new friends were exhausting. Were they friends? I didn't know. Bonny the brindled tabby was. She'd settled in my lap. I fitted my hand to the curve of her spine and closed my eyes again. I *did* know that I'd had socks on my feet and my feet in my shoes. My blue low-tops. Jeff called the color "island lagoon blue." His favorite color. Mine, too. They're old, but perfect for beachcombing. For getting wet. And traipsing.

When I'd closed the door to my sweet little garden shed abode, they'd been on my feet, and the frayed cuffs of Jeff's old University of Kansas hoodie had been rolled so the sleeves didn't hang to my knees. Then I'd walked to the point. Springer's Point Nature Preserve. No parking at all, including golf carts, according to the sign posted with the park's rules and regulations. No matter, I'd only planned to park myself on the beach. Take biologist E. O. Wilson's advice about spending time in nature to get my head right. Maybe take a quick reconnaissance-type beachcomb. See what treasures had washed up. Some of Blackbeard's booty? And be back home in my shed before dark.

"Before ghost time," I said to my two maybe/maybe not friends. *What the . . . ? Why on earth had that driveled out of my mouth?*

"Post time," Burt said. "A racing fan, are you?"

Someone snickered. If I'd had my eyes open, I might have known who. I opened them a tentative slit.

Glady clucked her tongue. "The *mud* on your feet, hon."

"And the blood," Burt said. "What about beer?"

"I don't think so." Glady leaned close and sniffed my breath. "No. You haven't been drinking, have you?"

I shook my head.

"I bet you'd like a drink, though," Burt said. "And I can sing a great song about mud, blood, and beer. Written by Shel Silverstein, of all people. Want to hear it?

"Don't encourage him," Glady said. "We should wash your feet and make sure you didn't step on something. No telling what a hurricane will blow in."

"A shell," I said.

"Bless you." Burt tut-tutted. "Now she's catching cold, Glady."

"When are you going to get your hearing checked? She didn't sneeze. She said 'a shell.'"

The shell. Had I lost it? Dropped it between . . . wherever and here? But no. It was under the table where the battery lantern stood. I pointed. "There it is. I saw it and went in to get it."

"Went in—you mean you saw it and came in here to get it?" Glady asked.

"No. I went in the water to get it. At the point."

"Afraid not." Burt picked up the shell, then cradled it in the crook of one arm. "This is Allen's. Pride of his collection. His baby. See the carving here? Beautiful example of scrimshaw."

"No, it's not," Glady said. "It's beautiful, but it's a cameo. Scrimshaw's done on ivory."

"It isn't a face in profile, so it isn't a cameo." Burt contracted his lips into a supercilious purse.

"Look it up, librarian," Glady snapped.

"Retired," Burt snapped back. "I don't have to look up anything if I don't want to. Ever again." He turned the shell, admiring it on all sides. If he heard Glady mutter *You're* the baby," he ignored it. "Plenty of people have tried to buy it off him over the years. Offered him boatloads of money, too, but good old Allen says nothing doing. Refuses to part with it. Sends them packing. Where'd *he* get it, Glady? On that trip to the Philippines?"

Glady shook her head. "He's never been to the Philippines. That's one of his stories. What's it doing out of the locked display case, Burt?"

What was it doing out at Springer's Point? I wondered. I *had* found it there. Caught sight of it as I sat on the beach above the surf line. Sat on sand wet from hurricane rain. With shoes wet from a hurricane puddle. Now with the seat of my pants wet from the sand. I hadn't cared. I was happy being hypnotized by leftover hurricane waves. Waves gray and foaming but not hurricane huge on this side of the island. Washing in, sucking back, shells and beach pebbles rolling and tumbling after, trying to catch up to the rollicking water. Sandpipers running back and forth on their tiny peg legs.

That's where I saw the shell. There, right where the waves curled over before racing up the beach. Ten inches long, easily. Twelve? Big around as a football. I'd never seen a shell that size on a beach. Certainly not one that intact. Was its critter still in residence? If not, what kind of self-respecting, shell-loving mollusk scientist would I be if I didn't want it?

But could I get it? Could I chase the next receding wave, grab that knobbed beauty, and scamper back up the beach like a quarterback without being tackled by the *next* wave? Without getting smacked silly by flotsam? Or worse, washed out into deeper water and caught in a riptide to the open Atlantic. Again, I was exaggerating the danger. Storyteller foible. But I had a vague recollection of a channel and treacherous currents not too far offshore. So why should I be a greedy ninny and do something irresponsibly stupid?

"Why should I risk my life for a shell?" I'd shouted at the taunting waves. The next wave, of course, splooshed in bigger than the rest, and I scooted back to avoid a soaking.

"Indeed, why should you risk your life for a shell?" Although the echo was almost lost in the susurrus of the receding wave, it didn't surprise me. When I wear Jeff's sweatshirt, it's like feeling his arms around me. And sometimes I hear his voice. Imagined advice, commiseration. His throaty chuckle over one of our inside jokes. Or the sweet nothings I long for. The grief counselor I'd seen in the weeks after his death assured me that hearing a loved one, especially one lost suddenly and unexpectedly, is a normal part of the grieving process for some.

The echoing comment about the shell had been *so* Jeff. The way he would try to make me laugh, using one of his stage accents. That had been one of the joys of being married to the director of a college theater department.

Resting my forehead on my knees, I imagined him sitting next to me, taking my hand in his. I didn't want to turn my head and not see him, but I put my hand on the sand, as though between us, as an invitation. Nothing happened, of course. Gulls cried overhead and my hand sat, by itself, getting chilled.

"Thanks a lot, Jeff. You were supposed to be chivalrous and put your hand on mine to make it warm." I sneaked a sideways peek to see what he thought of my complaint. And snatched my hand away from the shadow beside me. Then told myself not to be a goose and turned to look squarely at . . . nothing. Of course, at nothing.

But was that nothing a sign? Maybe? Talk about being a goose. But I straightened my spine and decided to take it as a sign, anyway. A sign that I couldn't, shouldn't hold on to shadows from the past. That I shouldn't take life sitting down, either. That life was about taking risks, especially the risk of loving and losing and ending up with nothing.

I got to my feet, faced the waves, judged the intervals between three of them, and dashed after the fourth to catch the shell before it disappeared back into the sea. Made it to the shell in time to scoop it up, lose my footing in the loose pebbles, and go under the fifth wave. Swallowed half of it, most of the sixth, flagons of foam, and a school of fish, and fended off the flotsam of foundered ships, then dragged myself up the beach, dug the pointy end of the massive shell into the sand like a climbing piton, and hung on for dear and gasping life. Something like that, anyway.

"Well worth the risk," Jeff said in my ear. "You were right to go after it, but come farther from the water. It'll be safer."

A hungry wave slid up the beach, licking my low-tops. They couldn't get any wetter, but the wave gave me further encouragement to pull myself off the sand and move.

How does memory work? Those details of finding the shell flashed into my head as clearly as if they were lit by a bolt of lightning. And here I was now, sitting on the floor of Allen Withrow's shop, the Moon Shell. With two, possibly three people, one of whom had switched from humming about a drunken sailor to quietly singing about him, and then, with an odd segue, moved on to something sultry. "Stormy Weather?" The crooner definitely wasn't my grief-produced Jeff. Jeff hadn't been able to carry a tune in a sand pail.

And sadly, none of that explained where I'd lost my shoes and socks. Or anything about the dead man.

Chapter 5

Glady and Burt were looking at me. What had I missed? They looked at the shell, back at me, and then Burt's glance skittered over to a glass display case with a telltale blank space on a shelf. Not just a space—an empty pedestal. Draped in midnight blue velvet. A bit showy for my taste. Glady and Burt didn't ask my opinion, though, and I didn't offer it. Instead, I made a statement. It would have been a question, but the sinking feeling in my gut wasn't going to let my voice rise to the occasion.

"You don't believe I found the shell at Springer's Point, do you?"

"Nonsense." Glady's brisk pronouncement broke the spell. "Burt, put the shell down. No, not back on the *chair*. Back in the *case*."

Burt followed Glady's order, sneaking another look at me on his way to the case. Jury still out, there, definitely. *That works both ways, pal,* I thought.

"It'll be safer out of his hands. He drops things." She said that out of the side of her mouth, as if he might not hear her, but she hadn't lowered her voice.

"Drop this in your pipe and smoke it, Glady," Burt said. "The case is locked. Like it should be."

"Except the shell should be inside it, not out here," Glady countered. "Get the key and—here, give me the shell. Now get the key, and while you're at it, find something to carry warm water in. And a towel. Two, if you can find them." Turning to me, she said, "We'll get those feet taken care of after we take care of the shell."

Burt used his phone as a flashlight and lumbered off through a door to the left of the locked display case, muttering what sounded like "a helluva swelluva shell."

"Don't be offensive," Glady nagged after him. "Brothers. I tell you. Some of them never grow up."

"I thought—"

"Burt's my brother, not my husband. Maybe I never married, but give me some credit. I've got better taste in men than that." She pointed a thumb after Burt.

"Oh."

"Ha! Don't worry. He says the same about me. We get along all right. We're peas in a pod."

"Twins?"

"Good lord, no. It's bad enough we live in the same house. I've always been grateful that I'm older. It gave me a couple of years on my own to make my mark on the family, set the tone, before he came along."

"But you left Ocracoke for a while and lost your island brogue?"

"I wasn't gone all that long. Burt exaggerates."

"How do you know Allen?"

"Easy as fig pie. We were all born here. Figs are a thing around here, same as knowing your neighbors." She turned serious eyes on me. "He told us he was going to check on Yanira. See if the water came up into the house. Yanira Ochoa and her little girl."

"Hey, look what I found." Burt, with a sloshing mixing

bowl, lumbered back into the room. The water was definitely warm; he sloshed some on me before putting the bowl on the floor. He hadn't brought a towel.

"No one *finds* a bowl of warm water," Glady said.

"They might. But I'm talking about these, not that." He took my shoes from under his arm, where he'd tucked them. "Found them under Allen's desk in the office. Side by side, sitting neat as a pin. Well, wet, sandy, and a bit muddy, but *sitting* neat as a pin, with wet, sandy, muddy socks inside. Shoes and socks both too small to be Allen's."

"Weird." I didn't have the breath to say anything else.

"Yours?" Burt asked.

I nodded.

"Why were they in there and you out here on the floor?"

I felt like I should know the answer to that. Should know the answers to so many questions. Simple questions. Harder ones. Questions out there wheeling like buzzards. Or like sharks smelling blood in the water. "Maybe—"

"Maybe what?" Burt said.

"Maybe—" I shot frantic looks around the shop. At the case, the shell, my shoes, the door still ajar, and back at Glady and Burt. They waited, watching me. Bonny rearranged herself in my lap to look at me, too. "Maybe we shouldn't touch anything else."

At Springer's Point, after tumbling in the surf with my prize, I'd scooched back up the beach, to *terra* not exactly *firma* but less briny. I don't know marine mollusks as well as I do freshwater mussels, but this shell looked more inflated, balloonish, more like a football than conch shells I've seen. Creamy white exterior blending toward pale salmon in its smooth opening. I'd turned it in my hands and marveled. This shell didn't belong in the water. It *had* belonged in the water, but the original critter-engineer had been evicted some time ago. Long enough ago for someone with time and skill to carve a picture in the shell's outer layers.

I'd turned the shell back around to its opening—the doorway. The owner wasn't home, but what about squatters? When the shell ended up back in the water, a scuttling crab might have moved in, delighted by its palatial find. I'd eyed the waves again, then went close enough to the surf to sluice interlopers and sand from the shell, spitting sand from my mouth, too.

Back up the beach again, holding the shell—hard and cool to the touch, its texture the language of an animal architect that must rank as one of the world's most amazing—somehow I felt more than the shell. Although what *more* meant I couldn't have explained. Maybe it was the carving. *That* was the language of an artist. It depicted an intricate, miniature, nighttime seascape with fish, jellyfish, sea anemones, and other sea creatures under the waves, a three-masted sailing ship on the waves, and a full moon shining from on high over them all. The shell couldn't have been back in the water for long. Not damaged in any way. Not sand-scuffed or sand-worn. It was altogether beautiful. Mesmerizing.

"Well worth the risk," I'd told the shell and immediately felt silly for talking to it. Then, I'd heard my words echoed again. As if someone stood next to me. I'd shivered.

"Do you need help?" This time the voice had come from farther away.

I'd closed my eyes, wondering what kind of trouble I was having. What kind of episode, if that's what it was, that I'd heard Jeff's voice so clearly. Then it occurred to me there might be people who really were in trouble. The shell and the flotsam might have come from a boat. I scanned the water from the surf line to the horizon. Nothing, except—for a moment, I heard voices. And for an odder moment, I thought I saw the masts of a sailing ship, a *galleon*? Nothing modern. But it disappeared into the fog. Fog rarely seen on the Outer Banks. A fog that, itself, disappeared.

Wet, chilled, and weirded out—clearly it was time for me to disappear, too. Time to find the path back through the woods and retreat to my shed away from home. So where was the path? No place obvious. Great. I'd come out of the woods and walked down the beach . . . a ways. I sighed and started trudging. The sand, while not dry or as vast as the Sahara, was just as void of features. I should have brought water. The woods, as they bordered the beach, gave no clues.

But then salvation. A man had appeared at the edge of the woods. He'd raised his arm and waved, then shaded his eyes and appeared to stare toward the same place where I'd seen the masted ship. I looked for the ship again but saw nothing. When I turned back, the man was gone, too, most likely down the path. Now that I knew where it was, I hustled. The wind was picking up. Then the rain came lashing. I'd run for the trees, had run down the path, darker than I'd expected and more disorienting. And I'd tripped over a log. Not a log?

But there was mud. Was there blood? I couldn't remember and I stifled a whimper.

Glady took my hand. "It's all right, hon. What *did* you find out there? Take some breaths and tell us."

"I think I found a body. I think I tripped over it."

"And that's not pleasant, is it?" Glady said.

"It's a nightmare." Burt crossed his arms. "And here we go again."

"Not helpful, Burt," Glady said. "It's not pleasant when it happens or when you *think* it happened."

"Who do we call?" I asked. "911? Do you have 911 here? Or, if the person's already dead, is it a nonemergency call?"

"Ordinarily," Burt said, "we'd start with Captain Tate."

"Captain of what? A boat?"

"Of the Ocracoke station of the Hyde County Sheriff's Department," Burt said.

"Okay. Good."

"He's off-island," Glady said.

"And that's a good thing," Burt said.

"Why?"

"Will you trust us?" Glady asked.

I didn't answer right away. Didn't know how to.

"There, you see?" Burt said. "First time she's showing that her head's screwed on right, even if her brains are addled." He took the shell from Glady, sloshed it around in the bowl of water, then dried it with his shirttail.

"Here's why I asked," Glady said. "If we call 911, we'll get everyone from here to Swan Quarter to Hatteras—"

"From here to hell and back," Burt tossed in.

Glady shushed him. He snorted. He took a small key from his pocket and used it to put the shell back on its pedestal, then relocked the case. Glady, holding her breath, watched his every move. He took the key back to the office.

Glady took a breath of relief and reverted to her complaint about calling 911. "A 911 call will get everyone all worked up," she said, sounding worked up. "Possibly over nothing."

"From then on, you'll be known as the woman who cried *body*," Burt said. "You don't want that. People pointing and whispering. Crossing to the other side of the street when they see you coming. It wouldn't be good for the business, that's for sure. Allen wouldn't approve."

Allen might be dead, and I knew manure when I heard someone shoveling it. *Why did I think it was Allen? How did I know it was him?*

"Burt's right," Glady said. "Up to a point. I don't think you're truly addled, but you're still not entirely with it, if you know what I mean, since . . . whatever happened. Now, with all that wind we had, a log or a downed tree in those woods is more likely than a body, don't you agree?"

"And 'in the woods.'" Burt made a very sarcastic set of air quotes. "Not to be nitpicky, but that isn't specific enough to go looking."

I shrugged. Sloshed more water on myself using my damp socks to clean my feet. Left the poor socks in the water. Wished I knew a way to put on my shoes to show these guys how aggravated I was. Jeff could have done it. He was a master at showing his theater students how to communicate understated emotions through actions. He would've shown this pair a thing or two. Doggone it.

"I'm going back there to look," I said. "To make sure the body's there. Or isn't," I added to show my grasp of the obvious, if not the entire situation. I didn't quite believe any of this myself, but I really hoped I *had* found a body, otherwise, I'd have to go looking for the mind I'd lost.

"Look where?" Glady asked. "There's more than one hundred and twenty acres of marsh and maritime forest at Springer's."

"Not far from Ikey D.'s grave," the fellow with the British accent said in my ear.

After a huge gulp and a thump to restart my heart, I repeated the words, wondering who the heck Ikey D. was. And who the heck had whispered in my ear. The unseen crooner? I tried very hard not to think *phantom* vocalist.

"A grave's as good a place as any to look for a body," Burt said. "Glad to see you're not bothered by the fact the woods are haunted."

"Haunted how?"

"Various ghosts," Glady said, "but primarily those of pirates."

I heard a low rumble that could be laughter or distant thunder. The humming started again. Had Glady and Burt heard the thunder? Did they hear the humming? Who knew? I didn't ask. Didn't want to know. I thumped my heart again for good measure and shakily got to my feet. "I'll find it, find him, the body," I babbled. Didn't care about babbling, either. "When I do, I'm calling 911."

"A first-rate plan," Glady said. "We'll come with you."

The humming broke off, and I heard the voice with the British accent again. "You, Mistress Nash, are not who they think you are."

Chapter 6

"The first rule of being prepared is bringing more than you'll need on any expedition into the unknown," Burt said. "Bring the first aid kit, Glady."

"The first rule of dead bodies," Glady said, "is that they don't need bandages or ice packs."

"This one was already cold," I said.

"There you go. The voice of experience." Glady patted my head, hitting a bruise I hadn't had B.W.H. (Before Whatever Happened).

"It's the voice of a woman who might or might not remember or know what she's talking about," Burt said. "We'll stop by the house and get the kit, anyway. If we take it, then we definitely won't need it. That's the second rule of being prepared. Now, you've been out that way already today," he said to me. "Are you up for a hike back there? In the dark?"

"She's in no shape for walking," Glady said.

"A minute ago, she was planning to hoof it on her own. So, okay, bikes it is."

"No better than walking, and she hasn't got a bike. You don't, do you?" Glady asked.

"No."

"Then the golf cart or the car." Burt's growl sounded like he'd put his foot down.

Glady wasn't taking his foot for an answer. "No parking allowed at Springer's."

"No one's going to see us, and if they do they won't care. You've ruled out everything but pushing her there in the wheelbarrow, and I'm not falling for that again."

Would you, could you take a hike? Could we, should we ride a bike? "Does it matter how we get there?" I asked, cutting through the drivel in my head and their argument. "Wait a second. What did you mean about not falling for the wheelbarrow *again*?" They didn't answer. "Okay, fine. I'm fine. I can walk. Why don't we do that? *I'm* going to do that."

"No, ma'am, you are not," Glady said. "Burt, we might regret this, but go get the first aid kit and the golf cart, and pick us up here. And we don't want nosy parkers wondering what we're up to now, so don't honk."

"Then don't keep me waiting."

When Burt left, Glady told me about his prostate issues and her anticipated bunion surgery. "Not that I'm looking forward to it, mind, but even a saint can only suffer in silence for so long."

"When is it?" I asked.

"I haven't thought that far ahead. I'm putting it off as long as I can. I know what hospitals are like. And doctors." She put a hand to her ear. "That might be Burt now."

"I don't hear anything."

"It's electric, so there isn't much to hear. You could be right, though. We'll wait till we're sure." She filled me in on the tribulations of sensitive hearing until we heard what sounded like an angry goose outside. "I know you heard *that*," Glady huffed. "And I know *he* heard me tell him not to honk. You have the key to lock up?"

"No."

She'd already stepped out onto a porch but turned around. "Then how did you get in?"

"Maybe it wasn't locked?"

"Could be." The look she gave me added skepticism to her otherwise flat statement.

I'd pulled the door shut behind me, so I opened it again to feel the inside knob. "There's no nub thingy in the middle for locking it that way."

"Old door, old knob, no thingy." Glady said. "The sooner we go, the sooner we'll be back. Clearly, Allen wasn't worried. Close it and let's go."

Allen's worries weren't at all clear to me. I closed the door, anyway, and thought I heard the *snick* of a dead bolt sliding into place. Burt laid on the anemic horn again. Glady shouted for him to keep it down and did he want to wake the dead. I stood there and tried to open the door. It wouldn't. I rattled the handle. No luck. Then I heard the British accent whisper through the door crack, "Standing by to repel boarders. Go and God be with you."

I turned tail and scampered to the golf cart. Wedged myself into a corner of the back seat. Hoping for invisibility, fearing for my sanity. Listened to the two in the front seat acting like best pals on a lark who'd never argued over travel plans or the need for first aid kits.

And who knew a golf cart's speed and turning radius could feel so dangerous? Burt's driving had my knuckles almost as white as they'd been on the boat trip over from Hatteras, with less to hang on to. "How fast are we going?" I asked.

"We've got a full load, and we're going full throttle," Burt shouted. Glady had been right; the cart made very little noise. No one needed to shout. "Minerva's a bit long in the tooth," he shouted, "so we're topping out at ten miles an hour."

"His cart's Minerva," Glady shouted. "Mine's Dorothy Parker. Because I can park her."

We were only tearing along at ten miles an hour. When had

I become such a basket case? Burt swerved for a pothole. We bounced through it. He and Glady laughed like loons.

"Would you like to hear some of the legends about the woods at Springer's Point?" Glady shouted over her shoulder. "The ghost stories?"

"No, thanks."

"Tell her about Teach's hole," Burt shouted. "Edward Teach and Blackbeard. One and the same."

"Shall I tell you about Blackbeard's headless corpse?" Glady asked.

"No, I'm good. Thanks, anyway."

"Okey-doke, but you're missing out," Glady shouted. "It swam three times around his ship before sinking out of sight. Burt can't swim at all, and he rarely loses his head."

Burt drove us in three tight circles in the middle of the road.

"I don't think you're taking this seriously," I said.

"We'll take it seriously when we find what you tripped over," Burt said. He started singing "Comin' Thro' the Rye," making up his own lyrics. "If a body finds a body when no one's drinkin' rye, or a six pack or hot toddy, would a body lie?"

"Or should a body cry?" Glady warbled.

Burt high-fived her, then slowed the cart. "Say, Glad, to show her how serious we are, maybe we should backtrack and head over to Frank's first. It's not like this so-called body's going anywhere."

"Who's Frank?" I asked.

"Sheriff's deputy," Burt said.

"He's on the island?"

Burt shrugged, sending the golf cart to the opposite side of the road.

"If that's a yes," I said, "then instead of *going* to Frank's, why don't we call him and ask him to meet us there?"

"I don't think you want to vote that way," said Glady.

"I think I might."

"No, Glady's right," Burt said. "If your body *is* a body, Frank is not your guy."

"We'll have to call *someone*." By now I was shouting, too. It did no good.

"Hit the gas," Glady shouted to Burt.

"Next stop Springer's Point," Burt howled into the rising wind.

Chapter 7

Burt flew us to Springer's Point, parked in a spray of gravel, and the three of us leapt out ready for action. Like ninjas who travel in golf carts. I could *almost* picture our arrival like that. Instead, our sedate ten miles per hour pace gave me time to ponder. Even with the excitement of Burt turning the road into a random slalom course, I tapped into enough of my wits to wonder why he and Glady seemed to have an uneasy relationship with the captain and his deputy. When he'd puttered to a stop, he and Glady had groaned their way out of the cart, stretching as if we'd driven for hours. Burt flipped open a hatch at the back and fished out a beach towel. Glady grabbed a flashlight. Who knew golf carts had trunks? Probably anyone who gave it a thought.

"To put over the body?" I nodded at the towel.

"What you can't see can't come back to bite you," Burt said. His remark turned out to be less cryptic and insensitive than it sounded when he draped the towel over the sign with the parking rules and regs.

Glady snapped on the flashlight, dazzling our eyes, then urged us to follow her. She led us down a path into a tunnel of woods, the woods pitch-black on either side with live oaks that caught at our sleeves and reached down from overhead to snatch at the hair on our heads.

Burt whistled a few notes of a ditty before Glady shushed him.

"Not this close to Ikey D. and Sam's graves," she said.

"There's more than one grave out here?" I asked.

"Those two at least," Burt said. "Possibly more."

"Not just possibly," Glady said. "Listen to that wind, will you? Gives me the shivers. Makes the branches sound like rattling bones."

An image I didn't need. "Who are Sam and Ikey D.?" I asked, hoping to distract myself.

"Sam is Sam Jones," Glady said. "Been gone, oh, not quite fifty years."

"Always wore white shirts with pleats down the front." Burt fingered invisible pleats up and down his chest. "A genuine, grade-A character. Born on a farm in Swan Quarter and left there to make his fortune."

"He did make it, too," Glady said. "And became a generous philanthropist."

"But eccentric in more ways than pleated shirts." Burt's fingers, running up and down his chest, looked jealous of those pleats. "He started coming to the island in the thirties or thereabouts. If he saw a need, he might dig deep in his pockets, but if you asked him for funds outright, he'd as likely ignore you."

"He and Ikey D.," Glady said. "They loved a good sing-along with friends and neighbors standing around the parlor piano."

"Ikey D. was his favorite horse," Burt said.

Did I believe that last bit? Frankly, it didn't sound any more far-fetched than a nature preserve full of graves and ghosts, and Glady and Burt gave no indication they were pulling my leg. So, sure, a horse joining the old gang at the parlor piano? I'd go to that party. It'd be cozier than creeping around a rattley-bone woods looking for a body.

The path led to a weathered, lichen-covered picket fence that enclosed a plot just big enough to bury a horse and a man.

"Sam and Ikey D.," Glady said. "That little rearing horse statue marks Ikey D's resting place."

"Another thing about Sam," Burt said. "He always wore a planter's hat. Guatemalan palm leaf. That man had style. Real panache. Shine that flashlight around, Glady. Do you recognize any of this?" he asked me. "Because I don't see a body."

I listened, kind of hoping to hear the British accent help out with a more specific location. Like *What you seek lies ten paces north of the rearing horse.* I heard nothing. Just as well. That might mean my brains were recovering from whatever blitz they'd experienced. But the voice had said *near* the grave, not on top of it. "Why don't we spread out?"

Glady lit her face from below with the flashlight. "Best stick together. Work our way around the cemetery in larger and larger circles. Rethink things if nothing turns up."

"Or if one of us sinks waist-deep in the marsh," Burt said.

"That almost never happens," Glady said. "Why do you insist on adding stress where we don't need it? Come on." She went first, sweeping the flashlight's beam slowly back and forth.

It only took a half circle around the picket fence. We found the body, face down in a churned-up mess of mud on the opposite side of the burial plot. The deep wound to the back of the victim's head looked garish in the beam of Glady's light. She crossed herself, then turned the light off to Burt's sharp protest.

"Hey!"

"Let's have a moment of silence," Glady said. "The poor man. This is terrible."

We stood without speaking, one of us barely breathing, as the word *victim* ricocheted around in my head and chest. Our silence magnified the preserve's night noises. None that I could identify for certain, except for the wind, the whisper of distant waves, and the crackle of twigs as feet shifted uncomfortably.

Mine were uncomfortable, anyway. No telling how their feet were coping.

"Amen." Glady flicked the light back on.

"Amen." Burt rubbed a hand over his face, scratched his beard. "We can't unsee this and go home, so what's the plan?" With a glance at my mouth hanging open, he added, "Thinking out loud."

"It's how his mind works," Glady said.

"We'd no more turn our backs on this than pick up a log and drag it back to the golf cart," Burt said.

"What do logs have to do with anything?" I asked.

Burt stood straighter. "A matter of integrity. It's against the rules and regs to harvest wood from the preserve." Said the man who'd parked illegally with his ridiculous beach towel ruse. "Some of us thought you were mistaken. That you'd tripped over a log instead of—" He waved vaguely at the body. Looked queasy or maybe uneasy. "Anyway, we should preserve the scene. Stay out of the mud if we can help it."

"The blood, too," Glady said. "Head wounds bleed plenty." For someone who hadn't been able to find a pulse and hadn't been a nurse for more than a wink, she was awfully composed.

"Is it Allen?" I asked.

"An interesting question," Glady said, "but it's not easy to tell in this light."

"It's not," Burt said. "Easy to tell, I mean. Even if I'd spent much time looking at the back of Allen's head, the back of *this* head isn't at its best anymore. Stating a fact," he said with a glance at me. "No disrespect meant."

"The blue jeans throw me off," Glady said. "I can't remember the last time I saw Allen in jeans. The hair color's right. What there is of it. What we can see of it through the mud. But gray hair? Hardly uncommon."

"What about the ring?" I asked.

"He doesn't wear one," Glady said. "Never did go in for jewelry. He called it male foolery."

"Then maybe that's a piece of grass or . . . shine the light on his left hand. There," I said. "It *is* a ring."

"Get a picture of that, Burt," Glady said. "Of the area around the body, too. Closeups of footprints in the mud if you see any. If you can do it without stepping in the mud and incriminating yourself."

"But why are we fooling around like this?" I asked. "He's dead. You agree it looks like a crime scene, right? So we should call someone. Another deputy if you don't like Frank?"

"Matt," Glady said. "He'd be a good choice."

"Then call him."

"He was fixing roof damage for old Mrs. Garrity." Glady shook her head. "Fell off and broke his femur. They airlifted him to the hospital in Nags Head."

"What about EMTs?" I asked.

"Another option," Burt said. "But as of this moment, we have confusing and conflicting evidence which makes it difficult to identify the body. I'd sure like to get a look at the profile. Turn the head enough to do that and get a picture."

"*Now*," I said. "We should call someone *now*, and we should *not* move any part of him." I pulled my phone out. "We don't need to identify the victim. That's what the experts do."

"Don't call yet," Burt said.

"*What?*" Who acted this way at a crime scene?

"We need to check for breath," Burt said. "It makes sense to look for signs of life. It's one of the first questions they'll ask."

"It's what we did for you," Glady said. "It's the least we can do for the body."

"Not *the body*," I said. "Him. He was a person."

"Oh, hon, calling it the body, or him, or the person, or Allen if that's who this is, doesn't matter now," she said. "The soul has already gone on somewhere else."

"We'll make the appropriate calls," Burt said silkily. If that silk was meant to soothe, then it had its work cut out for it. "The appropriate people will arrive. But for now, don't worry, and leave this to Glady. She's good in situations like this."

"I've solved any number of crimes over the span of my career," she said.

"Oh." Feeling like a dolt, I pocketed my phone and backed out of her way. "I didn't realize you were in law enforcement." On the other hand, I knew practically nothing about either of them, so how was I supposed to know she was or had been with the police? Considering her age, "had been" seemed more likely.

Glady's face beamed brighter than the flashlight. "Better than law enforcement," she said. "I write a long-running mystery series."

"Great," I said faintly. *Great.* When Glady turned her back, I took out my phone and held it behind my back.

"He's lying on his face because he was clubbed from behind," Glady said. "But what kind of weapon makes a wound like that? Hard and muddy, whatever it was."

"I don't see any good candidates nearby," Burt said.

"Then there's the state of his clothes," Glady continued. "Again, the mud. Was there a fight? Were they rolling around in it?"

"See how good she is?" Burt asked. "What's wrong? Are you going to be sick? Move well away from the crime scene if you're going to be sick. That's Frank's problem, too."

"Well away from *me*." Glady, who didn't want anyone getting sick near her, who'd had trouble finding my pulse, was practically crawling over the body looking for clues. But only in my antsy imagination. Neither of them had moved any closer to the body. No turning of the victim's head. No stirring of the already churned mud surrounding the body. But they still hadn't called anyone.

Rather than tear out my hair, I moved into the shadows. Pressed Patricia's number, hoping my phone had survived its ocean dip. It had, but Patricia didn't answer. I let it ring, heard that her mailbox was full. Hung up. Sent a text. Waited. Didn't get one back. Drat. Slipped my phone back into my pocket. And learned that footsteps don't always make noise in a wet, dark wood.

"Making a call?" Burt asked.

I took a step back, more like a frightened rabbit jump. "A park ranger I know."

He took a step forward. "There's no need for that."

I stood my ground. "We need to call. You didn't want to call 911. Patricia seems like a good alternative."

"That'd be Patricia Crowley?" he asked.

"Yes."

"Let me guess," Glady said. "You didn't reach her."

"*Do* you know her?" Burt asked.

"We're old friends."

"Really?" Glady said. "Then I'm surprised you thought you *would* reach her."

"Doesn't matter, anyway," Burt said, back to using his silken tones. "Deputy Brown is on his way. He should be here any minute."

This sounded more like it. But . . . in all the discussion of the captain and Matt being off-island and a desire to avoid upsetting Frank's delicate stomach, since when did they have a spare deputy kicking around? And what was up with these guys that they hadn't called Brown to begin with? Although, wait a second . . . "Why?"

"What do you mean why?" Burt asked. "You're the one's been bellyaching about calling 911."

"Different question then" I said. "How? *How* did Deputy Brown know he should be on his way here? *Now?* At *this* time? During this . . . this *situation?*"

"Calm down," Burt said. "It's simple."

"Turns out I'm not finding it simple to calm down *in this situation*."

"The answer to your *question* is simple," Burt soothed. "I sent Deputy Brown a text when I went to get the golf cart. Why do you think I practically stripped the gears and broke the sound barrier on the way here?"

"So we could check out the scene before he does," Glady said. "Take our own pictures. Good thinking, Burt."

Was it good thinking? With my mind sinking into a bog of confusing and conflicting information, I couldn't tell. I wanted to believe that Deputy Brown was galloping to the rescue, lariat twirling, ready to relieve me of this nightmarish mire. But I couldn't. The last smidgeon of my brain, still gasping for breath above the surface, glimpsed two clear and present dangerous thoughts: What else had Burt told the deputy in that text, and why did that worry me?

Chapter 8

A light bobbed rather than galloped toward us through the woods. Burt flashed his light that way. The bobbing light stopped. Its owner called, "That you, Burt?"

"You expecting someone else, Deputy?"

"Get your fool light out of my eyes."

Burt turned his light back to illuminate the body.

"He was cold to the touch when we got here," Glady said. "We think it's—"

"I'm not interested in what you think." The deputy's light bobbed toward us again. Bobbed in a sort of slouch that mirrored the rumpled, forty-something man carrying it. He stopped a couple of yards from the body. Sadly, he wasn't twirling a lariat.

"But we think—" Glady tried swinging her words at the deputy again.

"Stop. Nope. Not gonna listen, Glady." A huge yawn engulfed the deputy's face. He wrestled with it, then swung his light from Glady to Burt. "Hurricanes are hell. I haven't slept in two days. I really don't want to hear what you think right now. I'll let you know when I do. You might be interested in what *I* think, though." He shined his light on the body's split skull. "I think people without the good sense God gave them shouldn't wander around the woods during a hurricane."

"If you're talking about us—" Glady blustered.

"Settle down, Glady. The storm's over. I'm talking about this guy. Who are *you*?" He flashed his light in my eyes.

My knees turned to jelly, and the mud suddenly looked inviting. Glady's arm slipped around me, her bulk propping me up. I let my eyes close. Blessed dark.

The Moon Shell had been dark when I'd run toward it. In a rising wind that wailed like a family of banshees torn from each other's arms, with icy rain hammering down, I'd leapt the front stairs, lost my balance, and staggered across the porch to the shop's door. Clutched the doorframe to save myself from falling. The door stood ajar. I pushed it open and knew nothing more until . . .

"Welcome aboard," a British accent had murmured over me. A man? Who knew? I seemed to be floating on a sea between two places, neither of which I could see.

The murmur became a hum. The unseen person had untied and removed my shoes. Stripped off my socks. Then receded, like a tide, like my conscious thoughts, until I'd heard two other people arrive. What had they muttered to each other before they tried to find my pulse? That I'd gone toward the light?

I shook myself, opened my eyes.

"Get your fool light out of her eyes," Glady snapped at Brown.

Burt leaned close to Brown. If he'd planned to whisper, it was a fail. "She's the one I told you about. Maureen Nash. The one who found him."

Brown played his light over the scene again. "Is this the way you found the victim, Ms. Nash?"

"Except for . . ." All three stared at me, and my voice petered out.

"Except for what?" Brown asked.

"The um, a—" The word choked me until I coughed. A whack from the heel of Glady's hand between my shoulder blades dislodged it. "The knife. In his chest. He was lying on his back when I found him." Why did I know that? I was sure I knew he'd been lying on his back when I tripped over him. And he'd been stabbed. *Stabbed. Stabbed in the chest.*

"Well, that raises a few questions, doesn't it?" Brown said. "Here's a good one. Why did you turn him over?"

Me? I tried to remember if I'd done that, but the memory wasn't there. "I don't think I did."

"There shouldn't be any need to think about it," Brown said. "Either you did or you didn't. Which is it?"

Glady and Burt helped out by telling him they thought I'd probably been shocked by an electrical surge when I flipped on the lights at the Moon Shell while dripping a puddle of water on the floor.

"Still addled," Burt said. "From our porch, we saw—"

"Shaken." Glady put a hand on Burt's arm and spoke over him. "Sorry for interrupting. But it's perfectly natural for someone to be shaken after stumbling across a situation like this. I think we should avoid using words that will create a negative impression of Maureen before Deputy Brown has a chance to form his own."

"Fair enough," Burt said.

"Is it also perfectly natural for someone who's shaken to stumble back out of a situation like this without reporting it?" Deputy Brown asked.

"Do any of us really know how we'll react in a situation like this?" Burt asked. "I think not. I also think, given what we don't know about ourselves, much less what we don't know about Maureen, that *addled* might be a more accurate word than *shaken*."

"Point taken," Glady said.

I imagined the deputy's eyes rolling with the resounding thunder of a couple of bowling balls headed for strikes. He turned his light to the trampled morass of mud around the body and then played it over the mud clinging to our shoes. "I also think a herd or two of Ikey D.'s friends came through here to pay their last respects."

"The ponies got out?" Burt gasped. "We haven't heard anything about that."

"They didn't, Burt. That was sarcasm," Glady said.

"Ocracoke ponies don't deserve sarcasm," Burt said.

"They don't," Glady agreed. "And you can't blame Burt or me for the disturbed ground around the body, Deputy. We haven't gone any closer than this. But this *is* the first we've heard about the knife."

Burt fiddled with his phone, then held it for me to see. "Have you seen the ponies?" He showed me a picture of half a dozen pretty animals in a corral. "Back in the day, they roamed the island. We'd round them up every Fourth of July, and folks came from all over to buy them. These days, they live in pens. End of an era, but better for them, better for the vegetation."

Deputy Brown sucked in a hurricane-sized breath. "Better for all of us if you stop with the tourist orientation. If this was murder, *if*, then thanks to helpful citizens roaming the crime scene, it might not be worth my time investigating it."

"I told you," Glady said, a tsk in her voice. "We did not roam."

"My footprints will be there," I said. "From when I tripped." I hated saying that, felt sick about this poor man lying there. Surrounded by us, but alone in these woods, in death . . . A chilling thought slipped into my head. I'd tripped over *a* body. Who said it was *this* one? Some disembodied voice in a shell shop? A shiver tiptoed down my spine. I raised my hand to get Brown's attention. He wasn't looking, and this wasn't a classroom.

"Excuse me? Deputy Brown?" My tentative questions didn't catch his attention, either. I tried again, using storyteller's oomph. "Deputy Brown, what if there are two bodies? This one and another one lying on its back? With a knife."

Chapter 9

"He asked us to stay here because he needs us," Burt whispered. "*And* because he's afraid of the dark."

Deputy Brown had checked the ground inside Ikey D. and Sam's tiny cemetery enclosure. Deeming it untouched by crime, crime victims, or helpful citizens, he'd told us to stand in there, in the far corner, quietly, until he spoke to us again. He'd returned to his vehicle, then came back and put on the kind of crime scene suit I'd seen in TV shows.

"Two bodies and a *knife*," Glady whispered. "It ticks me off we couldn't get a look at this body's face before the cops swooped in."

"I'm not positive there are two," I said. "And Deputy Brown isn't much of a swooper, is he?"

"Let's forgive him for lack of swoop," Glady said. "That's Hurricane Electra's fault."

We watched as he jotted notes and took a few pictures. Mostly, he stood and stared at the body, scratching parts of his own.

"The other body," Burt said. "The one you say was on its back. Did you see *his* face?"

Glady grabbed my arm. "Was it Allen?"

"Do you have a picture of him?" I asked. "If I ever met him, it would have been years ago. Ten or fifteen at least."

"Then what put it into your head that you might've tripped over his body?" Burt asked.

"The circumstances?" I shrugged. "The coincidence of ending up in his shop? His absence? It sounds lame, but I honestly don't know what's going on. Or what's *been* going on."

Glady gave Burt a dirty look, then took one of my hands in both of hers. "You're having a reaction to fright, panic, and horror, hon. Try not to stress. But if we do have a picture of Allen, you might recognize him, and that's excellent. That's progress. Burt's always snapping away with his phone. I'll check mine, too."

Burt put a finger to his lips and turned his back to Brown and the body.

"You keep watch," Glady whispered to me. She turned her back, too, and they scrolled through their phones, looking not at all like a pair of fluffy geriatric amateur sleuths doing suspicious things under the nose of the local lawman. Oh, no, not at *all* like that. Especially when Glady giggled over a photo, nudged Burt with her elbow, and Burt snickered. Brown stayed busy, and didn't seem to notice.

"Here he is at last year's Pirate Jamboree." Burt showed me a picture of a man in a pirate costume complete with an eyepatch, a red scarf tied around his head, and a huge fake beard hooked on with loops over his ears. Like Blackbeard's famed beard, this one emitted smoke from the slow-burning punks twisted in it.

"Useless," Glady said. "He looks like any other person at any other pirate festival. Here. Look at this one." She pushed Burt's phone out of the way with her own. "Is this the man you saw?" She showed me a candid of a guy on a dock squinting into the sun. His face was clear enough, but to echo her complaint of Burt's picture, this could have been any other guy on any other dock anywhere. Except for the lighthouse.

"All I recognize is the Ocracoke lighthouse."

"If you want to sound like you're in the know, you should call it the Ocracoke Light Station," Burt said. "Or shorten it and call it the Ocracoke Light."

"Good tip. Thanks." Could I make myself believe the face in Glady's picture was the man—the body—I'd tripped over? In the dim woods as it rained and lightning flashed? I was pretty sure I'd tripped over a body. That I'd seen its—his— face. But something wasn't right. Okay, lots of things weren't right ever since I'd rescued the shell from the waves. I had no memory of this cemetery, where the deputy had us penned up with its hip-high, rearing horse.

"Do you or don't you, Maureen Nash, recognize the man in my photo as Allen Withrow?" Glady held up her phone. "I'll record your answer. Speak clearly."

"Record it? Why?" And what right did a mystery author have to sound so legal and officious?

"Let me see that picture," Burt said. "What are you doing with a picture of Allen, anyway?" He reached for Glady's phone.

"Low bat," Glady said. The phone disappeared into her pocket like a pebble dropped in a pond.

At the same time, Gene Kelly started belting out "Singin' in the Rain" from my phone. "Shh, shh," I said to the phone as I fumbled it out of my pocket. Then I said, "Sorry, sorry," to an entertained Glady and Burt and to Deputy Brown, who'd turned around looking aggrieved. "My son Kelly. He'll worry if I don't answer."

I'd meant to call the boys to let them know I'd arrived safely but had decided to wait until after I'd gone to the point so I could tell them about that. I knew they'd like to hear that I was already engaging with the island. *Engaged* is their most recent therapeutic word, and they're big on "therapeutic-ifying" my life. They're very nice adults, twenty-seven and twenty-nine, and don't mind that I still call them the boys.

"Hey, sweetie." I put on my upbeat, confident mom voice, wishing I could put some distance between this conversation and the three people watching me. Glady and Burt looked like they'd be happy to take the phone and introduce themselves.

Brown glared. "Does he have any reason to worry about you?" Even his words glared.

Glady saved me the trouble of answering by doing it for me. "Wouldn't you worry about *your* mother, if you knew that *she'd* tripped over a dead body in the dark woods?"

I hadn't planned on telling Kelly about the body yet. Glady saved me that trouble, too. I turned my back to them.

"*Mom?*" Kelly said.

"It's nothing to worry about, Kel."

"Was it a storm victim? That's horrible. Are you all right? Is it safe to be there?"

"It's fine. So am I. Let me go now. I'll call when I get back to the cottage. The deputy's here and he has questions."

"Or text. Texting is okay, Mom."

"I like to hear your voice." I didn't like texting with the boys anymore. Not since Jeff died. That day, after he'd kissed me goodbye and gone to work, he'd sent a text asking, "**1:00 lunch at the café?**" By one o'clock he was gone. I don't go to that café anymore, either. My need to *hear* the boys is silly, I know. Illogical. If Jeff's lunch invitation had been a phone call, would I now avoid the phone? Or was I operating more illogically than that, and did I believe that if he'd called, then that day would have ended differently? Wondering things like that is my own form of therapy. Not always the most positive.

I put my phone away. Turned back around. Glady, Burt, and Deputy Brown were still watching me.

"Short call. Good," Brown said. "Ms. Nash, will you stay inside the fence but step over here? *Just* Ms. Nash."

I did. Burt and Glady muttered under their breaths. Deputy Brown had turned the body over.

"Is this the man you say you tripped over?"

"His face wasn't so muddy then, but yes."

"Thank you." He walked around the fence to the corner where Glady and Burt still stood. I joined them. "I have information," he said. "Then I'll have questions. Then you can go. The victim, a male, is dead."

"We told you that." Glady gave an annoyed huff.

Brown continued as if she hadn't. "He was stabbed in addition to having his skull cracked. There is no sign of either weapon. I'll be contacting the sheriff, get the EMTs here. Springer's Point will be closed while a search is made for the weapons and further evidence. The victim is Allen Withrow."

Glady made a mewling sound. Burt hugged her.

"Can you describe the knife you saw?" Brown asked me.

"I only saw the handle sticking—" I sprinted for the other side of the cemetery enclosure and heaved up the little I'd eaten before landing on the island, in this mess.

When I dragged myself back to rejoin the others, Glady handed me a packet of tissues from the first aid kit. Burt left off hugging Glady and hugged me. Brown's eyes showed a flicker of sympathy.

"The handle seemed huge," I said. "It might not have been. Bigger than a steak knife, I think. But if this is Allen . . ." Confused, I turned to Glady. "The picture you showed me didn't look like this guy at all."

"What picture?" Brown asked.

"An experiment," Glady said. "I showed her a picture of one of the Farrow boys to get a candid reaction. Check to see how her wits are coming back together."

"Yeah? How's that going?" Brown looked at me as if Glady's "experiment" made sense and I might suddenly cross my eyes and drool.

I let him think whatever he wanted about Glady's gumshoe methods, then debated complying when he asked me to produce identification. Not for long, though, because I'm not much of a rebel or rabble-rouser. An interesting problem flittered in and out of my head as I took my wallet—wet but not sodden or lost in the waves, thank goodness—from the kangaroo pocket of my hoodie. Jeff's hoodie. What if my driver's license had a name I didn't recognize on it? What if my memories were so scrambled that I only thought my name was Maureen Nash?

Brown looked from my license to me and back at the license. "You're a long way from home, Ms. Nash. What brings you to Ocracoke, all the way from Johnson City, Tennessee, in the middle of a hurricane?"

Before I could answer, Burt blurted, "Tennessee? Her sweatshirt's from Kansas."

"And her license is from Tennessee," Brown said. "So, no, Toto, she isn't from Kansas, anymore." Brown left a space for us to laugh. We didn't. I gave Burt and Glady extra points for not even smiling. "Or she never was, if she knows someone who went to school there."

"Or if she picked it up in a thrift shop," Glady said.

Being talked about while standing right there didn't bother me. It gave my mind a chance to wander.

"Ms. Nash?" Brown asked.

Oops. Wandered too far. I stopped staring at Allen and stared at Brown. What was the answer to a question like *Ms. Nash*?

"This is my husband's sweatshirt."

"Where is your husband?"

"My late husband. He died a year ago."

"I'm sorry for your loss." Brown held my wallet open to a picture of Jeff and me on our honeymoon, the Ocracoke Light in the background. "This isn't your first visit to Ocracoke?"

"No." I didn't elaborate. Didn't tell him we'd brought the boys here quite a few summers when they were little. That I'd been here myself as a child. They were good times. And I didn't want those good memories floating innocently over this cemetery's picket fence, only to find the body of Allen With-row lying in the mud. And I didn't want to explain that kind of thinking to Deputy Brown.

"With all due respect for poor Allen," Glady said, "finding him has been a shock, for all three of us, and we don't want to stand out here any longer than we need to. Ask the rest of your questions so we can go home."

Brown asked me to tell him what I could remember about finding Allen the first time, and what I had and hadn't done. I couldn't tell if he believed the holes in my memory. He took down the address of my rental.

"There was an evacuation order," he said. "The ferry isn't up and running yet. How did you get here?"

"The people I'm renting from said as long as I could get here, I still had the place."

"And you got here when?" Brown asked.

"After the hurricane, not during. This afternoon. I caught a ride from Hatteras. One of the motels there let me leave my car with them until the ferries are running again."

"Who'd you get the ride from?" Brown asked.

"I didn't ask for a name." Not a lie. I didn't have to ask. "Sorry." Also not a lie. I didn't like holding back information, but I'd promised Patricia I wouldn't rat on her. I needed to get hold of her. Tell her what was going on. Tell her I might have to break that promise.

"Don't go back to the Moon Shell tonight," Brown said. "I'll need to go over that place, too. I would like you to meet me there tomorrow morning. You'll need to show me what you did there this evening. Let's say nine o'clock." He dismissed us and stood staring down at the body.

Before I followed Glady and Burt, I heard Brown mutter, "Allen, you've always been more trouble than you're worth."

When we got back to the golf cart, the beach towel Burt had draped over the no parking sign lay soaking in a mud puddle.

Burt looked at the cart, growled, and yanked a parking ticket from under a wiper blade. "This is what happens when you call Frank," he said.

"So who called him?" I asked. "Deputy Brown?"

"No," Burt said. "I did. Frank *is* Deputy Brown. You're the one who insisted on calling someone, so I did the best I could do. Called Frank."

"You did what you had to do." Glady patted his arm. "In fact, you did better, because you took all those pictures in case he screws things up."

"Not in case," Burt said. "When."

"Why will he screw things up?" I asked.

"Because," Burt said, "Deputy Frank Brown is an unqualified, cross-eyed, certified pain in the—"

Glady slapped a hand over Burt's mouth. "Simply put," she said, over his protests, "don't trust Frank Brown."

So now I had so many more questions in addition to the one no one knew I'd brought to Ocracoke with me. The one I'd let hitch a ride in my curiosity, that might have something to do with Allen Withrow's murder.

Chapter 10

Burt and Glady dropped me off at my garden shed home-away-from-home. Burt said they'd be happy to come in for a much-needed nightcap. Glady told him what I needed was a warm bath and a good night's sleep.

"Is there room in that place for a bathtub?" she asked. "Or a bed?"

"The bed's in the loft. There's a shower in the bathroom. I'll be fine."

After thanking them and waving goodbye, I locked my door. Then checked to be sure I had. Wow. What a day. Could I muster a rueful laugh? No. My phone encouraged me to, anyway, with Donald O'Connor singing "Make 'Em Laugh" as loudly as Gene Kelly had belted out "Singin' in the Rain" earlier.

"Hey, sweetie. How are you? What's up?" This sweetie was O'Connor, boy number two. We'd named our sons after two of Jeff's favorite song-and-dance men in one of his favorite movies. Relatives on both sides of the family worried that we'd name a third child Astaire.

"Kelly called me," O'Connor said.

"And he's worried. Oh, sweetie, I told him not to, and you shouldn't, either. I'm fine."

"But a *body*, Mom? And you tripped over it? Are you sure you're okay?"

"Sure as sure can be. A bit shocked, but who wouldn't be?" If he only knew. "I just got back from talking to the sheriff's deputy."

"Kel said he heard worry in your voice. I'll one-up him. I hear that shock *and* worry."

"Don't be silly." I checked the front door again. Still locked. "Don't worry at all about me worrying."

"Mm-hmm. Whatever you say. What'd you have for supper?"

I'd completely forgotten supper, and it sure didn't appeal to me now.

O'Connor pounced. "Aha! I deduce, with the aid of my little gray cells and from your hesitation to answer, that you did not eat any supper. That proves you're worried. Did you at least take groceries with you?"

"Not *groceries*, O'Connor. Food for feasting. Box o'cereal, box o'oat milk, bag o'bread, jar o'peanut butter." As a kid, he'd gotten a kick out of replacing the random *of* with an *o'*.

"Oh, yummy."

"I'll buy a few things when I can. I don't know if the store is open yet. Do me a favor?"

"Share your adventure? Catch the first ferry to the island?"

"You'd have to sleep standing up in the shower, the place is that small. Even then, there'd be no room in the shower for your nose and eyelashes, and we can't have you cutting them off to spite the shower."

"A likely story. Now I *am* worried. Spurning your favorite second son doesn't sound like you at all."

"I'd love to have you here. I honestly would. If I had a bigger place." Saying "honestly" like that made it sound like I might not have been honest to begin with. Semantics. Bother. "One more thing, sweetie. I should tell you before it hits the news, if it does."

"What?" Now I could hear the worry in *his* voice.

"The man, the body I tripped over, isn't a hurricane victim. He was murdered."

"*Mom!*"

"It's okay. There are good people here. The sheriff's department is right on top of it."

"Geez, Mom."

"I know. Do me a favor, will you? Call Kelly. Tell him about the—"

"The *murder*. Mom!"

"It's okay, O'Connor. It's all going to be okay. Tell Kelly I'll call him tomorrow and that I really am fine."

"You mean lie to him?"

"No, I'll definitely call him tomorrow." He laughed as I knew he would. "Sleep tight, Con."

"You, too. No nightmares."

"I'm pretty pooped. I'll sleep okay. No nightmares for me." Just weird waking hallucinations with charming accents.

"Mom?"

"Hmm?"

"Face it. There's a story here, and you love a good story. G'night."

I love a comfy bed, too, and the mattress in the snug loft met my Goldilocks standard of being just right. A few pages of the latest Richard Osman mystery hit the spot, too. When I'd yawned one too many times to remember what my glazed eyes read, I turned out the reading light and rolled over. Ow. The bruise on my head made me roll back. Phooey. I like sleeping on my right side so that I can see Jeff beside me when I wake up—that is, if this being a widow thing has all been a horrible mistake.

Another horrible mistake—tripping over a murder victim and probably doing irreparable harm to the case. Compounded by anything Glady, Burt, and I had done going back there. And by anything Brown would mess up, for all I knew. Could I be blamed for any of that? Another thought came to me. Could I be accused of murdering Allen Withrow? Sleep claimed me, though, and I slept soundly.

Until a voice in a dream said, "Death reaches out to you." That's the kind of dream to wake a body-tripper in the middle of the night. But had it been a dream or was it a memory? Who would say such a thing to anyone?

Like breakers battering the shore, more questions swept into my head, battering my sleep. What if the real story behind the bruise on my head was that it came from the same weapon that had cracked Allen's skull? What if he'd whacked me, then I'd wrested the weapon from him and given him one mighty wallop? The panic of that question made me sit bolt upright in a sweat—except I'd rolled closer to the wall where there wasn't enough room to sit bolt upright. *Ow.*

The new bump to my head shook sense into it. Let a clearer picture of what had happened in the woods filter in. I hadn't whacked or been whacked. I'd tripped over one body not two, and I'd seen the face. Allen Withrow's face. I curled onto my unbruised side, along the outside edge of the mattress, and fell into a sound sleep.

Until another panicked question woke me. *A* face? What if I'd seen two *faces* but not two dead bodies? Because what if I'd seen the face of one victim and the face of one murderer?

The rising sun blazed in through the east-facing loft windows too early, and I wondered whether I should stay in bed or hide under it. Oh, right. No room to hide under it; the mattress lay on the floor. Might as well face the day. The island shone outside those windows, freshly washed and basking under a clear blue sky.

I'd brought island-appropriate clothes in my duffle, having planned to blend in to the island vibe. Shorts with pockets for walking the beaches, camp shirts with more pockets. The jeans and the sweatshirt from yesterday. I put on khaki shorts and a blue shirt. An extra pair of shoes might have been a good idea, but my mysteriously disappearing and reappearing low-tops were fine with me.

Downstairs, I fixed a bowl of cereal and took a bite, surveying my comfy realm. Glanced out the window over the kitchen sink.

A face stared in at me.

Chapter 11

The face looking at me through the kitchen window opened its mouth and let out a mournful wail. Not that I claim fluency in meow-ese. But the bedraggled cat crouching on the bird feeder platform looked as pitiful as I'd felt in the middle of the night. The cat, a ginger tabby, looked at me with hungry, hopeful eyes. Again, I might not be the best interpreter of feline eyes. This one wasn't hungry or hopeful enough to be brave. When I pushed the window up to say "hi," it leapt down and ran off, belly low to the ground.

As promised, I called both boys, doing my best to reassure them, again, that I was fine. My best is pretty good with those two, and this morning was no exception. The sound of their tentative relief was a relief to me. Tentative because, as Kelly said, *murder* and *mom* are two words no one should use in the same sentence.

"It won't take long for the deputy to figure out who's responsible, Kel. The community's small and the island isn't big."

"A smart murderer would've cleared out pronto."

"Long gone before I showed up, I'm sure." Or after the first time I showed up. Hmm. I didn't tell Kelly that part. "Oh! I found the most amazing shell."

"*Mom* and *shell*. Now, there's a couple of words that *do* be-

long together. Have fun. The trip's got to improve from yesterday, right?"

"I 'shell' make it so. Call you again in a couple of days."

It felt good to leave him laughing, and O'Connor, too, when
I called him. Then I set out for the meeting with Deputy Brown
at the Moon Shell a wee bit early. Well, more than a wee bit.

The Moon Shell is on a short, unpaved lane made of sand,
oyster shell, and gravel. Called Howard Street because the
Howards put up the sign saying so, it's generally considered
the oldest street in the village. Trees, lichen-covered fences,
and houses line both sides. Many of the houses belong to de-
scendants of the original settlers. There are also small family
cemeteries on Howard Street, like the one where Sam Jones
and Ikey D. are buried. So well nestled in the trees are the
cemeteries, visitors don't always notice them. When Jeff and
the boys and I used to visit, it was our favorite street.

The Moon Shell had been one of our favorite shops, too. It's
in one of the houses—a dormered, one-and-a-half-story bungalow not nearly as old as some of the trees or graves. It might
be older than some of the fences, whose boards and pickets
take more of a battering from the weather. But the fences hold
their own, begging to be photographed, the skin of their
lichen-covered faces craggy and wrinkled with the island's lore
and wisdom.

That morning the pickets stood quiet, watching as I started
up the Moon Shell's front walk. A cloud slipped in front of the
sun as I did, and it was then I noticed someone standing on the
porch. A crow cawed and landed on the chimney top.

It wasn't *quite* someone on the porch. More like the shadow
of someone. A shadow standing there, on its own, without the
person who should be casting it. And this shadow had more
details than it should—details like a tricorn hat, full-skirted
knee-length coat, long waistcoat visible where the coat parted,
knee breeches, stockings, and buckles on his shoes. Some kind

of light show, I thought, and an actor. Cool. But how? Where had he been projected from?

The cloud moved on, and the shadow did what shade does when bright sunlight drenches it. Poof, gone.

He reappeared as he moved out of the sunshine and closer to the building. Huh. I climbed the stairs slowly, looking everywhere for a projector but didn't see one. And where could the flesh and blood actor possibly be? When I reached the top of the stairs, the shadow and I stared at each other, he looking as wary as I felt. What was going on here?

At that point, I began to wonder about the effects of electrical shocks and bumps on heads. Because the answer to the question about what was going on seemed so obvious and logical. This manifestation wasn't an actor. It—he—was a ghost.

Chapter 12

Was it too late? Could I turn around and go home? All the way back across the mountains to Tennessee? Of course, it was too late.

He seemed to be waiting patiently.

I glanced up and down Howard Street. No one out and about, so no witnesses. Good. If no one hears you ask a shadow if he's a ghost, then no one can say you sound like . . . like you definitely ought to go home.

"Are you . . ." Was I really going to ask this out loud? I steeled my nerve. "Are you a ghost?"

"Emrys Lloyd, at your service," he said with a lovely British accent and a slight bow.

He hadn't answered my question, and that left me in a pickle. Was he a ghost or was he the remarkably vivid result of the bump on my electricity-addled brains? Not that there was anything I could do about visions *or* ghosts. Not right this minute, anyway. I wanted to see if I could get inside the shop and look around before Deputy Brown and the Weavers arrived. Get in through the door that neither Glady nor I had locked when we took off in the golf cart last night. The door that a man with a British accent, inside the shop, had locked behind us.

I was glad I'd already called the boys. I wasn't feeling quite as fine anymore.

Someone had dropped a piece of white copier paper in front of the door. A flyer, maybe, and I stooped to pick it up.

"I put that there," the ghost said.

"Oh? Why?" I left the paper on the porch, thinking that "smug" wasn't a real good look for a ghost.

"A man spent several hours here last night," he—Emrys Lloyd, who was at my service—said. "He was dressed all over in white, including what looked like a baby's booties on his feet."

"The sheriff's deputy. Frank Brown."

"When he first arrived, I did not know that and was prepared to bar his entry."

"Repelling boarders?"

"Just so." The smug look again. "However, I saw his conveyance at the side of the street. It had an official emblem, done in gilt, on the door. I let him enter, then watched as he took photographs, collected mud from the floor, opened drawers, and made notes. He carried various items out of the shop to his truck—the computer, the lamp that was on the floor last night. He took the doormat, as well."

"Did he seem to know what he was doing?" I asked. Did I know what *I* was doing? My parents had always warned me not to talk to strangers, and this guy was strange up to the eyeballs. Up to the crown of his hat. "Did he seem to know what he was looking for?"

"I'm sorry. I have no idea. That could be because the deputy did *not* know what he was doing or because I am not versant in police methods, modern or otherwise."

This ghost sounded somewhat like a pompous twit, but I definitely wasn't versant in ghosts old enough to wear Paul Revere hats and their hair pulled back in ponytails.

"So why did you put the paper in front of the door?" I asked.

"Sometime after the deputy left, I heard another hand rattling the knob. A shoulder applied, too, if I am not mistaken. *This* scoundrel did not get past me. Shall we step inside?" Emrys opened the Moon Shell's door and stood aside for me to go ahead of him.

"Hold on," I said. "Did you know who was trying to get in?"

"No."

"But you were suspicious."

"Caution seemed the wisest course."

"Would you recognize the person if you saw them again?"

" 'Twas a moonless night and too dark to see without the lights inside or out. But I preserved the scoundrel's muddy footprints. Hence, the paper."

"Ah, very good." Okay, he'd earned his smug looks. I lifted the paper and looked at the footprints. They weren't terribly clear, but you could get an idea of the size—bigger than mine but not by a lot—could see some of the tread and where the tread was worn along the outer edges. I pulled out my phone and took pictures of the prints by themselves, then with the paper for size comparison. "You say this person showed up after the deputy left?"

"Not terribly long after."

"Waiting for him to leave, do you think?"

"A possibility."

I snapped two more pictures of the bottoms of my own shoes and laid the paper back over the prints. For someone whose brains might be pickled, I felt very CSI. "Thanks for covering the prints. I'll show them to the deputy—unless you'd like to?"

"Out of the question."

"Okay. That's fine." So he was haughty as well as smug.

"Let's go in," I said. "The deputy will be here in forty-five minutes or so and I'd like to—"

"Trespass?"

"Uh, yeah."

"Be my guest."

Heart pounding like a hammerhead shark trying to beat its way out of my chest, I stepped inside the shop. What was I hoping to see or find? The bowl of muddy water and my abandoned socks sat on the floor where we'd left them. Bonny the cat came and twined around my ankles. The lamp that had zapped me was conspicuous by its absence. Fingerprint dust covered what must be obvious surfaces.

I had very little doubt how suspicious it would look if Deputy Brown found me here. But I also had no doubt at all that he was already almost one hundred percent suspicious of me. Should I look around Allen's office? Go through his desk? Could I do it without putting my own fingerprints in the fingerprint dust? It wouldn't feel right. Not now, anyway. Maybe later.

Emrys closed the door. Are ghosts *supposed* to have kind, solicitous faces? "Are you fully recovered from the incident of last evening?" he asked.

"I'm not sure." I also wasn't sure I should be so trusting of this strange stranger with his pretty accent and manners. A smaller voice, sounding a lot like my mother, called from a nook or cranny of my mind. *Ask questions first,* the mother voice said. *Trust later.* Not a bad suggestion. "Um, Emrys? May I ask why you're here? I mean, here in this shop?"

"I'm not sure. I think that you and I are alike in that respect. Do you know why *you're* here?"

"My perception of what happened last night is off," I said carefully, thinking that a figment masquerading as a ghost might echo my thoughts like that. "My memory's iffy, too."

"Then we might suffer from similar memory issues. Mine, obviously, an affliction of longer standing. Gladly, the salt water at Springer's Point revived me. When you rescued the shell, you also rescued me, and for that I am much obliged."

"I'm not sure I understand."

"Yesterday, at some time past midday, I was kidnapped from the shop along with the shell and taken to Springer's Point."

"How?" I asked. "How is that possible?" Or any of this. I backed up against the door and leaned against it. My left hand strayed to the doorknob.

"Again, I cannot explain. No more than I can explain why I am now a mere ghost of myself." He smiled.

"You like jokes," I said.

"I do. A wise man once told me that there is no humor in heaven. Perhaps that is why I am as I am." He stood with a shoulder against the fancy display case, arms casually crossed, one ankle cocked against the other. There was nothing threatening in the pose or his words. "I also like cats."

Bonny flopped on her side and gazed in the ghost's direction.

"So you haunt this shop?"

"More accurately, I haunt the shell. Where it goes, there go I."

"You live in the shell. Like a genie?"

His back stiffened. "You make it sound ridiculous."

"Sorry, that could be my affliction speaking." I twiddled my fingers next to my ear. "Not to be rude, but *you* might be a symptom of my affliction."

"I beg your pardon?" No more cocked ankle. No more Mr. Casual.

"It's like this," I said. "I have an important question, and I need an honest answer." I put my right hand on my heart, kept the left on the doorknob. "And I'm being completely honest with you when I say that I don't mean my question to be insulting."

"I shall endeavor to be as *completely* forthright and honorable as I am able."

"Are *you* haunting *me* or am *I* hallucinating *you*?"

"I shall now endeavor to move past the implied but possibly understandable insult," he said. From the tone of his voice, he wasn't endeavoring much. "I am a ghost. A specter. A phantasm. An incorporeal being."

"But if you're a hallucination, wouldn't you say the same thing?"

"I have never been a hallucination, so I would not know." He massaged his forehead for a moment, then smiled. "Let us start anew by introducing ourselves properly." He bowed with a flourish of his hand. "Emrys Lloyd, merchant, from Rhuddlan in Wales, late of Edenton by way of the Virginia colony." It was a lovely bow and flourish for a hallucination *or* a ghost.

"Maureen Nash of Johnson City, in the state of Tennessee, west of here and over the mountains." A curtsy from a fifty-two-year-old in khaki shorts would look ridiculous, so I didn't.

"Mistress Nash, it is a true pleasure to make your acquaintance."

"It's Mrs. Nash, but Maureen is fine."

"Are we expecting Mr. Nash?"

"He's . . . he's also late. He died last year. Um, how late are you? How long have you been dead?"

"You would think that I would know. I used to keep track. A macabre pastime, but as it happens, much about being a ghost is macabre. To answer your question, I haven't counted that high in a very long time, but I died in the year of our Lord 1750."

"Wow." I did quick mental math. "Two hundred seventy-four years ago. Wow. This house isn't that old."

"The shell is older. I was a merchant by vocation and a conchologist by avocation."

"A shell scientist? That's similar to my profession. I specialize in freshwater mussels. But not just the shells. The animals that create them, too." Wait, did I believe this conversation? What were the odds of a conchologist ghost appearing to a malacologist concussion victim?

"Fancy that connection," he said. "I trust your experience with shells is happier than mine. I lost my life in my pursuit."

"Oh! I'm sorry."

"Thank you," he said with a somber half bow. "I died pursuing this magnificent helmet shell." He reached into the case—through the glass—and stroked the shell. "The situation gives new meaning to the word *attached*, for I now seem to be attached to the shell."

"Do you mind if I ask how old you were?"

"Thirty-seven. I was the younger of three brothers who left our father's home in Rhuddlan to seek our fortunes."

In defense of the insensitive question I asked him next, I had never heard anyone, in real life, say *We left our father's home to seek our fortunes*. "To seek your fortunes? Like the three little pigs?"

His face went from confused to annoyed.

"I'm sorry," I said. "That wasn't meant to be an insult, either. It was a reference to a children's story that might not be as old as you are. Not in its current form, anyway. It's a fun story. Exciting. It has a wolf."

"Apology accepted. I like a good literary reference, myself."

"Did Allen Withrow know about you . . . being here?"

"Oh, yes. Allen and I were great friends. Friends of a philosophical nature, that is, meaning that we enjoyed each other's company, but often disagreed."

I'd put my hands in my pockets, and the doorknob was digging into my backside. I was getting cold feet about Deputy Brown finding me in here, too, but I had more questions. I thought I'd better wrap up my info-gathering fest.

"You told me where to find Allen's body, so you knew he was dead. Do you know who killed him?"

He bowed his head. "No."

"I'm sorry you've lost a friend."

So odd to hear a ghost draw breath in a sigh.

"Do you know how the shell ended up in the water yesterday? Who would be stupid or mean enough to throw an amazing piece of art like that into those waves?" I went to the case and stared in at that marvel. Then I remembered what I'd thought, yesterday, was my own conjuring of Jeff's voice. "You spoke to me at the beach."

"I did."

"I heard other voices and saw a ship in the fog. But there was no fog yesterday. Is *any* of this real?"

"Would you rather it is or it isn't?"

I was trying not to hyperventilate, so I didn't answer.

"I know of no way to convince you that I am not an emanation of your fevered brain," he said.

"I do. I know how," I gabbled. "It's easy. If someone else sees you, then I'll be convinced."

"Mmm, no." Lips pursed, he shook his head. "Not such a good idea. One I would steer clear of if I were you."

"Why?"

"You still wouldn't know. They might only be humoring you."

He had me there, and then he did something interesting. Not that everything about him wasn't interesting in a jarring, alternate reality kind of way. He flickered, as if reception for ghosts was suddenly bad. Then he disappeared.

"Are you still here?" I called. "Can you lock the door behind me?"

No answer.

Now I had *so* many questions and so little time before Brown, Glady, and Burt would show up. One of the questions shouldn't have been foremost in my mind but rose up and stuck there, anyway. "How old is the word *conchologist*?" I called to the emptiness.

All that came in reply was a lilting hum.

Chapter 13

By the time I closed the shop door behind me, I was in such a tizzy, afraid Deputy Brown would find me inside, that I didn't just have cold feet. I'd become one with the abominable snowman, shedding icicles, hail, and drifts of sleet. What was I thinking? What a *stupid* chance to take. And to do what? Mince around the shop to learn something? Learn *what*? Well, I had learned something. Two somethings. That it was a *stupid* chance to take and that I might believe in ghosts. Or hallucinations of ghosts. But what if Brown had shown up early to crawl all over the shop again? Or brought a whole team of deputies? What a *stupid* chance to take.

But he hadn't.

So I got a grip, calmed down, and felt the icicles and whatnot melting and trickling away between my toes. My phone said it was only eight-thirty. That left thirty minutes to spare before Deputy Brown or the Weavers arrived. Fifteen or twenty if any of the three sneaked over early, too, but that still left time to enjoy the relief.

I sat on the steps. Alone but not feeling completely alone. I didn't hear voices, though, and nothing shadowy crept close. Maybe it was the sun keeping me company. It felt good. I leaned against the stair railing and closed my eyes.

At a screech and the sound of running feet, my eyes flew open. Glady and Burt hurtled toward me. A slow hurtle. Glady's was more of a concerned lurch. Burt, phone at the ready to make an emergency call, came at an amble.

"Maureen Nash, don't you *ever* close your eyes for that long around me again." Glady, breathing hard, plopped down next to me, a hand to her heart.

"Oh, I'm so sorry. I just closed them for a minute. Kind of a rough night."

"You, too?" Her heart forgotten, Glady squeezed my arm. "Stick with us. We'll get through this."

"Look at the picture I got of her taking her catnap." Burt held out his phone.

Glady grabbed it. "Honest to Pete. You were supposed to be ready to call Frank. Oh . . ." She looked at the picture. "Burt, this is really good." She handed the phone to me.

"See how the sunlight filtering through the leaves sort of co-alesces?" Burt said. "It almost looks like someone watching over you."

"Yeah, almost. Very artistic." I handed the phone back.

"Come on, Burt." Glady patted the step next to her. "Might as well be comfortable."

"Not sitting down there I won't. There's something about the light this morning." He wandered away as he spoke, his words trailing after to catch up.

Glady turned her smile to the sun. Last night, I'd thought she might be halfway between my mother's age and mine. Now, with my first good look at the siblings, I recalculated. Glady didn't have the skin of someone who'd tanned her whole life, but bright daylight showed more soft wrinkles than I'd seen the night before. She might be closer to Mom's seventy-five than my fifty-two. Hard to say. She wore her gray hair short. She was short, too, in capris, an embroidered shirt, and flip-flops.

Burt had the heft and build of a formerly big man. He'd faded, like his overalls, and frayed a bit, like the short sleeves of his checked shirt. He didn't move fast, but his feet looked comfortable without socks in a pair of scuffed loafers.

"Frank just turned the corner," he said. He gave Glady a hand up, and the three of us watched Deputy Brown's black pickup roll to a stop in the small gravel parking area.

Frank Brown climbed out of the truck and proved, again, how poor my age calculating skills had been the night before. Not a rumple in sight and plenty of lean muscle. The forty-something I'd guessed became thirty-five, tops. Maybe a bit of sleep, a shower, and fresh clothes had been the tonic. His uniform consisted of a black ball cap that said SHERIFF HYDE COUNTY, short-sleeved khaki shirt with two breast pockets, black pants, black belt with holster and various cool-looking leather pouches attached, black shoes, and a shiny badge. He surveyed the sky, then us, then showed dazzling teeth in a shiny smile.

The dazzle made me wonder. I'd been wrong about his age. Would I be wrong to trust Glady and Burt's sour opinion of him? Or was it those shark-grin teeth I should keep an eye on?

"Deputy?" I said, stopping him before he reached the shop's door. "There are muddy footprints under the paper in front of the door."

Brown quirked an eyebrow at me. "You just happened to have a sheet of paper with you?"

"Always prepared." I turned and patted my shoulder pack. I really did have paper in it. "Did you take the doormat last night?"

"Yeah. It's a long shot, but we might learn something from it." He crouched and lifted the paper. "Another long shot. These weren't under the mat last night or here when I left."

He took pictures of the prints. Picked up minute samples of mud from the prints with tweezers and dropped them in a small plastic bag. That done, he rose to unlock the door. He had trouble getting the key in the lock, then trouble turning it. While he fussed with the key, I thought about Burt's picture of me on the steps. I'd sat there because they'd been in full sun. So what tree had suddenly sprinkled its dapples into my nap and Burt's picture? None that I could see, and the stairs were still in full sun. What a wit this hallucination was to play tricks on Burt and Deputy Brown.

"Frank, stop fiddling and open the door already," Glady said. "Maureen is shivering."

"Let me try, Frank," Burt said.

"Nope. Nope. I got it, I got—there. Finally."

We trooped inside on Deputy Brown's sigh and Glady's tut-tutting like a hen when she saw the fingerprint dust. Bonny came to meet us, and Glady scooped her up, holding the cat so that Bonny's head fit under her chin.

"Frank," Burt said.

"Hold on. Something I gotta say first. I want to apologize for the way I must've come across last night. Seeing Allen like that . . ." Brown stopped, then shook his head as if that could erase the image. "On top of no sleep for forty-eight hours and with Matt and Tate gone, it was a shock for me, too. Even more, I don't mind telling you, because this is my first murder. Anyway. Sorry."

"A sorry business all the way around," Burt said. "That's why I want to ask you this. Are you sure us being in here is okay? Shouldn't there be crime scene tape around the whole place?"

"That's the thing. This isn't the crime scene. I went over the place last night top to bottom. Took pictures *and* video. I took away the lamp, Allen's laptop, the doormat to be sure, but the place appears to be clean."

"Except for the fingerprint dust everywhere," Glady said.

Frank nodded in agreement. "I did go through a lot of it."

Glady took a tissue from a pocket and wiped Bonny's paws. "And I suppose we'll have to clean it up?"

"Par for the course. Sorry." The teeth dazzled at her. "Where are you going?"

"To feed this poor orphan. First the hurricane, then Allen is taken from her and the trauma of you and your hurricane of fingerprint dust. Come along, Maureen," Glady said over her shoulder. "You need to learn where the food and bowls and litter box are."

I followed her into the small office, where it wasn't hard to find any of those things. Bonny watched our ministrations from the desk. She showed her approval of my skill with a litter box by jumping down and immediately using it.

"Bottom line," Brown said when we rejoined him and Burt. "Allen's golf cart is missing. Beyond that, I found no evidence of a crime taking place here. No forced entry. No violence. No evidence that Allen left against his will."

"Would there be evidence of him leaving against his will?" I asked.

"There might be. The lamp, for instance." He scrolled through pictures on his phone and showed us one with the lamp on the floor. "Say the lamp got knocked over if Allen put up a fight when they tried to get him out the door. That could be evidence."

"They?" Glady's cheeks went pale. "What kind of evil are you talking about? Did more than one person come after him?"

"Glady." Brown looked at her, his hands directing her eyes to his face. "I said there isn't any evidence indicating that happened. I don't know what happened yet. That's why I'm investigating, okay? It's a shock for all of us." He included Burt and me with a glance, and we nodded. Glady swiped a tear with the tissue she'd used to wipe Bonny's paws. "Back to the lamp," Brown said. "Where was it when you came in last night?"

"Already on the floor," Burt said, "but with all the excitement—well, I guess I could've cleared it up."

"We didn't bother with it because we didn't want Maureen going back out to the point and looking for the body on her own," Glady added.

Brown looked at me. "How's your memory this morning? And your head? Do you remember where the lamp was when you came in?"

"On the table. I'm pretty sure."

Brown made notes on his phone. "Here's what I'd like from all of you. As best you can, let me know if anything is missing or misplaced."

"You already checked the cash box?" Glady asked.

"Intact and easy enough to find, if someone had wanted to," Brown said. "I took it last night, too. Everything I took is in the evidence room."

"Did you look for a note?" Burt asked. "Anything to indicate why Allen went to the point?"

"You mean did I do my job?" Brown didn't apologize for the snark or the yawn that followed it. "There was no note."

"What about his phone?" Glady asked.

"Missing," said Brown.

"Have you looked at the computer yet?" she asked. "At his emails?"

"Believe it or not, I haven't had time. I also don't know his password. Do any of you?"

We didn't.

"Now, to repeat, can you tell if anything in the shop is out of place? Is anything that I didn't take missing?"

Glady and Burt wandered around shaking their heads.

"Ms. Nash?" Brown said.

"I wouldn't know. Oh! But I do. The shell was missing." I pointed to the cameo shell, basking on it's dark blue velvet in the display case.

"We don't actually know that it was," Burt said, with the tone of correcting a small child's imaginative answer.

Brown looked at me.

"I found it in the surf at Springer's Point. Before I found Allen."

"If she did, then she brought it back here," Burt said. "It was here when we found her."

"On the floor," I said. "Like me."

"With the display case locked," Glady said. "The mystery isn't how the shell ended up here, with Maureen. It's who took it to the point and threw it in the water."

"Maybe I should take it as evidence," Brown said.

"I don't see why," Glady said.

"If you want if for fingerprints, forget it," Burt said. "I rinsed it and dried it and put it back in the case."

"I'd like to take it, anyway," Brown said, with an unreadable glance at me. "Where's the key?"

"The desk," Burt said. "Kneehole drawer."

I thought I caught a flicker moving ahead of Brown into the office. He pulled at the drawer, then rattled it.

"It isn't locked," Burt said.

"It isn't opening, either—ah. Got it."

The flicker again. This time ahead of Brown as he went to the case. He tried and couldn't get the key into the lock.

"Blast Allen and his lousy locks," Brown said.

"Do you have the right key?" Burt asked.

Brown looked. "The label says, 'big display.' "

"That's the one." Glady held her hand out. "Let me try."

Glady and then Burt tried to fiddle the key into the lock. As they did, I saw a reflection in the glass. A reflection? No. It was a shadow of the shadow—Emrys holding his finger over the keyhole. How was a ghost able to do that? But if there could be a ghost, then why not?

I went closer until I saw my own reflection, wondering if

that was what I would look like if I were a ghost. Except that I reflected in full color and Emrys's look of triumph showed in watery grays.

"I don't know what's wrong with it," Burt said. "Take the key with you. That way you'll know where it is and where the shell is."

"So will whoever took the shell, and they might come back for it. Tell you what," Brown said. "Why don't I snap the lock with a screwdriver. Take the shell with me for safe keeping even if it isn't evidence."

The triumph on Emrys's face dissolved into—what? Was it fear? Horror?

"I don't think the thief will be back," I rushed to say. "Think of me as a monkey wrench in the original plan. The person who took the shell and threw it in the water didn't expect anyone to find it, much less bring it back here."

"Maybe," Brown said. "But how much is that thing worth?"

I heard a low growl. The kind I would have been tempted to make if someone had maligned one of Jeff's theater productions by calling it a *thing*. The kind of growl that should make someone think carefully before saying anything else rude or dismissive about the shell. But not the kind of growl that anyone else in the shop heard.

"It's never been for sale," Burt said.

"Then it can't be worth all that much or Allen would've had better security." Brown grabbed the top edge of the display case door between a thumb and index finger and gave it a shake.

"This is Ocracoke," Glady said, with the air of summing up her worldview and the answer to all of life's problems in those three words.

"Last I checked, Ocracoke is part of the big, bad world." Brown bent to wrinkle his brow at the shell. As his nose approached the glass, his shoulders were taken by a visible shiver.

"What's the matter, Frank?" Glady asked. "Ghost walking on your grave?"

"Close," the British accent said, with an audible sneer. But like the growl, only audible to me.

"Anything in the shop might have something to do with Allen's death," I said. "The shell's one of those things, but you can't move the whole shop into your evidence room."

"I could seal the shop," Brown said.

Burt made a rude noise. "With the crime scene tape I asked you about? Do you know how long that stuff will keep anyone out?"

"Okay, we'll do it your way," Brown said. "The shell's location yesterday seems to be a matter of circumstantial evidence, *if* it's evidence at all, and *if* it was anywhere but here. It can stay here, and the key comes with me."

I caught a flash of teeth in a wide smile over Brown's shoulder. I gulped.

"Yes, Ms. Nash? Is there a problem with that?"

"No."

"It's splendid," Emrys said.

I wasn't so sure.

"How well did you know the deceased, Ms. Nash?"

"Not at all."

"You never met him?"

"We brought our boys into the shop when we were here on vacations. The last time would've been more than ten years ago."

"Ten or fifteen. That's what you said last night," Glady said.

"I remember the man here was kind to the boys." I flapped a hand that meant *time flies and so do memories*.

Brown might not have read my hand flap that way. He scratched a finger along his jaw, mouth slightly open, one eyebrow raised. Jeff would have wanted a picture of that look for his theater classes. He would have called it "How to Not Merely Portray Cynical Suspicion but Also Exude It."

Did I want to slap Deputy Brown? No. I'm not much of a slapper. But I did want to know why the hand not involved in cynical scratching kept straying to one of the buttoned pockets on his shirt. Unconsciously tracing the outline of something hiding there. What was it?

Chapter 14

Brown pulled a key ring from a back pocket. He slipped one key off and handed it to Glady. "Thanks. The keyhole needs lubrication."

"Allen didn't have keys on him?" I asked, wondering why Glady had a key to the building. Sign of a good neighbor? Probably.

"He did," Brown said. "But you saw how stiff Glady's key was. I couldn't get the door open at all with Allen's last night."

"Huh." I'd let that slip out. Tried to look nonchalant. Normal. Not like I'd heard a dead bolt snick into place last night, followed by the voice of a person prepared to repel borders. Then heard that same person admit he'd, at first, repelled Deputy Brown.

"You shouldn't have had any trouble," Glady said. "We were in a hurry, and I didn't have the key on me."

"You didn't lock it?"

"Not when we went to the point," Glady said.

"What about later?" Brown asked. "When you left the point?"

"No." Glady looked at Burt. He shook his head.

"Who else has a key?" Brown asked.

"No idea," Glady looked at Burt again. He shook his head again.

"And you two didn't wonder why I came to borrow your key last night?" Brown asked.

"Frank," Burt said, "do you think it's our habit to question local law enforcement?"

"I think you see yourselves as Ocracoke's answer to late night TV." Brown looked at me. "What about you?"

"Did Allen have any relatives on the island he might leave a key with?" I asked.

"No," Brown said.

"Maybe he keeps one outside somewhere," I suggested. "Under a rock, in the gutter."

"And you think what?" Brown said. "That a volunteer door checker, passing in the dark, found this one unlocked, took the key from its hidey hole, and remedied the situation?"

"I'm guessing stranger things have happened." I heard applause no one else did. "Or that Allen gave one to another friend."

"As a matter of record, Ms. Nash," Deputy Brown said, "I'd like you to know that your presence and involvement in this matter raises questions, and so far, I'm not finding answers to many of them."

"I wish I could help you better. Some of the questions wouldn't be here if my memory was all here."

"So the door was unlocked when you arrived yesterday?" he said.

"Not only unlocked but ajar."

"You didn't think to tell me this last night?"

"I'm not sure I remembered it last night." Also, he hadn't asked me.

"Think of her memory as an exotic martini," Burt said. "Shaken, addled, and stirred."

"Did you get Dr. Allred to look at her?" Brown asked.

"He left before the storm," Burt said.

"He's back."

"*Is* he," Glady said. "Interesting. What about Captain Tate?"

"Back tomorrow." Brown lifted his hat and ran his hand over a brush cut. "I don't know about you, but I need to get off my feet." Poor guy. His uniform still looked laundered and tidy, but his voice was beginning to rumple. "Not enough room or chairs in the office. Anyone mind if we go up to the apartment?"

"Allen won't," Burt said.

Allen had lived in a shipshape apartment in the half-story above the shop. We reached it by a steep staircase behind a door—a door behind another piece of the white beadboard paneling covering the shop's walls. I wouldn't have known the door was there if Deputy Brown hadn't slapped his fingerprint powder along its edge. Bonny trotted up ahead of us. The stairs opened in the middle of the apartment, with a kitchen to our right and living room to the left. I guessed that the door at the far end of the living room led to a bedroom.

Bonny leapt to the window seat of a dormer that looked out onto Howard Street. I sat next to her and watched Burt try to commandeer a mellow-looking leather recliner. Brown pulled rank, and Burt joined Glady on an antique settee covered in deep green brocade. The green was picked up and joined by browns, blues, reds, and golds in the geometric patterns of an almost room-size woven carpet. There was no hint of haunting. Except for the fingerprint powder on various surfaces, the room looked ready for a photo shoot.

"Tell me about finding Ms. Nash," Brown said. "From the beginning. How you knew something was going on."

I was eager to hear this, too. I made myself comfortable, Bonny on my cross-legged lap, and hoped their story would jog my memory. Jog it and not fill my memory holes with a questionable version of events. Thinking they might tell a questionable version sounded better to my ear than thinking they'd tell lies. Lies could be a problem.

"From our porch, we saw a flash and heard a pop," Glady said. "Flash and pop pretty much simultaneous and electrical in nature, as best we could tell."

"Both came from the direction of the Moon Shell?" Brown asked.

"Not from the *direction of*," Burt said. "From the shop itself. Inside. We wouldn't have seen the flash except it lit up the windows."

"So, naturally, we went to see if Allen was all right," Glady said. "Instead, we found Maureen. Out cold."

"We thought *she* was dead," Burt said.

"After coming all this way to help Allen run the shop." Glady's voice faded off for a moment, then continued with a hitch in it. "It's beginning to sink in. Allen's gone." She gazed around at his living room, his crowded bookshelves, the photographs and watercolors he'd hung over a small desk that looked impossibly fragile and impossibly expensive. "And you were nearly gone, too, Maureen."

Brown called our attention back. "This flash and pop. What time?"

"Just after dark?" Burt looked at Glady. She nodded.

"You didn't see Ms. Nash arrive at the shop or go in?"

Burt shook his head.

"We'd just stepped onto the porch," Glady said.

"Why?" Brown asked.

"Because it's our house and our front door," Glady said with a good amount of squelch in her voice. "We go in and out of the door as the whim takes us, and when we do, we either step out onto or step in off of our porch."

"Why so prickly, Glady?" Brown asked, his voice softer.

"The stress is hitting home," Burt said. "We came out because of the crows. You know how Glady is about crows."

"No, I don't."

"Should I tell him?" Burt asked Glady.

"I doubt he's interested, and I don't see that it's any of his business."

"Well, anyway," Burt said, "They were raising a ruckus."

"Confess," Glady said. "It's because you threw pine cones at them. Again."

"I want to know how you feel about crows, Glady," I said.

"*I* don't." It was Brown's turn to squelch. "But Ms. Nash, do you still want me to believe you found the shell in the water, you found Allen's body in the woods, and you found the door to his business open for you to wander in?"

"It'd be nice if you did."

"We would like you to believe it, too," Glady said. "Right, Burt?"

"Not only yes, but shell yes," Burt said, then to me, "One of Allen's favorite exclamations."

Glady wiped a tear. "Oh, I'm going to miss the old so-and-so. Frank, who makes the decision about when the shop can reopen?"

"There's no rush," Brown said. "The ferry isn't running. And, to be blunt, it isn't your business."

"All that aside, who makes the decision?" Glady's eyes glinted with more tears, but her voice was clear and steady.

"I do," Brown said.

"You or the department?"

"It's the same thing. Thanks for meeting with me, folks. I'll see myself out. Don't forget to lock up."

"Speaking of." Burt held his hand out. "Can you leave Allen's keys?"

Brown didn't look happy about it, but he pulled the key ring from a pocket.

"Let Maureen have them," Glady said.

"Why?" Brown asked.

"Because," Glady said, sounding exaggeratedly patient, "she came to help run the shop. The shop will need to be cleaned.

She will need the key to clean and run the shop." She nudged me and I held out my hand.

"I've just explained my suspicions of her," Brown said.

"And if your suspicions bear fruit you know where to find her," Glady said. "And if you need to get back into the shop, you know who to ask for permission."

"Or, if you'd rather give the keys to me," Burt said, "I'll give them to Maureen as soon as you leave."

Looking way less happy, Brown handed the keyring to me and left. We heard him stop on the stairs, yawn, then continue down.

"Do you want to know what I think?" Glady asked after we heard the front door close behind him. "Frank's word and the department's word are not the same thing at all. *That's* what I think."

"I think we should . . ." my voice trailed off as I wondered who we needed to ask for permission.

"Should what?" Burt asked.

"Get the locks changed."

Chapter 15

None of us immediately followed Brown out of Allen's apartment and down the stairs. Glady, Bonny, and I sat silent, maybe fumbling with the emotions and realities surrounding what had happened to the man who'd lived here. Burt gently snored.

Being the building's half story, the apartment had sloping ceilings. They met the walls at about my shoulder height. Walls and ceiling were paneled in the same beadboard as the shop. Up here, the beadboard had been left unpainted, and the bare pine gave the place the feel of being in a log cabin.

Glady roused herself first. She roused Burt by reaching over and holding his nose until he startled awake for air. "Speaking of changing the locks," she said, "we should check the fridge for lox or anything else that will spoil." She levered herself up, and we heard her exclaiming over cheese, fruit, eggs, milk, a couple of chops, fresh scallops—

"Forget the list," Burt said. "Find me a couple of bags, and I'll cart it home. Unless you want some, Maureen?"

"Thanks, you go ahead and take it." The idea of eating from a dead man's fridge didn't appeal. Browsing a dead man's bookshelves, on the other hand . . . I crossed the room to a bookcase with old hardbacks. Some spines were faded or frayed, some had dust jackets in varying condition, some were leather. There were books in slipcases, too. Many of the titles I could read had to do with shells.

"Oof," Glady said from the kitchen. "I was going to ask when Allen started eating Brussels sprouts, but he obviously didn't start soon enough. These are going in the garbage, Burt. You can tie up the bag and take it out. And I've changed my mind. We have plenty at our house. We'll offer this to someone else. Let's go see what it'll take to get the shop ready and sparkling for when you reopen."

Glady started down the stairs. Burt followed with the garbage. Bonny and I brought up the rear.

"Should I reopen?" My words fell down the stairs after Glady.

"You came all this way, and it's what Allen would want you to do. It's what the island needs you to do. The Moon Shell is an institution." Hands on her hips, Glady looked around at the fingerprint powder. "Black powder on light backgrounds. White powder on dark. One of the tips I picked up at a mystery writers' conference." With one of her ever-present tissues, she swiped at some of both colors. "This will be easy. Won't take us any time at all."

"I wonder if it's legal for me to run the shop," I said. And how could I do it without knowing the basics and the financial and tax situation? "Did he have a lawyer?"

"The only likely suspect in Ocracoke is Daniel Umstead," Glady said.

"But Allen could have had any number of lawyers in other places," Burt said.

"Really?" What smalltown merchant has any number of lawyers in places other than nearby? And why?

"Cleaning supplies are in the stockroom," Glady said. "Grab some cloths on your way back from dumping the garbage, Burt."

"Let me do that," I said. "I need to learn my way around. Garbage and cleaning are a good place to start."

"Excellent." Burt handed over the bag and opened a door to the right of the locked display case. "This room and the office were bedrooms in the old days. Identical, except this one has an outside door. Garbage tote's to the left when you go through it."

I opened that outside door, and as I stepped through, I froze with one foot in the air. I knew who Glady and Burt thought I was, but who did I think *I* was by going along with it? I was at a point of no return, I told myself. Step through the door, dump the garbage, and keep on going, or come back inside and continue this deception. This charade of being the person Allen expected. But if I wasn't up-front about why I was on the island, didn't that make me dishonest? Untrustworthy? Was this an existential crisis, or was running the shop the practical decision anyone would make?

I dumped the garbage. Went back in. Found the cleaning supplies and grabbed a stack of dust cloths. Wondered if Glady expected to help run the shop. Decided I wouldn't mind the help.

"We forgot to tell Frank you were in the office last night," Glady said when I handed her a cloth. "We also forgot to tell him there's a second key to the display case in the desk."

"Does either slip matter?" I asked. "We might want to open the case, and he decided this isn't a crime scene."

"I like to be truthful," Glady said, heading into the office.

"More often than not," Burt added. He took a cloth but made no move to use it.

"Anyway, I don't think I did go in there." I set the rest of the cloths on the table by the door and started wiping down the woodwork.

"Then how did your shoes get in here?" Glady called. "Not to mention your socks."

"Pshaw, Glady," Burt said. "We both know the answer to that."

Together they sang out, "I don't know, but I wish I did."

"You see the problem, don't you?" Glady came out of the office. "If you didn't put them in there, then someone else was here before Burt and I got here. And we got here lickety-split. But if you did put them in there, then you were here longer than we thought you were, and then we have to wonder what you were doing."

I sighed out loud for her benefit. "I see the problem."

"There's another problem with the theory of another person," Glady said. "Why would someone else take off your shoes and put them in the office?"

"In the office and tucked under the desk," Burt said. "I would've missed them, but the reflective stripe on the heel winked when my flashlight caught them."

"Well, I'm sorry I don't have the answer." I tried not to snap at him but definitely heard snip in my voice.

If Burt heard the snip, it didn't bother him. "You also said that you and Patricia Crowley are old friends."

"We are."

"So have you heard back from her yet?" he asked. "You said you left her a message."

"I left a couple—" Patricia! I *had* tried to report the body. When I'd found Allen, I'd sent a text to Patricia. And like the one I sent later, got no answer. Then I'd heard a noise. A voice in those woods. Coming closer. And closer. And I panicked and ran like I've never run before. Ran through the woods, but not to my rental—no, not to that tiny place with only a mattress on the floor that I couldn't crawl under to hide. No, pursued by screaming visions of the dead man, I'd leapt like a winged deer over logs and tangles of vines and raced toward town. Ran to the only other place I could think of—the Moon Shell. And then I'd electrocuted myself. Instant end of panic.

"I *remember*," I said. "I remember why I came here last night. What *drove* me here like a runaway horse. It was nothing but pure, unadulterated panic. I tripped over Allen, heard something in the woods, and ran."

"Nothing routs us but the villainy of our fears."

"Who said that?" I demanded. Surely, they'd heard it, too.

"Who said what?" Burt asked.

"It sounded like a quote. 'Nothing routs us but the villainy of our fears.'"

"Shakespeare," Burt said promptly. "From *Julius Caesar*."

"You're rarely right about lines from Shakespeare," Glady said. "You're not right this time, either. That's from *Othello*."

"They are both wrong, you know," Emrys's voice said from somewhere near the display case. "The quotation *is* Shakespeare but not from either *Othello* or *Julius Caesar*. The line comes from *Cymbeline*."

I kept that information—about the correct citation and the guy doing the correcting—to myself. Wondered if Glady or Burt ever saw ghosts. Wondered how long I could expect extremely realistic aural and visual hallucinations resulting from a concussion to last. Wondered if ghosts can be called extremely realistic.

"You're looking peaky," Glady said.

She said that to me, not to Emrys, who'd appeared again. As a ghost, did he ever look anything *but* peaky? He leaned against the display case, arms crossed, smiling. This was all so strange, but curling into a ball and babbling didn't seem like the option to take. Maybe if I'd been alone in the shop but—

"What do you think, you two," I said. "If you're alone in a haunted shell shop, are you truly alone?"

Was this the kind of philosophical discussion Emrys and Allen had engaged in up there in that cozy living room? Glady and Burt were more interested in staring at me than answering my question. Staring in a way that made me uncomfortable. That might be on me and the way I react to people staring, not on them. So instead of trying them with another philosophical or apocryphal question, I resorted to my refuge when anxious in public—a bad joke. Eying the guy who couldn't really be watching and listening to us with such undisguised interest, I said, "Do you know why I wish I could touch a big rock right now?"

"Now you're *sounding* peaky," Glady said. "I didn't know that was even possible. Burt, bring a chair from the office. We can't have Maureen fainting and hitting her head again."

Burt wheeled a desk chair from the office, rolled it around behind me, and knocked it into the backs of my legs so that I plopped into it. Glady took my hand. I let her hold it for a second or two, then took it back, deciding it was time to stop being so needy.

"What's wrong with her?" Burt asked.

"She wants to touch a big rock." Glady leaned close, peering at one of my eyes, then the other. "Whatever for, hon?"

"Because I'm being a wimp and I want to feel a little boulder."

Emrys groaned and flickered out. Burt, an easy mark, guffawed.

Glady shushed him, then rounded on me. "You're no more a wimp than any of us. Possibly less so and more sensible to boot. The reason you ran here last night might include fright, but the rest of it is simple. Allen invited you. He expected you. He's your contact here on the island. It made *sense* for you to come here in your panic. That's more than my theory of this situation, it's the truth."

I liked the sound of that but had a question. Because when don't I have questions? "I ran here even though I thought I'd just tripped over his body?"

"Ah. That's the next part of my theory. I also think he was

alive when you found him. But I don't think you killed him. I think he told you something."

Was he alive? *Had* he told me something? "But I don't remember that at all, and is that something I'd forget? Glady, do you have Dr. Allred's number? I think I should go see him."

In patented Glady fashion, she screwed up her face and said, "Mmm, no. You really shouldn't."

Chapter 16

Burt went upstairs to wipe Allen's apartment clean of Deputy Brown's avalanche of fingerprint powder.

I cornered Glady, and in case a certain ghost was lurking and could still hear me, I told her why I wanted to see Dr. Allred—loudly. "I want to know that I'm okay after whatever happened happened." But saying it like that, in itself, didn't sound as okay as it should. I tried again. "I don't want anything else abnormal to happen."

"Shh, now, shh," Glady said in an annoyingly placatory way, as if she knew I wasn't normal. "The island will get back to being itself. It *is* getting back to being itself. It always does. And you'll get back to being yourself, too. Shh. It's okay. What abnormal thing do you possibly think will happen?"

A sudden, sharp rapping sounded on the door. We both jumped. Glady's eyes were huge. She'd jumped higher than I had, but she recovered first, laughed, and opened the door. A small, waifish figure stood there—a girl with serious brown eyes, a thick brown braid down her back, and a tiara in the shape of a purple octopus on her head.

"Hello, Corina," Glady said. Before stepping out of the girl's way, Glady looked up and down the street.

The ghost flickered into view. Looking unhappy, he eyed

Corina and flickered out. Bonny, who'd been napping on the stack of dustcloths, hopped down and disappeared behind a display table. Those were a couple of interesting reactions to a child who didn't look to be more than six.

Corina knew what she wanted, though, and Glady wasn't it. She pushed her way past Glady into the shop, then stopped when she saw me. I wasn't what she wanted, either.

"Hi. Nice octopus," I said.

"I'm not supposed to talk to strangers."

"Sorry, my name is Maureen."

"Miss Maureen," Glady said brightly, "this is Corina Ochoa."

"But my real name is Coquina," the child said. She hadn't moved.

Glady left the door open and came around beside me. "Your mama named you Corina. Does she know where you are?"

"Yes."

"Coquinas are beautiful shells," I said. "So tiny and colorful. They're almost my favorite."

"What's your favorite?" Coquina asked.

"I can't make up my mind, so I only have almost favorites," I said. "But I have tons of those."

"See what I can do?" Coquina twirled. If she'd been wearing a skirt instead of purple leggings that matched her octopus, it would have blossomed around her.

"Coquina's mother teaches first grade at our school," Glady said.

"And I'm short like a kindergartner." Coquina twirled again. "But I'm in third grade."

"Tiny like a coquina shell," I said. "And they're practically perfect."

"That's why I changed my name."

"May I call you Coquina?"

"Of course. Want to know why I wear fancy headbands?"

"I do. I can hardly take my eyes off that one."

"That's why I wear it." Coquina touched a finger to her lip, where a cleft had been repaired. "Otherwise people stare."

"Lots of people don't think," Glady said, "and you give them something better to think about. You're a smart girl."

Coquina tried to catch hold of Bonny, who was now slinking toward Allen's office. Bonny got away. Coquina followed the cat to the office door. "I'm looking for Mr. Withrow."

Glady's face started to crumple, but she recovered before Coquina turned back to us. "Mr. Withrow isn't here today, Corina."

"That's what my mother told me. I'm checking because sometimes adults make mistakes, too, and sometimes people come back."

"Come back how?" I asked. Had my voice quavered?

"In a different golf cart. Mr. Withrow wants a new one. He says his has a bad *sol-ehn-oid*. I had two bad *ad-en-oids*, and they had to come out. Do you want to know a *fact-oid*? I like *oid* words."

"Bugs Bunny would call them 'oid woids,'" I said. "*As-ter-oid's* a good one."

"And *hoi-toid*," Glady said. "Speaking of high water, did Mr. Withrow stop by yesterday to see how you and your mom were after the storm?"

Coquina was making a tour of the shop, touching her fingertip to the shells she could reach as she passed. "I couldn't keep track. I cried during the hurricane every time the wind tried to blow our house down, and Mommy cried *after* the hurricane every time someone came to see if it *did* blow down. But it didn't. Mommy said it made her happy-weepy that so many people love us. We had to open the trapdoor."

Horrified, I asked, "To get on the roof?"

Coquina looked at me like I was a *noid*. "The trapdoor is in the floor. We open it to let the water in so the water doesn't make the house float away."

That sounded even more horrifying. "Glady? Is this a thing?"

"Yes, ma'am, it is," Glady said. "I've heard stories of past hurricanes where people broke holes in their floors with axes. A trapdoor saves the trouble of mending the floor."

"Opening the trapdoor made *me* happy-weepy," Coquina said. "I didn't want to float away, but I was afraid of what else might come in with the water."

"What did you think might come in?" I could see shark fins circling in the hole in the middle of my living room floor. The great mouth of a great white gaping wide in the gaping trapdoor of my nightmares. Coquina had other worries.

"Ghosts," she said.

My hand went to my cheek.

"But they'd be better than snakes," she said. "And if it was fish or crabs, we'd catch them and eat them."

I brushed aside the idea of a free seafood dinner. "Why would ghosts come in your trapdoor?"

"If the cemeteries got flooded, the ghosts would have to swim somewhere to be safe. They couldn't fly in through the windows because we closed them. It was raining."

I liked her calm, reasonable explanation. "Makes sense," I said, glancing around. I didn't see or hear anyone ghostlike to corroborate Coquina's theory.

"Do you have a message for Mr. Withrow?" Glady asked.

Coquina made another circuit of the shop before answering. "I'll come back another time. It was nice meeting you, Miss Maureen." With a twirl, she was gone.

"Cute kid," I said. "This trapdoor thing is interesting. Do many houses have trapdoors?"

"Not so many. Not this one or ours."

"It'd be an interesting way to exit a house, wouldn't it?" I asked. "Either on your own or against your will."

"If the villain knocked you out, it would be easier to do it against your will. There isn't much headroom under a house. You'd have to crawl or slither."

"Like the snakes Coquina worried about. Let's turn on the lights," I said, "so we see every bit of the powder." And snakes.

Deputy Brown had used so much fingerprint powder I wondered if we could report him for wasting supplies bought with taxpayer money. The work was mechanical, giving me time to think. There was a lot to think about. I continued wiping surfaces after we'd cleared the last of the powder away and after Glady had gone upstairs to see how Burt was getting on.

I met them at the bottom of the stairs when they came down. "I've been thinking," I said, crowding them a bit so they couldn't ignore me or my thoughts, "and I want to know why *you* don't think I should talk to Dr. Allred. And why you didn't want to call Deputy Brown last night."

"Oh, Frank." Glady flapped a hand. "He just wouldn't have been our first choice."

"But why not?"

"You have to understand that Glady has trust issues," Burt said. "In general. Not just when it comes to Frank."

"I do not. There now, see? I can't even trust my own brother not to malign me in *front* of my back."

They looked at each other and burst into laughter. A couple of jokers. To prove it, Burt gave my shoulder a light punch and laughed again. I was beginning to like them. Kind of.

"Don't worry," Glady said. "Any issues we have with Frank are personal quibbles, not professional ones."

"They sounded professional last night."

Glady cocked her head like a bird. Like a crow eyeing a shiny object. "You've got more than changing the locks worrying you. Spill."

"Even if he searched the shop and apartment last night, and took video and pictures, how could he be so sure there isn't evidence he missed?"

"He collected everything he needs," Burt said. "He asked us about anything missing or misplaced."

"But would you know if something small is missing?" I asked. "A thumb drive? Cash? Or something big that you didn't know Allen had or he'd recently bought? Why is Deputy Brown letting us stay here to wipe away fingerprint powder he spread around by the boatload? Why does he trust us not to mess up potential evidence?"

"He knows us," Burt said.

"He doesn't know me, though, and I don't know him."

"You're with us," Burt said. "The luster of our good intentions rubs off on you."

"Stop preening and listen to what she's saying," Glady said. "She has an outsider's view. Go on, Maureen. What's your worry?"

"What if, judging by our actions last night, he let us come in, stay, and rummage around because he trusts our good intentions to be so thorough, or bumbling, or both, that we contaminate or obliterate evidence he purposely left behind? Or what if he's hoping we leave fingerprints on something?"

"All the better to accuse you with, my dear," Glady said. "Not you specifically you, Maureen. Any one of us."

"Frank as the Big Bad Wolf?" Burt asked. "I'm not sure he's that crafty. What do you think, Glady? Is this the latest manifestation of the zap and the bump on her head, or do you think she's always been this paranoid?"

"Either way, it's further proof her mind's working," Glady said. "But I do agree with you, Burt. There's no way Frank is that cunning."

I wasn't going to try to change their minds if that's what they wanted to believe. I, on the other hand, would try to keep my fingers off incriminating items, although it was probably already too late, and my eye on Deputy Frank Brown. "What about Dr. Allred? Is he the only doctor on the island?"

"He is," Burt said. "And speaking of *All*red, I am *all* out of time for this morning." Looking as though he did it every day, he nonchalantly pulled out his shirttail and used it to turn the doorknob. "See ya."

That left Glady alone with me and my question about Dr. Allred. "Glady, I'd really like to know—"

"Look at the time." Glady headed for the door like she had skates on. "I'm famished. You must be, too. I'll make lunch and bring it over for the two of us. Back before you know it."

Deputy Brown came back even before that.

Chapter 17

Deputy Brown arrived as I started searching the desk in the office. By no stretch of the imagination did Brown's eyes show even a glint of friendliness. My own eyes watered, the last speck of fingerprint powder floating around having landed in one. I blew my nose.

As if that had been a signal, Emrys appeared. "You weep. Are you in distress, Mrs. Nash?"

Brown showed no such curiosity about the state of my eyes or emotions.

"Sorry," I said to Brown. "Something in my eye." I blew my nose again to prove it and so I could study the two men, now standing side by side. They were roughly the same age. Frank Brown was taller. Emrys, despite being a washed-out gray and dead, had a livelier face. A better hat, too.

"Ask the deputy why he went slinking like a fox along Glady and Burt's porch but neglected to knock at their door just now."

I most certainly would. Not a great opening line, though, so I started with something lighter. "Nice to see you again so soon, Deputy." Then I sank my teeth into the ghost's question. "That was you on the Weavers' porch, just now, wasn't it? You should have knocked. Glady and Burt are home."

"There was no need to bother them," Brown said. "I was

verifying part of their story. Checking to see how clearly they can see the windows over here from their porch."

"And can they?" I saw Emrys lean closer, waiting for the answer.

"Their story checks."

Emrys, in the moment before he flickered out, looked disappointed.

Brown glanced around him. "It didn't take you long to get the place cleaned up. So, if Glady and Burt left, why are you still here?"

"That was a whole blizzard of fingerprint powder to deal with." I smiled. He didn't, so I stopped. "We didn't finish that long ago, and I have plenty of other things to do. Get to know the place. Clean a bit more." Watch for flickering ghosts and wandering deputies. "Glady went to make lunch. She's bringing it over. If you didn't expect to find me here, then why did you come?"

"I saw the lights on when I was checking Glady and Burt's story."

"The proof you needed. Good."

"And I was on my way to see you at your rental, anyway."

"I'm still a bit turned around. Howard Street isn't on the way between the sheriff's office and my rental, is it?" It *isn't*. I wasn't *that* turned around.

"I take circuitous routes through the village," he said. "Keep my eye on things. Especially at times like this. Post hurricane. Post murder."

"Post arrival of a stranger."

"All part of my duties. Here's another part. I picked up information for you about reopening the shop."

"That was kind of you. Thanks."

"Don't thank me until you hear what it is. You'll need to talk to Allen's lawyer. He's expecting your call." He handed me a business card for Daniel Umstead, Esquire.

"Glady thought Mr. Umstead might be the lawyer."

He didn't make a move to leave.

"Do you have more questions?" I asked.

"It's like this." His feet shifted. "I'm still trying to piece things together about last night. Do you remember anything more? Like why you were so frightened?"

"Why wouldn't I be? It was getting dark and starting to rain. I was already drenched from the waves. I had trouble finding the path through the woods. That's enough to scare someone, but then I tripped over a guy who'd been stabbed." All that came out in a string of sound like one very long, increasingly shrill word. I took a couple of breaths. "Wouldn't any decent person be frightened out of their usually sane wits?"

"So frightened that you bypassed your rental and ran here?"

He hadn't answered my question, so I didn't answer his. I took out my phone. Brought up my texts to Patricia. "Here. See the time? I did try to get hold of someone. I sent a text to Patricia Crowley. She's a park—"

"I know who she is. Was Allen still alive when you found him?"

"What? No."

"I think he was."

"Why?"

"I have my reasons."

"He was cold when I found him." And now I was cold. Was one of his reasons that Glady had told him *she* thought I'd found Allen alive?

"He was cold when you *say* you found him. I think he was alive until you came along the first time. An *earlier* time. Before your convenient text to Ranger Crowley, who conveniently didn't respond."

"No!" Emrys had been right. Brown had been slinking. Slinking and waiting until he knew I was here alone.

"And I wonder," he said, "why you would kill a man you say you've never met."

"I *didn't*. I would *never*."

"Allen had an envelope in his pocket—stamped and addressed to you."

"Oh, is *that* what you had in your shirt pocket?"

He didn't need to answer. The hand he'd let stray to his shirt pocket over and over, earlier, now tried to sneak around to a back pocket. He caught it in time. Crossed his arms to show that traitorous hand who was boss. "Why would Allen still be writing to you? If he'd hired you and was already expecting you, why would he write another letter? Surely, you exchanged email addresses, phone numbers."

Calm, I thought. Be calm. "If he didn't mail the letter, then I haven't read it, so how would I know what he wrote or why?" That seemed like a reasonable, mostly nonconfrontational question. "When did he write it? Is there a date on it?"

"The envelope was torn open. The letter wasn't inside."

"Then how do you know it was a letter?"

"Call it an enclosure of unknown description then," Brown said. "Did you look through his pockets and take it?"

"No. I didn't take anything from his pockets or anywhere else." I didn't add *eeuw*, but I was sure my face did, then decided to verbalize it, anyway. "That would've been horrible. Horrible to do, to think of doing, to experience, and a really awful, horrible thing for you to suggest I did."

"So who did take it?"

"*I* don't know. He might have taken it out himself."

"Why would he do that?"

"If he thought better of sending it. If the information in it was redundant."

"Or you found out, after driving five hundred miles, that he'd changed his mind about hiring you, and you didn't like that."

"And killed him? Over a long trip and a job as a clerk in a shop? A job that, for your information, I don't need? Please feel free to check my financial situation on that, Deputy Brown. Come on. That's a lame reason to kill a person. *All* reasons for killing someone are lame."

"Not everyone feels that way," Brown said.

"Thank goodness most people do. If you find someone who doesn't, Deputy, they'll make a better suspect."

"Who?"

I looked for patience in a corner of the ceiling, noticed cobwebs I'd need to get down, sighed, and looked back at Frank Brown. "I don't know the people Allen knew. I don't know who killed him. I don't know if you're looking for two people or one person with two weapons. I only know that I didn't kill him. Wait . . . wait . . ."

Brown's turn to seek patience. He did a good job of it.

"There's another reason I panicked. I heard a voice. After I sent the text to Patricia."

"Why didn't you mention—"

"My memory of last night is Swiss cheese. I wish you knew how awful that is and how sorry I am that it's making things harder for you. But parts of it keep flickering back." Like ghosts. Weird.

Brown took out his phone, tapped in a few notes. "Did this person say anything?"

"Maybe. I don't know. I remember hearing the voice coming closer. I absolutely freaked, so maybe it did say something. That's why I didn't go to the rental. I thought I was being chased and was afraid to be caught in that tiny place with no one else around. So I ran here."

"Good stamina. You must be a runner."

"I keep fit enough." I appreciated that he hadn't looked me over when he said that. He tapped steadily on his phone.

Emrys flickered back into view, behind Brown and reading

over his shoulder. "He has taken down your words almost ver-
batim."

Heartened, I mustered the courage I hadn't had in the
woods the night before. "Deputy Brown, at the point last
night, as the Weavers and I were leaving, you spoke to Allen.
May I ask why?"

He screwed up his mouth, as if it might want to answer but
his brain didn't. His mouth won the argument. "It's what I'd
tell anyone who went and got themselves killed on my watch."

To the door that closed behind him, I said, "I don't think so."

"You don't believe him?" Emrys asked. "What did he say?"

"It sounded more personal. For Allen in particular. He said,
'You've always been more trouble than you're worth.'"

Chapter 18

"Mr. Lloyd," I said. "Emrys. Will you do me the favor of joining me in the office? I'd like some information, and I'd like to sit down. It's been quite a morning. Quite an evening and night, too."

"Then it will be my pleasure."

It was then I learned a lesson in Ghost 101. They don't just disappear when they flicker. They reappear somewhere else within the twinkling of that flicker. Emrys had been standing next to the locked display case when he agreed to join me. When I turned toward the office, he smiled at me from behind the office desk. Disconcerting and annoying. I might have complained, but what did I know of ghost tempers and the results thereof? At least he waited until I brought a spindly spindle-back chair from the corner for myself before seating himself, with a flip of his coattails, in the more comfortable desk chair.

Allen's office, like his apartment, had the understated, mellow look of money. The desk, a couple of bookcases, and my chair were antiques. Different woods, different eras, but the muted finish on each of them glowed. It was interesting to see the modern ergonomic desk chair *through* Emrys. Another beautiful woven rug covered the floor. A lovely, large seascape hung on the wall behind Emrys.

"What sort of information are you looking for?" Emrys asked. With his elbows on the chair's armrests and his fingers tented, he looked like a bank manager or therapist about to leave for a costume party.

"Do you ever take your hat off?"

The bank manager was affronted.

"Sorry. That was a real question, though. I want to know how ghosts work. You can understand that, can't you? You've had two hundred and seventy-four years to get used to this. It's all new to me."

"I am sorry, as well," Emrys said. "Being asked questions about what I now am is new to me."

"Allen didn't ask questions?"

"It's curious, but he seemed incurious." Emrys tapped his fingertips together. "Sam Jones used to quote a fellow named Ward. 'Curiosity is the wick in the candle of learning.' So to answer your question, my hat comes off"—he lifted it—"but it does not have a separate existence."

Made sense. I've never heard of separate sightings of phantom clothes or accessories. "Did Sam Jones see or hear you?"

"No. Ikey D., on the other hand, enjoyed my singing around the piano. A capital horse. Good company."

"You have a beautiful singing voice."

"I'm Welsh. We're known for our singing."

"I've heard that, but I guess I thought it was a myth."

"You didn't think ghosts existed, either."

"Did you believe in ghosts before you died?"

"I heard credible tales of hauntings. My own grandfather took to drink after confronting the ghost of his grandfather."

"Maybe it's genetic and your family is prone to ghostiness."

"We're Welsh, not Genetic. But you may be right and it is a family peculiarity. There are certainly more things in heaven and earth, Mrs. Nash, than are dreamt of in our philosophies." He smiled. "I might be embellishing the original quotation."

And I might still be hallucinating. "Can you appear and disappear when you want to?"

"Oftimes, but a ghost is not an agent of free will," he said. "Please understand, however, that I can only speak from my own experience."

"You don't know other ghosts? Do you see other ghosts?"

"Only a very few." He looked more matter-of-fact about it than "woe is me."

"So you aren't free to choose who or where you haunt?"

"Neither where nor when."

"That sounds so limiting."

"As would be a grave."

"But what about *who* you haunt? Who else sees you or is aware of you? Can you control that? And if not, then why me?"

The crux of the situation. I sat forward. He pondered. Then he shrugged. A *tsk* escaped me.

"I cannot give you information I don't have. I can only surmise. That we are sitting across from one another, conversing, might have something to do with your recent bereavement."

"I feel like it's recent. There's a tendency for people to think a year is enough time for grieving."

"Continue listening to your heart," Emrys said. "Ignore the tongues of those who do not know the depth of loss. If I could speak to my wife one more time, I would tell her that."

I took a moment with a tissue.

Emrys offered another theory. "The jolt of electricity might have created our connection."

"It might." I nodded, thinking about that. There was a problem with his first theory. This one made more sense. If anything made sense anymore. "If the connection is through bereavement, what about people on the island who've lost loved ones? Have any of them seen you?"

"Not that I am aware. But I don't always know what is true

or what has happened. I am of this time but sometimes . . . not. It's an inconvenience I live with."

What a pickle. The second pickle since meeting Emrys. Here we both sat, neither of us knowing truth from figment or fantasy. The mirrorlike quality of this fellow was unsettling.

"Here's something *I'm* not aware of," I said. "Burt found my shoes under that desk last night, and I don't know how they got there."

"Then I must confess. I removed them and placed them under the desk."

"*You* took my shoes off?"

"I thought you'd be more comfortable. Lying on the floor in a heap, as you were."

"And your first thought was 'How tragic. Her shoes must come off and go under the desk in another room?'"

"It was a moment of some alarm for me. Perhaps I wasn't thinking clearly. But if you knew how uncomfortable my own shoes are . . ." He brought his foot up—through the desk—and showed me the stiff sole of his shoe.

"Real torture, huh? You might say your shoes feel like hell?"

"A tasteless joke and worth remembering. Thank you. My father was a cobbler, you see, so I know what a good shoe should feel like. These, I can tell you, ain't them, and I'm apparently destined to spend eternity plagued by them."

"That's an aspect of ghosthood I've never considered," I said.

"I also have not previously had the opportunity to study modern footwear such as yours."

"The Moon Shell's customers don't wear shoes?"

"Study them at my leisure," he said. "Without the feet inside them. I imagine some of those feet are nearly as unpleasant to smell as old cabbage."

"So you can do that?" I mimicked untying shoes. "You can manipulate objects?"

"To some extent. Small items. Over short distances. Open and shut a door." If he'd been embarrassed by his shoe confession, he'd recovered. He was pleased, to no end, that he could close a door or move small items.

He flickered away again, without a goodbye, leaving me to wonder if he considered a chef's knife small.

My stomach rumbled. Glady hadn't come back yet. Perfect time to find Dr. Allred's phone number myself. She and Burt did an awful lot of telling me what I shouldn't or didn't want to do. Now I wanted to hop online and . . . yes. A few taps on my phone revealed a number for Dr. Irving Allred, physician, Ocracoke.

"I'm going out on the porch," I announced to the possibly empty shop. "I'd like some privacy to make a phone call." I backed through the front door, saw no flickers, heard no humming, no singing. I turned around to find Emrys sitting on the porch railing.

"I thought you might like time and space alone to turn matters over in your mind," he said.

Was he naturally this considerate, or had he heard me say I wanted privacy? Or were all the coincidences between us part of . . .

"Thank you." With a shuddering breath, I stepped back inside, closed the door, and called Dr. Allred's number. Allred answered, listened to my request for an appointment to see him, and said he wasn't taking new patients.

"I've had an accident," I pleaded. "Storm related. I'll only be a temporary patient. Short term. I don't have any way to get to Hatteras or the mainland."

"If bleeding or broken bones are involved, call the helicopter," Dr. Allred said. "My office is a hurricane victim, too." He sounded testy, but anyone with hurricane damage might.

"No blood or broken bones. It's a good bump on my head. Probably from whatever happened."

"You don't know what happened? Then how can you expect me to help you? Let me be clear. I do not prescribe drugs of any kind over the phone."

"I wouldn't take drugs you prescribed over the phone." Two can be testy. "I don't know what happened, but apparently I was shocked when I turned on a lamp and I hit my head when I fell on the floor. I don't know if I blacked out before or after hitting the floor."

"Did this happen at the Moon Shell?" His voice had brightened.

"Yes."

"Are you the Nash woman? The one who found Allen Withrow's body?"

"Yes."

"Are there any obvious burns to your fingers from the shock? Or burns anywhere else?"

"No."

"Then at a guess you have a concussion. Try not to do too much. Stay quiet. Get some rest. I wouldn't worry. You sound lucid. Now I really must be go—"

"Wait. Please. Can concussions result in hallucinations?"

"They can."

"Wow. Okay. That's a relief." And, oddly, a disappointment. Intellectually, concussion made more sense, but my storyteller's mind wanted to believe . . .

Allred interrupted my disappointment. "Tell me about your hallucinations. Describe them."

"I hear voices. *A* voice. See a person who sort of flickers in and out."

"Does anyone else see or hear this person?" Allred asked, his voice excited. "What does he look like? How is he— But I'm getting ahead of you. Is it male or female?"

Now that I was talking about it, I didn't want to. I didn't use the word *ghost*.

"Ms. Nash, are you familiar with tokens of death?

"No."

"Some people see them shortly before a death. The token might come in a dream. It might be an unusual occurrence, like a rooster crowing at noon."

"Sounds interesting." Sounded creepy. "How does this tie in—"

"I saw one before Allen died. When did you arrive on the island?"

"Yesterday."

"Ah, yes. I should have guessed. I would like to meet you, Ms. Nash. I would like to see you for an appointment."

"I thought you weren't taking appointments." He was leaping at me through the phone. If I was using a landline, and I were in a cartoon, I'd see a bulge in the wire and he'd spurt out the receiver and land on the floor at my feet. Instead, I pictured him erupting from the "home" button on my cell like a genie from the spout of a brass lamp.

"Are you still there?"

"Yes, sorry."

"I was saying that I will happily make an exception with an appointment for you."

"Well, I don't—"

"Tell me, are you familiar with the term *paramnesia*?"

"No." It didn't sound like anything I wanted to be familiar with, either. Garden variety hallucinations were enough to contend with. I peeked out the window. My recently bloomed hallucination was nowhere in sight.

"Do you know what a jellyfish is?" Allred asked.

"A *what*?"

"Oh ho! You don't know the word? Extraordinary. What about *kayak*?"

"A jellyfish is type of cnidarian and a kayak is a narrow boat. Why are you asking me this?"

"To paraphrase," Allred's voice quacked in my ear, "paramnesia is a condition sometimes characterized by a sufferer not remembering the proper meaning of words."

"Then I think we can skip a diagnosis of paramnesia. Thanks for your time, Dr. Allred—"

"Forget the jellyfish and kayaks and hear me out. Please," Allred said, trying to squeeze through the phone again. "Paramnesia also manifests in distorted memories. Confusions of fact and fantasy. Confabulation and déjà vu. That sort of thing."

"Oh."

"Yes. Fascinating stuff. A psychiatrist, a German, coined the term in the late 1800s. One of the three varieties of paramnesia he identified is called simple memory deceptions, that is, the sufferer remembers, as genuine, events she imagined or *hallucinated* in fantasy or dream. It is not uncommon in confused and amnesiac people. It also occurs in paranoid states."

Par-a-noid. There was a good word for Coquina.

"Would you characterize yourself as suggestible, Ms. Nash?"

"Not that I know of." Although I was tempted to tell him yes, now that he'd suggested it.

"I ask because suggestible personalities are more prone to confabulation. Do you consider yourself an introvert?"

"Pretty much. What's that got to do with it?"

"An introvert who can hold her own in social situations, even if somewhat superficially?"

He streamed on without waiting for my answer, maybe guessing that he'd gotten it in one.

"From what I've read online, that is, through my research," he said, "superficially sociable but basically secretive personalities are particularly prone to confabulate. Now, what suits you best? I can fit you in this afternoon or tomorrow morning, or if you prefer, I can make a house call. Where are you staying?"

At that question, I made a snap decision—possibly a flaw in

my basically secretive personality. My current hallucination, I decided, the one with the lovely accent and beautiful singing voice, suited me more—an astronomical number of times more—than an appointment with the overeager Dr. Allred. Glady had been right. I did not want to talk to him. Hoping I'd made the right snap decision, I hit the disconnect button.

Chapter 19

Lunch arrived via bike, with Glady wheeling it over. "The bike's for you," she said, propping it against the porch railing. "Until you can get your car over on the ferry."

"You're so kind." I was sitting in the sun on the front steps again, Dr. Allred and his tokens of death having put a chill in my bones.

"Come and see her." Glady patted the saddle. "You won't win the Tour de France with her, but she's got good tires, brakes, and—" She rang a bell on the handlebars, then handed me a small key. "There's a cable lock in the basket."

It was an old blue Schwinn with balloon tires and coaster brakes, the kind made for girls decades ago. A metal market basket hung from the handlebars. A wicker picnic basket sat in the market basket.

"She's perfect, Glady. I already feel free and easy." Also wary. Should I let myself become more entangled with the Weavers? On top of being entangled in a murder case? Not to mention—I looked at the porch, at the shop windows, and the dormer window above. No ghost, no flickers, no one singing or humming about drunken sailors. I sighed. Keeping myself to myself seemed prudent.

"Grilled cheese with fig jam," Glady said, picking up the picnic basket. "Still warm when I left the house."

Prudence is for sissies, I decided. Besides, as Jeff liked to say, always trust neighbors bearing warm, great-smelling food.

We ate in the office, Glady taking the desk chair while apologizing for not inviting me across the street to the house she and Burt shared.

"He's in the middle of a project," she said. "Another boat in a bottle. Excuse me a moment." She shouted in the direction of their house, "*Ship* in a bottle." She took a healthy bite of her sandwich. After washing it down with tea she'd brought for us in a thermos, she said, "He hates it when I call them boats."

"He makes the ships himself and puts them in bottles?"

"It's not quite as simple as 'putting' but yes, he does, and he makes the mess to prove it."

"I'd like to see his work sometime, and I don't mind mess. Jeff used to build parts of his stage sets in our living room."

"Well, you don't want to see Burt's mess. Correction. *I* don't want you to see Burt's mess. Ask him to show you pictures next time you see him. Of the boats and bottles, not the mess," she said with a shudder.

I was glad she corrected herself because the recurring theme of her or Burt telling me what I did or didn't want to know or do irked me. My phone buzzed with a text. I glanced at it. Allred. My turn to shudder. Point to Glady for her warning about Dr. Allred.

"Glady, about Dr. Allred."

She stopped with her sandwich halfway to her mouth. "What about him?"

"Is he all right? I mean, as a doctor, is he kind of—"

"A quack?"

"I didn't want to say that." I *did* want to, but if I didn't like the idea of him judging me by our phone call, then extending him the same courtesy seemed only fair. "I just wonder what your beef is with him."

"Pussyfooting around a label for Dr. Allred is very kind, and kindness is a plus in your favor. I think I do like you."

"Was the jury out?"

"It'll be out for years," she said happily. "That's the wonderful balancing game between newcomers and communities, isn't it? Newcomers working like mad to fit in—trying to be so agreeable, volunteering for this and that, bringing interesting salads to potlucks—and the jurists of the community endlessly deliberating. Why did you ask about Dr. Allred?"

My phone buzzed again. I looked at it. Oozing guilt.

"What have you done? Oh, dear." Glady shook her head. "Will it help if I say I told you so? Probably not. Well, come on. Out with it."

I told her about the phone call.

"You didn't make an appointment, did you? You didn't tell him where you're staying?

"Glady, wait. You can't ask me those questions without telling me what you know about him."

"Dr. Allred, Irv to his friends—" Glady stopped with an exhausted sigh. "By the way, no matter how many times he asks me to call him Irv, and no matter how good the macaroni and cheese is that he brings to annual meetings of the Library Friends, I will never call him Irv. He's putting out feelers about opening a side practice in alternative medicine and parapsychology, so I've heard."

"You might have heard right. But if that's a new sideline, what *is* your beef with him?"

"It's new as a business venture, but he's always had tendencies in that direction. He gravitates toward people who are hurting."

"Isn't that a good quality for a doctor to have?"

"It's the *way* he gravitates," she said. "As if he can smell misery. He looms over the suffering. Which is hard for him because he's no taller than I am. It isn't good for his medical practice. Maybe that's why he's branching out. Burt and I call him the Shroud."

"He said he saw a token of death before Allen died."

"Of course, he did."

"You believe him?" I asked.

"Of course, I don't."

"He asked when I arrived on the island. I told him yesterday, and he said he should have guessed."

"He'll know some superstition associated with Mondays and bad luck and death. I wouldn't worry, though. Stay away from him, if you can, but he's mostly harmless."

"Speaking of superstitions, I'd still like to hear how you feel about crows."

"Simple," Glady said. "I love them. Did you know they use and make tools? We have an old bird feeder platform out back. I put shiny objects on it. The crows come and take them and leave me twigs in exchange. It irritates Burt. He says the crows cheat me on the exchange rate."

"Maybe they haven't found the right shiny thing to bring you yet. There's a bird feeder platform out the kitchen window at my rental. I mean right outside. There was a cat on it this morning looking in at me. A pretty ginger tabby."

"With one docked ear?" Glady brushed a hand across the tip of where her ear would be if she were a cat.

"I didn't notice."

"Didn't notice or don't remember?" Glady asked.

I didn't like my new termite-ridden memory and dug for details. "I waved at it," I said, proving that not all details were slippery. "I thought about inviting it in for breakfast."

"Don't," Glady said.

"I didn't."

"It wouldn't have come in, anyway," Glady said.

"You're right. It looked happy sitting there in the sun until I opened the window to say hi."

"*If* it had a docked ear, it's an Ocracat," Glady said. "A cat from one of the feral colonies on the island. The dock indicates it's been live-trapped and spayed or neutered."

Glady stopped talking and stared intently at a spot some-where in front of her. I looked over my shoulder to see if Emrys had joined us. I hadn't seen or heard him since I'd seen him sitting on the porch railing. Before I talked to Dr. Allred.

"What is it, Glady? What are you looking at?"

"Nothing." She gave herself a shake. "Thinking of a young man, Noah Hampton. Horning. *Horton*. That's it."

"What about him?"

"Your Ocracat made me think of him. He's big into the Oc-racat scene. Not a local. A summer visitor who seems to be staying. It's more than Ocracats, though. He's concerned with animal rights in general. Nothing wrong with that. At all. But you won't want to get on his bad side."

Another warning about what I should not want. "Can you explain why?"

"Not really," she said. "And I know—that's not helpful and maybe proves I don't know what I'm talking about. But in a small community you see things and hear things and they don't always mean anything until you add them up."

"What's your addition coming to on Noah?"

"I wonder if Allen got on his bad side."

"Any idea how?"

"Various possibilities," Glady said.

"That's not very specific," I said, thinking of her *various ghosts* remark the night before. "But if you know something, you should tell Frank Brown.

"That's just it. I have nothing concrete. I've barely spoken to Noah. He might have left the island before the storm."

"Glady, do you think I killed Allen?"

"What? No. Where did you get that idea?"

"Deputy Brown came back, after you and Burt left, and ac-cused me of killing Allen."

"Why?"

"Because I found Allen. And because Allen had an empty

envelope, addressed to me, in his pocket. That's opportunity and motive."

"That's poppycock," Glady said. "Now, why are you smiling at a time like this?"

"I'm an optimist. We agree that's poppycock. We see that Frank Brown is happy to investigate poppycock. So, you can tell him your worry about Noah Horton. If it turns out to be poppycock, no harm done."

"And if we happen to run into Noah, we can pump him for information."

"I don't know, Glady. Do you really think that's a good idea?"

"Don't worry. I was exaggerating. We won't pump him. We'll ask artful questions to elicit the information we're looking for from our suspects. Do you know how many scenes I've written like that in my books?"

"Sus*pect*," I said. "You said suspects. Noah is one suspect."

"There's always more than one suspect in an investigation. Oh, wait until I tell Burt."

Glady left, leaving me feeling the way I'd felt so often since landing on Ocracoke. Correction: the way I'd felt so often since the wallowing, floundering, near-foundering boat ride over. That feeling? Shell-shocked. And that thought set me laughing to the point of tears until I heard my phone buzz with another text. Probably Allred reporting another token of death. *Woooooo,* I thought. *Ooga booga booga.*

The text was from Patricia. "**Heard about Allen. Sorry. Remember our agreement? Hope nothing else awful happens during the rest of your stay.**"

So then I had to wonder how paranoid I really was and how much Patricia regretted giving me that boat ride. Because was that a threat in her text, or was she sorry she'd seen me?

Chapter 20

The snarky and the profane—I composed three texts of the first variety and two of the second in response to Patricia's possibly threatening message. I deleted each one without hitting send. Temper and nerves under control, I sent **"No worries. Agreement remembered. Take care**." Now, if she'd sent "**take care**" to me, would I have seen *that* as a threat? Very possibly, because it turns out that tripping over bodies and being electrocuted, accused of murder, and flickered at by ghosts makes me jumpy and irritable. As the ghost might say, "Fancy that!"

I jumped when the ghost himself flickered into the desk chair as I was adding sarcastic to irritable and jumpy. "I wasn't sure you were coming back," I said.

"I was here. Around," he said airily. "I heard Glady say that you are embarking on an investigation of Allen's murder and will soon be questioning suspects. I believe I can make a valuable contribution to the effort."

"You mean you were in the other room listening to us the whole time we ate lunch?"

"No. I was . . . otherwise occupied. I do hear conversations from time to time, though, and phone calls. Allen had several recent phone conversations that left him spitting oaths not fit for womanly ears."

"You also read texts over people's shoulders. Did you listen to my call to Dr. Allred?"

"I gave you privacy for your call." Emrys leaned across the desk—through it—to peer at me more closely. With concern? Worry? I didn't know. The emotional capacity of ghosts, so far, escaped me. "Don't you remember?"

"I do. Sorry. These phone calls could be important. Do you know who Allen was talking to? What he said?"

"The oaths were quite blasphemous. Beyond his anger, I'm afraid they're all that stuck in my mind. However, I was aware that Allen had plans underway to make some sort of change that meant a great deal to him."

"Glady and Burt think he was hiring someone to help him run the shop."

"I cannot say what the change was."

"Can't say because it's a secret or you don't know?" I asked.

"I don't know if hiring someone was the change. I do know that he had not hired you."

"How do you know that?"

"You never once volunteered the information that he had, yet when others brought it up, you let them assume such is the case. As far as secrets are concerned, I am good at keeping them, if you ever want to tell me why you really came here."

We stared at each other, unblinking, for a moment. He could do that longer than I could. "Thank you. Did you come with us to Ikey D.'s grave last night?"

"No."

"Why not?"

"I am somewhat of a homebody," he said. "Without the body. Why do you ask?"

"You might have seen something the rest of us missed. Did you see anyone come in the shop yesterday?"

"Alas, no. I don't keep track of the custom flowing in and out."

"There wouldn't have been much flow, if any. Everything's still closed because of the storm."

"There is also the issue of being caught in a pattern." He cocked an eyebrow. "You really are not familiar with ghosts?"

"Only cartoon ghosts and ghosts in books and movies. So far they pale to the real thing."

"The tales I heard described specters that repeat a pattern. A gray lady will be seen to walk a corridor over and over, never varying.

"I have heard stories like that," I said. "It sounds like being caught in a film loop."

He raised the eyebrow again.

"It's like a circle of—I'll tell you about it another time. So what's your loop? Your pattern?"

"The shell."

"Walking back and forth to it?"

"Nothing so active. My entire focus is on the shell, with no conscious awareness of anything else. As though the shell is my lifeline, my source of breath and heartbeat."

"Wow. That's intense. Somehow I don't picture the gray lady having such a compelling need to walk down her corridor. Any idea why that's your pattern?"

"I can't be certain, but I've had several centuries to contemplate the phenomenon. The shell was meant to be a present for my wife."

"And she was your source of breath and heartbeat."

"She was the prevailing wind in my life."

"That's beautiful."

"It's a paraphrase from a recent obituary I particularly liked."

"You read obituaries?" I asked.

"And I like literary quotations. As my father said, it is the sign of a well-read man."

"Previous question," I said. "You read obituaries?"

"Every morning. I suppose that's another pattern. A *loop*."

"How? The Ocracoke paper's a monthly."

"I go to the library. They subscribe to several papers."

The idea charmed me, but . . . "How do you read them without people seeing the pages turn?"

"I go before they open for the day and have the place to myself. I also read the *New York Times*."

"But if you're attached to the shell, and the shell is locked in a display, how does going to the library work?"

"Shell if I know."

"What else do you do? When you're not looping on the shell?"

"Watch Glady entice the crows and Burt shoo them away as soon as her back is turned. My wife liked crows. I think of her when I see them."

"Feeding them is supposed to be good luck."

"That's what she said, and it must be true for I was never shot and drowned in Virginia."

"*That's* how you died? I'm so sorry." I felt bad that I hadn't asked for those details earlier. Then again, when had I ever asked anyone how they'd died?

"An unfortunate business," he said. "The bitterness eventually wore off. And now I have no need to lure crows with food or trinkets. They have a natural affinity for my, shall we say, spirit." His gaze strayed to the office doorway. To the corner of the locked display case, visible from that angle. No flickering, but I rushed to ask a few more questions.

"When Glady and I left the shop last night, you said you'd stand by to repel boarders. Were you expecting them?"

"A phrase." He waved it off. "I did not know that anyone would try to get in, but evil walked the woods, and I thought it best to prepare for it to leave the woods and climb the front stair. 'Be wary then; best safety lies in fear.' That's *Hamlet*."

"You were right, too. The person who left the footprints came along. But wait a second. You said you don't know who came in the shop yesterday, but also said you were kidnapped along with the shell. Do you know who took the shell? How it got to Springer's Point?"

He sank his forehead into his hands. "It was the pattern. The confounded loop. They happen at inopportune times. I would call it a weakness, but I seem helpless to break the hold."

"Think about other days then. Can you remember anyone who paid a lot of attention to the shell?"

"The child. Corina. She likes hearing the ocean in it."

"So Allen let people hold it? Did he take it out of the case often?"

"No, and I found it upsetting when he did."

A thought flickered through my mind. The ghost of a thought. Did Emrys kill Allen in a fit of rage over the shell? Could he do that? How safe was this guy?

Chapter 21

I rode my borrowed bike to Daniel Umstead's office the next morning. The route took me cruising past the lighthouse and in a swoop around the man-made harbor called Silver Lake, past businesses shaking off the damage and debris left by Hurricane Electra. Seagulls cheered me on as I headed toward the Ocracoke Island Discovery Center, then laughed after me when I turned left onto Water Plant Road. I'd called lawyer Umstead after leaving the shop the afternoon before. He'd cordially invited me to be his first appointment of the day.

Umstead's office was in a small, white clapboard outbuilding in the yard beside his house. It looked as crisp as a well-starched shirt, like the shirt Daniel Umstead wore. He met me at the door, his manner as cordial as his voice had been on the phone. He looked old enough to have retired from a practice somewhere inland. Slim, slightly stooped, and unsurprising. The surprise was Captain Rob Tate of the sheriff's department, already there, joining our meeting.

Tate looked as fit as Deputy Brown but a decade or so older—maybe midforties. He stood when Umstead ushered me in. When Umstead made introductions, Tate shook my hand without trying to crush it. He had a soft, calm voice, and I pictured him talking that way to skittish island ponies.

"I'm sorry for your loss," Tate said as we took our seats.

"Thank you." I couldn't help feeling like a skittish, mistrusting pony. As a policeman, maybe he was used to that reaction. From suspects. He'd obviously talked to Brown. Confirming that, he said he knew the story of my finding Allen's body and me arriving to help run the shop. But did he lean heavily on the word *story*? Heavily enough that the poor little word carried extra baggage, including the words *Do you have anything to hide?* His voice remained calm, though, with no undercurrents.

Umstead's resting face was the picture of congeniality. "You said you have question for me, Ms. Nash. What can I do for you?"

"The Weavers and I are wondering about reopening the Moon Shell. Can we do that? How does that work, legally?"

"Unless Captain Tate objects, the decision is yours."

"It's that simple?"

"You look surprised, and I'm not surprised by that." Umstead smiled. "I'll explain. Captain Tate wants to hear the details of Allen's will. I have information that will be of benefit to you beyond opening the shop. I like efficiency, so here we three are."

He perched a pair of half-moon tortoiseshell reading glasses on his nose. "I'll skip the mumbo jumbo part of the will and read the important part. 'I, William Allen Withrow, being of sound mind and body, hereby bequeath my business, legally incorporated under the name Moon Shell, and the rest of my estate to Jeffrey Cullman Nash, or his legal heir or heirs, should he precede me in death.'" Umstead looked at me over the tops of his glasses. "The building isn't part of the business. I'll give you information about the building's owners before you leave. The rest of Allen's estate includes a piece of sound side shoreline property. Is this what you expected to hear?"

I slowly shook my head while madly thinking, *This makes me not only the stranger in the village who says I tripped over Allen's body, but also the owner of his business with its valuable inventory. Holy moly.* Out loud, I asked, "Is there an explanation in the mumbo jumbo you skipped?"

"There isn't," Umstead said, "and I didn't ask for one."

"Did it surprise you that he made no other bequests?" Tate asked.

Umstead blinked his eyes. "How often are you surprised in your line of work, Rob?"

"At least once a day. Sometimes twice," Tate said.

"Wait until you're my age," said Umstead. "I almost never am."

"When did he make the will?" I asked.

"It's signed fifteenth June 2023."

"Ms. Nash?" Tate asked. "You have no idea why he did this?"

"I'm completely floored."

"I can see how you might be," Tate said. "But I have to ask you again—Do you have any idea why Allen Withrow left his estate to your husband and, by extension, to you?"

Giving me a motive to kill him. "I have no idea at all, but—" I grabbed the small bottle of water Umstead moved across the desk toward me. Wrestled with the lid, drank half of it. "I have no idea what connection existed between Allen and my husband, but it might be why I'm here. Why I came to Ocracoke."

"We are all ears," said Umstead. He offered a bottle of water to Tate and opened one for himself. He sat back, his ears perked.

"I have something," I said. "I don't know what's going on, but I have something you need to see." Without taking my eyes off the two men, I pulled my shoulder pack off. Unzipped the pocket. Slid my hand in, brought out three letters, in their postmarked envelopes, and put two of them on the desk. "These two arrived three months apart. The first one is postmarked the day after Allen signed that will. The second arrived a month before my husband died." I set the third letter beside the others. "This one came six weeks ago."

Tate and Umstead looked at the envelopes without touching them, then at me.

"From the Moon Shell?" Umstead asked.

"From Allen. Jeff thought they were a joke or a scam."

"But he didn't throw them away," Tate said.

"Read them and you'll see why," I said. "They're like a story in an old novel—claiming to be Jeff's uncle with information to his advantage. Jeff loved stuff like that. The letters tickled him, but not enough to answer them. He had no uncles named Withrow. No relatives at all by that name."

Tate read the letters in order, passing each one on to Umstead as he finished it. When he'd passed the third letter to the lawyer, he sat back with a single word. "Interesting."

Umstead started to return the letters to their envelopes, then stopped. "I'd like to make copies of these if no one minds."

"Make two sets," Tate said without waiting to see whether I minded or not. "Give one set to Ms. Nash. I'll keep the originals for the time being. Copies of the envelopes, too."

We waited, silent, until Umstead returned.

"Presumably, what your husband would have learned 'to his advantage' is the contents of the will," Tate said.

"I wish he was here," I said. "This would have blown his mind."

"What do you make of it, Dan?" Tate asked.

"The letters don't offer any more explanation for the bequest than the will," Umstead said. "It makes me think Allen expected Jeff Nash to know the reason."

"Why do Glady and Burt think Allen hired you to help him at the shop?" Tate asked. "Did you contact Allen? Did he know you were coming?"

"They assumed that when they found me out cold in the shop Monday. I had no idea what had happened or was going on. I even wondered if I knew who I was." I shrugged. "It was easier for my head to go along with them. But no, I didn't contact Allen, and he didn't know I was coming."

"When they're worked up," Umstead said, "Glady and Burt Weaver are a force of nature."

"Truer words were never spoken," Tate said. "So if Allen's letters brought you to Ocracoke, what were you planning to do when you got here?"

"It wasn't necessarily a good plan," I said.

"Indulge me."

"I wasn't going to tell him who I was. I hoped I could figure out what his game was."

I sat at a picnic table near the Ocracoke Preservation Society building, digesting what I'd learned from lawyer Umstead. Too much for me to take in on my own. With seagulls bossing each other in the background, I called Kelly and then O'Connor to share with them.

Kelly was quiet for a short moment, then said, "Dang."

"That's a good, concise summary."

"But first, Mom, how are *you*? Things are coming at you from all directions. I can hear seagulls in the background. Next thing you know, they'll be after you, too. So, really, how are you?"

"It's a lot to take in. *Everything's* a lot to take in. But I'm okay."

"Come home if it's too much. Or give the word and Con and I will be there."

"Thank you, sweetie. I know you'd do that."

"So, then, to be clear. Dang, Mom. And why? Who was Dad to this guy? Spell his name for me."

I did, then told him I'd let him know the why of it all when I knew.

"Will you sell the shop?"

"It's the business, not the building. There's the shoreline property, though."

Kelly must have immediately searched Ocracoke property

values while we talked. "There isn't a lot of property available. And shoreline property along Pamlico Sound? The question is, Do you hold on to it until its worth even more, or sell it now for a really nice retirement? Wow."

"The whole situation here is definitely 'wow.'"

"Don't make any rash decisions."

"Or rushed. I won't, Kel."

O'Connor was excited about the property, too, but less about selling it than exploring it and having a foothold on the island.

"Is the Moon Shell solvent, Mom? Can it be a going concern?"

"Too early to know. We're talking it over."

"Who's we?"

I gave him a quick sketch of Glady and Burt.

"How does all this impact the murder investigation," he asked. "How do Glady and Burt fit in with that?"

"If you mean are they suspects, then I'm not sure. Glady's happy to say she doesn't think *I* killed Allen, so that's nice."

"Yes, it is," O'Connor said. "There's nothing half so nice as hearing that people don't think your mother's a killer. So why aren't you returning the favor?"

"I don't think they had anything to do with it. I don't. But—"

"There's reasonable doubt?"

"Unreasonable, I'm sure. They're kind but kind of odd at the same time. For now I'm going to be careful about sharing information with anyone."

"Except the police, I hope. Or your sons."

"Goes without saying."

"How are the police treating you?"

"Captain Tate seems straightforward. I'm not sure Deputy Brown trusts any of us. He probably trusts Glady and Burt more than me. I did wonder if he'd ask them to tell him if I do anything suspicious."

"Oh, yeah?"

"He's nice enough, though. Overworked."

"How's your mousehole?"

I laughed. "That's a perfect description. Come to think of it, maybe that's why there's a cat who comes to sit on the bird feeder platform and look in the kitchen window every morning."

"Why didn't you tell me?" O'Connor said. "That's perfect. If there isn't room inside, then I can come down and sleep on the platform with the cat."

"Talk to you later, goofball."

"Mom? Seriously, are you sure you should be in business with your new buddies?"

"No, I'm not, Con, but it can't be helped. According to the lawyer, they own the building."

Chapter 22

I leaned my elbows on the picnic table and rested my chin on my fists. Why hadn't Glady and Burt told me they owned the Moon Shell's house? Where Allen had lived. Where they'd grown up. Umstead said it was the original Weaver house. The house they lived in now, a two-story with a generous porch, was built by an uncle on family land across the street.

The seagulls offered their cranky opinions of the matter. I agreed with them, on principle, but couldn't bring myself to condemn Glady and Burt. I might be the only one on the island who *didn't* know they owned the building. They assumed I'd been in contact with Allen, why not assume he'd told me he rented from them? This explained their key to the place and Glady's desire to reopen the shop—keep the rent money coming in.

The explanation could be that neat and simple. Would things be so neat and simple if I had a more official and legal connection to them? Or a permanent connection to Ocracoke?

A car pulled up beside the Ocracoke Preservation Society building—a beautiful big old Ocracoke house. A woman got out and took a heavy-looking box from the back seat. From my spot at the picnic table, I could see more boxes in the car. After struggling up the stairs to the porch with the first box, the woman came back and popped the car's trunk. Even more boxes.

"Can I give you a hand?" I crossed the sandy grass to the car. "Do they need to come out in any order?"

"None at all. If you don't mind, I'll unlock the door and we can take them right on through to the storeroom."

We moved back and forth between car and storeroom with little breath for chitchat. When we stowed away the last two boxes, she thanked me.

"My pleasure. I'm looking forward to coming back when you're open."

"Don't wait," she said. "I'm proud of this place and happy for your help. I'll be here for another forty-five minutes. I'll find you when I need to lock up."

"Wonderful. Thanks."

The first exhibit that drew my eye was . . . wait for it . . . wait for it . . . shells! The fabulous specimens of North Atlantic seashells belonged to the Ocracoke Shell Club. Scotch bonnets (the state shell), olives of all types, sand dollars, whelks, scallops, razor clams, angel wings—ah, shells. One would think, with my nose pressed to the glass, that I'd never seen shells before and hadn't spent the previous day surrounded by excellent specimens in the shop. My own loop, I guess.

I left the shells to skim a series of panels introducing the island to visitors with an overview in text, maps, and old photographs. Pirates were, of course, mentioned. Blackbeard, his compatriots, his death. Our boys—as so many others did, including Glady and Burt—loved the pirate history of Ocracoke. But visitors reading beyond pirates learned that Ocracoke is also known for figs, wild ponies, feral cats, shipwrecks, hurricanes, the oldest continuously operating lighthouse in North Carolina (and second oldest in the nation), a fast-disappearing accent peculiar to the island, small cemeteries, and ghost stories.

Figs and figments, I thought. Ghosts and ghost stories. Well.

I wandered into another room that featured a more in-depth pirate exhibit called "On Beyond Blackbeard—The Unknown Story of the Crime of the Century." It proved eye-opening.

It seems that in September of 1750, the *Nuestra Señora de Guadalupe*, a Spanish treasure ship suffering hurricane damage, limped to Ocracoke Island. Afraid his ship would break up, the Spanish captain contracted with two respected merchant captains, brothers, to remove the cargo to their sloops so that it wouldn't be lost. Those respected merchant captains loaded the cargo—spices, silks, and fifty-eight (some said fifty-two) chests of silver doubloons—into their two smaller ships to ferry it to safety. Giving in to a sudden piratical urge, the merchant captains waited for dark (or until the Spaniards were eating lunch—stories differed) and then took off for the West Indies in their very fast sloops with more treasure than Blackbeard and all his compatriots had ever amassed.

The crime was reported in newspapers all over the world. One brother's sloop ran aground not far from Ocracoke, and he was captured. He had a wooden leg. His brother, however, got clean away, making it to Norman Island in the West Indies, where he buried his part of the loot, with plans to return for it. Most accounts fail to mention the two captains' unfortunate younger brother. The only fatality, he was shot, fell overboard, and drowned as his brothers sailed away.

Some researchers think Robert Louis Stevenson was inspired, after reading about the brothers' adventure, to write the story of peg-legged Long John Silver and buried treasure in *Treasure Island*.

The names of the merchant captains and their brother? Owen, John, and Emrys Lloyd.

Chapter 23

Pedaling to the Moon Shell, I thought about perspective. The story about the Lloyd brothers put small details like Glady not telling me she and Burt owned the building into brilliant perspective. Details like Captain Tate almost certainly telling Deputy Brown about Allen's letters to Jeff and that I hadn't come to Ocracoke because Allen offered me a job. All of that was good. Uncomfortable for me in the short run, but good to clear the air. Clear the muddy waters. Give my troubles perspective as crystalline as the blue sky above me.

Which darkened when I turned into Howard Street and saw Deputy Brown driving slowly, craning his neck as he passed the shop. When he looked forward, he saw me. I waved and for good measure rang the bell. He backed up, then pulled over. I didn't want to deal with this guy right now. I wanted to confront an eighteenth-century pirate.

"On your way in?" Brown asked as I propped the bike against the porch. "Getting comfortable in your new domain, I see."

I patted myself on the back for not answering, not rising to the bait. Then I stooped low. "Oh, gosh," I said, pulling Allen's key ring from my shoulder pack, "we still haven't lubricated the lock. Let's see if I can get it open." The key turned with ease. "No problem at all. Come on in, Deputy Brown." Not waiting to see if he followed, I gave Bonny some attention, promising lunch, and glanced quickly around the shop for piratical flickers. Seeing and hearing nothing, I went into the office and sat in the desk chair. I could see why Allen had it, why Glady and Emrys always opted for it. Very comfortable. Bonny hopped into my lap. Very comfortable, indeed.

Brown sat on the spindly spindle-back. Not as comfortable. He lowered himself gingerly. "Nice place you suddenly own. I wonder how that happened."

"So do I."

"Smells like motive to me."

And there it was. The accusation I thought Tate might have made but didn't. Maybe they used a good captain, bad deputy routine.

"I know it does. That's one of the reasons I want to know why Allen left his estate to my husband. The other is—" I lifted my open hands and shook my head. "The other is total bewilderment."

"But you're more familiar with Ocracoke than you've let on. Too familiar for your story to ring true."

"How? What story? I told you we used to come here with our children."

"How you happened to be lucky enough to 'find' that shell at the point. Your story about being here for a job."

"The job story isn't mine, but with everything else going on Monday night, telling Glady and Burt they were wrong about that seemed like the least of anyone's worries."

"Nothing is least in a murder investigation, and one lie, even by omission, makes me wonder about others. Like your story of being in the right place at the right time to find a valuable shell and its newly dead owner."

"I don't mean to sound glib, but being in the right place

happens. I came to Ocracoke because I wanted to see Allen. I wanted to see if I could figure out what his letters to my husband were all about."

"I wonder if you gave Tate all the letters Allen sent."

"I gave him all the letters we received."

"Hear me out." Brown laced his fingers behind his head and started to lean back. The chair creaked. He retaliated by getting to his feet and leaning across the desk at me. "Say Glady and Burt are right. Allen was expecting someone. Someone who arrived, lured him to the woods, and killed him." He breathed horrible coffee breath at me. Bonny noticed it, too. She gave him a look of pure cat disdain and abandoned me.

"Why would they kill him if he was giving them a job?"

"He wasn't giving them, meaning *you*, a job. He was giving you his business and its valuable stock."

How could this nightmare be happening? I forced myself not to back away from his breath.

Brown sat down again, his mood shifting. "Word on the street is that Allen was getting ready to retire and move inland." Smiling, tipping his head, he sounded like a friend who'd stopped in for a chin-wag. "Took himself all the way to Tennessee. Or so I've heard."

I sat very still, hoping this word on the street—his hunting hound of a story—wouldn't see me or smell my fear.

"What I think is, what his trip was all about, was scoping out your husband, your family. And if that's true, then he would have recognized you when you showed up here. So maybe you did know about Allen's will, and *voila*. We have motive."

"But not for me. I'm perfectly well set. I don't need this business or the shore property."

"What about your sons?"

I was on my feet before he'd added the question mark, finger pointed at his heart. "Leave them out of this. They aren't here. They haven't been near here for years. They don't know Allen. They don't know any more about the letters or the will than Jeff did or I do."

"Sit down, mama bear." He hadn't lost his smile. "What about this guy at the edge of the woods. Could that have been a woman?"

"I'm pretty sure it was a man. But the voice I heard before I ran—I don't know. I was in full panic. It could have been male or female."

"Did you see his golf cart when you reached Springer's Point?"

"No. Have you found it?"

Brown shook his head. "How long were you on the beach?"

"I'm not sure. At least fifteen minutes. Maybe half an hour?" This was making my head hurt. "Where are you going with this?"

"Why didn't you see Allen on your way *to* the beach?"

"You know where the body was. Even if I'd taken the path to stop at Ikey D.'s grave, I might not have seen Allen. And I wasn't at the beach long enough for him to be killed and grow cold."

"And on the way back, you got disoriented. It happens."

"But you don't believe me?"

"I didn't say that."

"Your tone did."

"In my line of work, disbelief happens. You could have arrived earlier on Monday."

"I didn't. You know what, Deputy Brown? Your accusations sound personal. To you, I mean. Like they mean something to you personally. So did what you said to the body. Why is that?"

"Because Allen was nothing but an old pirate."

* * *

I crossed the street when I heard Brown's truck take off. Burt opened the door when I knocked. In one breath, he invited me in and shouted for Glady to put the kettle on. She was right. The place was a shambles. I felt immediately at home and trailed after Burt to their cluttered, sunny kitchen.

"I need to come clean," I said, and while they drank tea and mine got cold, I talked. I told them the truth about the letters and why I'd come to the island and then about the will. They listened with bright eyes, with no interruptions or comments until I finished and sat back.

Glady nudged my cup toward me. "I knew all along you weren't the person Allen was expecting."

"You did? Then why did you go along with it?" I asked.

"Well," she said, "I didn't know it at first. But I've been thinking it over and putting things together and—"

"And when you told us, Glady realized she knew it all along," Burt said.

"That's not it at all." Glady rapped the table. "Something told me. Something didn't feel right."

It was that kind of answer that made me not want to trust Glady. It also made me like her.

"Could Jeff be who Allen expected?" Glady asked.

"Unlikely, I think. Jeff never answered Allen's letters. What do you remember Allen saying about it?"

"He dropped hints about expecting someone," Burt said.

"And you interpreted them to mean he was hiring someone?"

"I'd been bugging him for so long it made sense," Glady said. "There's no way we could have figured out what he really meant if he was expecting Jeff to come and hear about the will. Maybe, rather than really expecting Jeff, Allen was *hoping* he could expect him."

"That's a possibility," I said.

"You have no idea why Allen left everything to him?" she asked.

"None at all."

I'd had no idea I was consorting with a pirate, either. I went back to the Moon Shell and looked for him. Shouted for him the way I used to shout for the boys if they'd gotten up to something and were lying low. No answer.

Ghosted by a ghost.

Chapter 24

That day, I finally had the time to do what I'd been wanting to—look through Allen's desk, his files, his apartment for anything that would tell me why he wrote those letters to Jeff, what connection lay between them. But I came up with nada, zippo, zilch. I didn't catch a hum or a flicker of Emrys, either. Then I heard him before I saw him.

"I trust you've had a useful day." He came into view perched atop the bookcase I was searching in the apartment. "I witnessed some of your exchange with the deputy this morning. I was glad to hear you sounding more *spirited*." He looked pleased with himself.

"I'd like to be able to count on you." My tone had his attention. "When I went after the shell, after I got it, you told me to move farther up the beach. You said, 'It'll be safer.' You didn't mean it would be safer for me. You meant it—the shell— would be safer. And it was your voice I heard in the woods. That scared me into running like a—"

"Like a bat out of shell," Emrys said. "Another one of Allen's favorites."

"I would have liked him, but I'm still annoyed with you."

"I saved you from exposure by leading you to the Moon Shell. It was self-serving, I'll admit. I wanted the shell returned to the shop. It's where I feel most comfortable, most at home. Safest."

"It wasn't that cold. I wouldn't have died of exposure."

"But no harm done," he said.

"You scared me half to death."

"As one who is one hundred percent dead, I don't see the problem."

He wasn't the picture of a cutthroat pirate. Didn't look like any of the reproductions of period illustrations I'd seen at the preservation society. "Come downstairs with me, will you?"

I took the cameo shell from the locked case and held it between us. I moved it to the right. His eyes followed it, and his chest swelled with a phantom breath.

"Should I drop it?" I asked.

If it hadn't already, his heart would have stopped, and I felt a stab to my own. I'd caused him pain he had no control over. "Emrys, forgive me. That was horrible. You can count on me to never do anything like that again." I put the shell back on its blue velvet. "*But.*" I waited until he took his eyes from the shell and looked at my face. "*But* I need to be able to count on you. At least somewhat. You've spent years with Allen. You must know him better than anyone. I need help proving that I didn't kill him."

Emrys flickered, then turned to face me.

"Do you know why Allen was writing to my husband?"

"No."

"Were you really friends with Allen?"

"Of course."

"The kind of friends who sit and talk to each other over tea or coffee? Or beer?"

He looked blank.

"Over whiskey? In a bar? At an alehouse?"

"We were the best kind of friends. We left each other alone most of the time."

"So I can assume you won't be much help figuring out why someone murdered him. Right. Glad we got that straight."

"And I can assume you're angry about my limitations."

"You can assume that I won't bother you or your shell with my problems."

"Thank you. I'll return the favor, but first I feel I must tell you that you seem to have a problem with making assumptions." He opened his mouth to say something else. Closed it and looked at the floor between us. "Why are we angry with each other?"

"Because I believed you when you told me you were a conchologist. Even though the word didn't exist when you did. Come to find out, *days* later, you aren't just a prevaricating conchologist, you're a pirate.

"Not a very good one."

"Are you kidding? You and your brothers pulled off the most audacious and lucrative heist of the century. It was covered in newspapers worldwide. In 1750, that was quite an accomplishment."

"I'll admit it was a bold plan," he said, then hurried to add, "but I was not one of the planners, and it was not without bloodshed."

"Yeah. Great. Something to be proud of. You aren't just a pirate, you're a *bloody* pirate. You know what? The word *pirate*, and everything it stands for, kind of gets in the way of me accepting your excuses. Let's address *pirate* first and then see if we can move on."

"It's hard to know where to begin," he said. "What questions do you have?"

"Only one. You were a *pirate*?"

"Only one?" Emrys chuckled. "Only once."

"Yes, I see what you did there. Ha, bloody pirate, ha."

"I see that this is difficult for you. I want you to know that it is difficult for me, as well, and has been since shortly before my brothers and I made off with the Spanish treasure. Sit down, why don't you, and I'll tell you."

"I don't think so. Sit down with a pirate? Nope. Pass."

"But not a very good pirate, and my crime still haunts me." The sidelong look he gave me seemed more about gauging his story's effect than atonement. "Will you pick up the shell again?"

"Why?"

"Trust me? Please?"

"This better be good."

I took the shell from the case again and—saw Emrys standing at the rail of a two-masted ship with the shell I held in *his* hands. *How?* Somewhere a man called his name. Emrys glanced up, then back at the shell. The other man shouted his name, crossed the deck, grabbed the shell from Emrys, and dropped it over the side of the ship. As Emrys leaned over the railing to watch the shell disappear, I heard a fainter shout and a shot rang out. There was an instant where red bloomed on Emrys's shoulder, then because he'd leaned over the railing, he toppled into the water. He didn't come up.

A teardrop hit the shell in my hands. I wiped it away, but it was another moment before I could speak. "You were shot but you might have lived. I'm so sorry."

"I never learnt to swim," he said, "and with the bullet in my shoulder, I couldn't have. So, yes, I drowned. An ignominious death. A poltroon's death. A pirate's death. Now I'm a pirate ghost with a deathly fear of the sea."

"Who shot you? The guy who grabbed the shell?"

"A Spaniard on the the *Nuestra Señora de Guadalupe*. You didn't hear? He shouted '*Pirata!*' just before the shot."

"Do you know that you were the only fatality?"

He shook his head.

"Who's the jerk who grabbed the shell from you?"

"My brother Owen. He was sick of seeing me "playing" with shells, so he threw it overboard."

"That's appalling. How did Allen get the shell?

"His mother had it before him."

"Do you know where she got it, where it's been since 1750?"

"I'm unable to account for every minute of my existence. I do remember that Allen's mother was the first to give the shell a name. She dubbed it the Moon Shell."

"And named the shop after it."

"Yes. For a number of years, I planned to add more to the carving."

"*You* carved it. You're an artist." And a pirate. I wondered how truthful the average pirate was.

"I carved it for my wife, who waited for me to return to her in Edenton."

"Did you have a shell collection of your own?" I asked, thinking that surely a shell-collecting, shell-carving pirate couldn't be all bad.

"I did," he said. "Some as fine or finer than the shells for sale here, which I don't mind telling you I covet. In my time, shells from the far reaches of the world fetched prices at auction to make the Dutch masters blush."

"Did you have any that valuable?"

"A few. My untimely death was a tragedy. Not of Shakespearean proportions to me. I am not so conceited as to think that. It might have been of Shakespearean proportions, though, for my wife. I hope she was able to sell my collection for good money, that it did not end up down the hole in the privy with the broken crockery. The lives of women have always been hard. I've seen that over the years, but I've also noticed that they have improved in the past century and decades."

I put the shell in the case again and locked it. "You know what I think? I think the loop that gripped you, so that you don't know who took the shell from the shop, happened because you were worried about the shell. Afraid for it and for yourself."

"Terrified into a loop." The gray of his face paled. "Forgive me if I have not thanked you enough for rescuing it and me."

"My pleasure."

"No longer angry?" he asked.

"Not angry. But I'm not sure about the logistics of working with a ghost or about the ethics of working with a pirate."

"Look at it this way," he said, pushing his hat to a cocky angle. "You'll be working with an accidental pirate in the same way that I shall be working with an accidental murder suspect."

Chapter 25

The next morning, someone knocked on my mousehole door before I'd finished a restless night's sleep. I went down the ladder and peeked out the window over the tiny kitchen table. Glady.

Rather than return my "Good morning" when I opened the door, she said, "We need to start our list of suspects," then pushed inside past me. "Where can we sit? Ah." She took the few steps to the table and made herself at home.

"Coffee?" I asked.

"Please. Now, Monday afternoon, Allen told Burt and me that he was going to check on Yanira and Coquina post-hurricane. Why, then, was he at Springer's Point? Or did he go to the point after seeing them? We need a timeline *and* the list of suspects. To be thorough, a list of people who *did* go to see if Yanira and Coquina were okay, too." She pulled a pen and legal pad from a large purse.

"Sounds like a good start. I'll go get dressed."

"You're wearing shorts and a T-shirt," she said without looking up to take in my frowzy glory.

"Pajamas. Be right back." The difference between my pajamas and my shorts plus T-shirt being the lack of pockets in the pajamas and the lack of romping, plaid-ribboned Scotties on my shorts and shirt. As I shucked the Scotties, I wondered whom I should trust more—Glady or the ghost of a pirate? Or was it safer to wonder whom I should trust less? *Whom* had such a gloomy sound to it. I studied Glady from above before going back down. Scribbling away at her list of suspects, she was far from gloomy. And Emrys, who had every right to be gloomy, never seemed to be, either. Why not trust both?

Glady looked up when I put two mugs of coffee on the table and sat opposite her. "Are dark circles under your eyes part of your natural morning look," she said, "or did you sleep badly?"

"Slept badly. Also it's only six-thirty."

"Well, I wanted to go over this with Burt, but he's busy. Do you think the cameo shell is connected to the murder?"

"I do."

"Then how's this for a scenario? Someone takes the shell, runs with it, Allen gives chase, they end up at Springer's Point, the culprit panics, knifes Allen, then is afraid to be caught with the incriminating evidence and hurls the shell in the sea."

"That's a long foot chase. How old was Allen?"

"Eighty-three," Glady said. "In good shape, but not a marathoner or sprinter. I see your point."

"But Allen could have been *meeting* someone at the point."

"Went there in his golf cart," Glady said, "to meet someone who wanted money to return the shell, and the deal turned ugly."

"Like ransom for a kidnap victim." Emrys had said he was kidnapped along with the shell. "That scenario's plausible. And the killer ditched the shell, then took Allen's cart and ditched *it* somewhere."

"Or this," Glady said. "The two incidents are separate. Someone saw an opportunity, took the shell, then lost it. Not necessarily the same day Allen was killed."

"Here's an interesting problem I have with that theory. Before I came to see you yesterday, Deputy Brown came by the shop to accuse me of the murder—"

"What? Again?" Glady slammed her mug onto the table. "Honest to Pete."

"That's how I felt, too, and part of why I slept badly, but he's doing his job. Trying to rock me, find a hole in my story, see if I've remembered anything else. One of the things he has trouble believing is the coincidence of me finding the shell *and* Allen's body. Someone finding either one was a long shot considering where they were. But finding both?"

"You did, though." Glady had picked up the mug but put it down again. "Didn't you?"

"I did. But now I'm having trouble believing the coincidence of the shell disappearing and someone else killing Allen."

"I'll write it down, anyway. Part of brainstorming. Oh."

"What?"

"What if someone told him the shell was taken and lost and he went to retrieve it? Then along comes the person or persons unknown, unbalanced in some way—stress from weathering Electra—and killed him before he got to the beach to find the shell." Glady made notes of that theory, too.

"I'm having cereal. Can I get you a bowl?"

"No, and don't get one for yourself. I forgot to tell you. You're invited for breakfast." She looked at the time on her phone. "Burt was busy making muffins. They should be out of the oven by now. Let's go."

Burt welcomed us into their kitchen wearing a faded and patched apron made of blue denim that Glady said she'd made for their father fifty years earlier. The house smelled of baking and coffee. A dozen corn muffins sat cooling on a rack in the middle of the table, joined by jars of jam, a carton of orange juice, and more coffee. Between bites, Glady read her notes to Burt.

"Your last theory, about someone taking the shell and losing it, sounds like something a kid might do," Burt said. "Coquina?"

"No," Glady said. "That's not like her."

"Do we spend enough time with her to know that?" Burt asked.

"I watch her for Yanira," Glady said stoutly.

"Occasionally," Burt said. "And I'm not saying she did it." He put a conciliatory muffin on Glady's plate. "But you know she's a kid with a mind of her own."

"How would she get the shell from the case?" I asked.

"Allen was always letting her hold it to her ear," Glady said. "She would see where he got the key. But why would she run off with it? He let her see it almost any time she asked. No. It's not Corina." She put jam on her muffin, then noticed that neither Burt nor I had said anything. "But," she said with a sigh and a note on her legal pad, "we'll have to find out."

"We'll do it carefully," Burt said. "This murder can't help changing the way people look at each other. Let's not forget we're all neighbors."

Allen's murder had brought all kinds of change, I thought. Certainly to my life. "We need to consider his will," I said. "I didn't know about it, but someone might have. Tate and Brown are right. The will could be a motive."

Glady wrote. Burt sipped coffee. I wondered about this man with whom I shared acquaintance with a pirate ghost. The gloomy *whom* again.

"Yesterday Deputy Brown called Allen an old pirate," I said. "And Monday night, didn't one of you say that Allen told stories? I'd like to know more about Allen. I need to if I'm going to be any help with an investigation. What can you tell me about him?"

"Oh, my," Glady said. "How to sum up a life?"

"Start with the shell," I said. I tried to remember if I'd seen it when we'd brought the boys to the island. But, no. I was sure

I'd remember that amazing shell if I'd seen it before. "How long has it been on display?"

Glady and Burt looked at each other. "Do you remember Mrs. Seashell having it out?" Burt asked.

Glady's eyes lost focus as she thought.

"Who's Mrs. Seashell?" I asked.

"Allen's mother," Burt said. "Sort of an honorary name."

"Sweet. I've been called Ms. Mollusk."

"I'll remember that." Burt pretended to pluck it out of the air and tuck it in his pocket. "The name suited Dottie. She had that delicate pink and white coloring you see inside some shells. She revived the island's shell club."

"She named the shop for the cameo," Glady said, coming back from the search through her memory. "I don't think she ever had it on display before she retired and Allen took over. He kept it and a few other special shells in the locked case, but I don't think he put the cameo on display before Dottie passed."

I poured each of us more coffee and listened to their memories of Mrs. Seashell.

"She was an O'cocker, born on the island, like us," Burt said. "Married Whit Withrow right out of college."

"Another O'cocker?" I asked.

"Dingbatter. Like you," Glady said. "From somewhere other than here. Raleigh, maybe. He became a foreign service officer and diplomat. They traveled the world. Dottie beachcombed wherever they went and made connections among shell collectors. She came to stay with her mother when she was expecting Allen. She wanted her baby to be born here. Growing up, he spent his summers here with his grandparents, flying in from wherever his father was stationed, stepping out onto the wing of the little plane like a movie star."

"Baloney," Burt said. "You never met him at the airstrip."

"But all the girls knew that's exactly how it would be," said Glady. "Dottie came back to live here when Whit died. She rented our old house and opened the shop. She'd ask us, every few years, if she could buy the house."

"Did she live in the apartment upstairs?" I asked.

"Couldn't," Burt said. "No room. She pretty much turned that into a fire hazard, cramming everything in that she'd picked up on her travels. She lived with her sister in the house where they grew up."

"She never pestered us about it," Glady said, "but she had a hankering for the cachet of living on Howard Street."

"Allen pestered us." Burt took a vicious bite of muffin.

"The money wouldn't have hurt," Glady said mildly.

"But we don't want to sell." Burt finished the muffin with a second chomp.

I watched Glady doodle spirals on the legal pad. Was she thinking about what they could have done with that money? Burt scowled into his coffee cup.

"When did Allen move here for good?" I asked.

"A long time ago now," Glady said. "In the early seventies. Dottie died in her eighties, and he's owned the shop since then."

"He had it about twenty years," Burt said.

"Was he *Mr.* Seashell?" I asked.

"Nah." Burt's anger had faded. "He was all right, just not as approachable as Dottie. Not as involved with the community. Even after all this time, a fish out of water."

"Not quite a fish out of water," Glady said, "but the wrong kind of fish for these waters."

"Or the critter who takes over a shell after the original critter is gone?" I asked.

"That makes him sound kind of sneaky," Glady said.

"It does," said Burt, "but he had more sneak in him than we knew."

"Frank Brown told me a story about Allen," I said. "That he was planning to retire and move inland."

"*Inland?*" Burt said at the same time Glady said. "*Never.*"

"He said it was 'word on the street.' "

"Not on this street," Glady said.

"Frank cruises down streets we don't get down too often," Burt said. "I wonder how old that word is. Or how new?"

"Or how made up," I said. "He might've been trying to get a rise out of me. Part of the story is that Allen took a trip to scope out Tennessee as a place to relocate. But Frank thinks Allen took that trip to check out my husband and family. Did Allen ever talk about a trip to Tennessee?"

"No," Glady said.

"He didn't just have more sneak in him. He had more secrets, too." Burt shaking his head reminded me of a bear trying to sniff something out. He found it. "This whole thing smells bad, and it's going to smell worse before it's over."

"Since when are you a fortune teller?" Glady asked.

Burt shook his head again and drank coffee.

That night someone broke into the Fig & Yaupon Bakery and Beer Garden.

Chapter 26

Gene Kelly, singing in his blasted rain, woke me out of a groggy sleep Thursday morning. I looked at the time. Ugh. Another too early morning. "Kelly? What is it? What's wrong?"

"Mom! Are you kidding? What the heck is going on there?"

"I don't know." My hair didn't want to be up yet, either. I pushed it out of my eyes. "Wait—why?" I sat up. "What have you heard?"

"There was a break-in at a restaurant there. The Fig and Pompom. No. Sorry. Fig and *Yaupon*. What's a yaupon?

"A tree. What happened? No one was mur—"

"No, no, no. At least, nothing in the article online. I . . . Mom, are you sure you're safe?" Losing the dad he'd idolized stitched that worry into his voice.

"I am. I'm fine. Snug as a mouse in a mousehole. What else did your online article say?"

"Let's see. They specialize in pies, tarts, cakes, and bagels. After five o'clock, they also serve beer. They're known for their fig specialties and yaupon tea. Never heard of that, but this says it's similar to green tea or yerba mate."

"Did a reporter write that article or a restaurant critic?"

His voice relaxing, Kelly read, "It's owned by Tracy Garber. The place is still closed since the hurricane. The burglars got away with a few cases of beer. Sorry for the panic, Mom."

"You can panic to me anytime you want. You know that."

"Any progress on figuring out why that guy left everything to Dad?"

"Not yet."

The bike and I pedaled along Back Road. We followed a curve past the library, the health center, cottages and houses, and a few other businesses. Up ahead, a herd of golf carts congregated, some haphazardly in the road. Glady, standing next to one, spotted me and waved me to a stop. I'd arrived at the Fig & Yaupon. People stood talking in small groups, most sipping from travel mugs. I put my kickstand down, took my own travel mug from the bike basket, and joined them.

"This is a shell of a thing, isn't it?" Burt said. "We don't get many break-ins on the island."

"Rentals sometimes," Glady said. "Off-season." She nudged me. "There's Tracy coming out with Frank."

Tracy Garber's teeth and artfully tousled hair looked like they were trying hard to be perky. The stress of the burglary definitely had the edge. She looked anywhere from thirty to forty, but if she owned the restaurant, then closer to forty made sense. Despite the cool morning, she wore a sundress that showed off toned, tanned arms and legs. Deputy Brown spoke to her, and she put her hand to her mouth, then to her heart. He squeezed her shoulder and walked to his truck.

"Tracy, honey," a woman called out, "what can we do to help?"

"We're here for you," a man said.

"Ya'll are too sweet," Tracy said with a Southern accent not native to the island. "I can't do anything at all until the insurance agent gets here and sees the mess these jerks left. Stealing is one thing, but this was ornery."

"You put out the call when you're ready," a man near Glady said. "We'll round up folks and have a cleanup party."

"Ya'll are *way* too sweet," Tracy said. "But you're on. I'll see you later. Boy howdy, do I have phone calls to make." She waved and went back into the restaurant.

Burt nodded to the man who'd suggested the cleanup party. "Round us up, too, when you have that cleanup party, will you?"

"Count on it," he said. "Besides trashing the place, what were the yahoos after?"

"Beer," Burt said. "And if they were planning a party, they were in luck. Tracy has a generator for the walk-in, so what they got was nice and cold."

Glady pulled me aside. "Here's our reason to drop in on Yanira. She works here in the summer."

"It isn't too early to go calling?" I asked.

Glady checked her phone. "Nine thirty? Not at all. There's a rack at the back of Dorothy Parker for the bike."

We dropped off Burt and picked up some of his muffins for Yanira and Coquina—the girls, as Glady called them. Dorothy Parker took us at a sedate speed the mile or so to Yanira's. She lived in one of the old, square, single-story island houses with a deep porch on three sides. It sat a few feet off the ground with a wood lattice skirting for air flow. Water flow, too, in times of storm surge. Narrow white clapboards covered the house. Bright green and blue paint rioted over the porch.

Coquina sat swinging and reading on a sunflower-yellow porch swing. She waved when she saw us and ran into the house, letting the screen door slam. Yanira, early thirties and a taller version of her daughter, welcomed us in to sit in a tidy living room.

Glady introduced me to Yanira.

"You're the one who found—" Yanira stopped with a quick glance at Coquina.

Coquina eyed the plastic container of muffins still in Glady's hand.

"*Niña*," Yanira said. "Have you been invited to look at Miss Glady's box?"

"Not yet."

"Well, if you'll bring four plates," Glady said, "then you're invited to open the box and put one muffin on each plate."

Coquina was off like a shot.

"I *am* the one who found Allen," I said. "Luckily, I found Glady and Burt, too. And Coquina when she stopped by the Moon Shell. She's a cutie."

"Please, may I ask that you not indulge Corina by calling her Coquina? I encourage her to face the world as she is. Scar and all. She needs to be able to do that. I've taught for over ten years, and I've seen what children do to each other." Her request was warm and friendly but firm.

"Oh, of course," I said.

We heard a noise and saw Corina standing in the kitchen doorway. She stomped into the room and handed the plates to her mother. "I am going to my room," she announced. The next thing we heard was a slamming door.

"I'm so sorry," I said.

"Don't be. I told her if she still wants to be Coquina when she's fifteen, she can change her name for her quinceañera. What I'm more worried about now is what adults do to each other."

"Allen?" Glady asked.

"How can I believe he's gone?" Yanira glanced down the hall where Corina had disappeared and lowered her voice. "And murder? Not here."

"Allen told us he was coming here to check on you and Corina after the storm," Glady said. "Did he?"

Yanira shook her head. "That's so like him. He had a soft spot for Corina. But we didn't see him."

"I hope other people came by," I said. "I can't imagine weathering a hurricane."

"Noah came by." Yanira's brown face grew rosy. "Do you know him, Glady?"

"Sandy hair, gangly legs, early twenties?" Glady asked.

"That's the one. He has a crush on me. He worked at the restaurant this summer. He told me he took the job so he could be near me. He thought seeing me every day would make up for the restaurant being vegetarian but not vegan. It didn't. He quit after a couple of weeks."

"What about the crush?" I asked.

"*That* hasn't quit. I told him I'm old enough to have been his babysitter." She took a bite of muffin, said, "Oh, but—" She put a hand over her mouth to chew and swallow. "Speaking of the restaurant, you heard about the break-in?"

"Yes," Glady said. "Terrible. Tracy's going to organize a cleanup party. If you want to go, I'll be happy to keep Corina."

"Perfect. Thank you. Tracy's sick about this. Not the mess or the stolen beer. We can deal with that."

"What else?" I asked.

"She's a realtor, too, and runs that business out of the Fig & Yaupon's office. They took employee files, documents, and keys."

"New theory," Glady said on the way back to her place. "The same person or people who did the Fig and Yaupon got into the Moon Shell. Allen scared them off and got clouted."

"Taking the shell?" I asked.

"Scared off before they could grab anything else," she said. "Tossed the shell after hitting Allen because they realized the shell is too recognizable."

"The stabbing wouldn't be spur of the moment. That was face-to-face."

"In a rage," Glady said. "Maybe drugged up."

"And carrying a big knife. I wonder if any knives are missing from the Fig and Yaupon? Either from before Allen's death or after the burglary?"

"Why would it matter after the burglary?" Glady asked.

"If our person in a rage used one of the restaurant's knives, returned it, and then got worried about trace evidence," I said. "And then everything else about the break-in was camouflage."

Chapter 27

Who knew the ghost of a pirate could be such a prima donna? After the visit to Yanira and Corina, I stopped at the Moon Shell and learned that interesting tidbit.

"All other aspects being equal," Emrys said, taking up quite a lot of room in the office doorway, "I am approximately two hundred and sixty years older than you and I am a man."

"You were born two hundred and fifty-nine years before me, but you stopped aging at thirty-seven. That makes me fifteen years older than you."

"I think the years since my death should count," Emrys said. "I'm sure I've continued to mature over those two hundred and seventy-four years."

Not much, I said under my breath. He was miffed because Bonny and I had sat down in the desk chair before he could. Aloud, I said, "To your second point, how does the fact that you're a man make you more qualified to be lead detective?"

"Not just a man but a British man. Surely, you agree that all the best detectives, whether found in movies, television, or literature, are British men."

"Most of them uber good-looking, too."

"Uncanny, isn't it?"

"I was being sarcastic about their looks," I said. "Even

Bonny got that." She looked up at me with a slow cat wink of approval. "And sorry, I don't agree with your best detective theory. But I also don't think we should argue over who's the detective and who's the sidekick. If the detective title means that much to you, I'll call myself a sidekick. You'll have to accept being a Nero Wolfe–type detective, though. He rarely leaves his apartment, and he has loops. Every morning, he disappears to his orchid room, where he must never be disturbed. He always wears yellow shirts and always has two bottles of beer after dinner. Archie Goodwin, the sidekick, acts as Wolfe's eyes and ears. That's what I'll do. I can go places and round people up for you. Have you read the Nero Wolfe books?"

"I've not had the pleasure."

"Then you're in for a treat. I'll take some out of the library for you when it reopens."

"As the detective, do I get to sit behind—"

"Yes." I lifted Bonny from my lap to the desk, then, before getting up, fixed Emrys with my eyes. "But *not* because you're a man and I'm a woman. Got it?"

"Understood. Thank you." Emrys sat behind the desk, looking, for a fleeting moment, like a child allowed to sit at the grownup's table. No, not like that. Like the younger brother who'd been bullied by his older brothers.

"What's our first move?" I asked.

"A list of suspects."

"Do you mind if I take notes?"

"An excellent idea," he said, then asked with wistful hope, "May I ask you to call me Sir?"

"No, and may I suggest that you not press your luck?"

"As I thought. Glady started a list, you said, then became diverted. I shall not be diverted."

"We," I said. "We shall not be diverted."

"Forgive me." A darker gray rose up his ghostly neck, suffusing his cheeks. "*We* shall not be diverted. Do you think the child, Corina, might be responsible for the disappearance of the shell?"

"Possibly. Why do you think she might be?" I took my notebook and a pen from my shoulder pack.

"She makes me uneasy. Not a good reason, I realize."

"But considering your attachment to the shell, your unease carries weight." I made a note. "Burt wondered about her, too. Do you have anything more concrete than your unease?"

He shook his head.

"Have you felt uneasy about anyone else? You said you heard Allen's end of an angry phone call. Did you ever hear shouting or arguments in the shop or apartment? Any other angry phone calls?"

"Such exchanges make me tense, which, although I cannot tell you why, is different from the unease I feel around Corina. Perhaps because the child's whims are unpredictable, whereas with arguments and shouting, in my experience, threats are predictable and often inevitable." Emrys traced the wood grain of the desktop with a fingertip.

"What happens when you hear arguments and shouting—besides getting tense? Do you blip out if you hear someone flip out?"

"I do." He looked up with a smile. "Blip out. I like that."

"Who else should we be suspicious of?" I asked.

"Not that I dislike either of them, but I believe we should include Glady and Burt."

I hated being suspicious of them, but I still wasn't completely sure of them, either. Possibly no surer than I was of Emrys. "Did you hear what they muttered to each other before they tried to find my pulse Monday night?"

"Sorry, I was humming a song I'd forgotten about since the late 1800s."

"First Glady and Burt muttered and then Frank Brown. A

whole lot of muttering went on that night. Tell me why you're adding them to the list."

His eyebrows drew together as he thought. "I once had a prism glass. When I looked through it at my cat, it gave me many multiples of the cat. A myriad of cats. That made me wonder what each of those cats would be like. The same? Or would some scratch me and some be better mousers? I had similar ruminations about my brothers. After our 'incident,' I had more time for reflections like these, and it occurred to me that each brother's body and mind contained many more people than I'd dreamed. We're all a myriad. That's my long-winded way of saying I'm never sure what to think of Glady and Burt."

"That captures the conundrum of them."

"This might be a clue," Emrys said. "Do you remember Burt saying that you were the one Allen was expecting? *Was* expecting—past tense. That could that mean Burt knew Allen was dead."

"It might," I said. "People don't always speak grammatically, though. And a suspect slipping up and using past tense is almost a cliché in books and TV shows. Also, because I *was* there, he *was* expecting. So it wasn't ungrammatical. Maybe."

"I think you're caught in a loop." Emrys, snickered. "Burt also said he and Glady couldn't afford for you to drop dead on them. One wonders why not? That is hardly an ordinary worry. An innocent worry. Might they have a criminal history?"

"The sheriff's department must be looking into all that," I said. "But there was also that odd remark about not falling for the wheelbarrow again. What did that mean, and when did Burt fall for it before?" I made a note to ask Glady about it. Again. "Glady and Burt own this building. Allen's mother wanted to buy it. Allen wanted to buy it. They don't want to sell, even though Glady says they could use the money. Did you ever hear Allen argue with either of them about the building?"

"I never witnessed him shouting at Glady or Burt," Emrys said, "and shouting is how Allen showed his anger. I don't know how Glady or Burt show anger."

"Burt bites muffins in two when he talks about Allen's pressure to sell. Glady doodled spirals when Burt talked about the pressure and bit his muffins."

"Then it's right to have them on the list," Emrys said. "Do you know that there are no pine cones in their yard? If Burt throws them at crows, where does he get them? One possibility is Springer's Point."

"There must be other places with pine cones."

"Undoubtedly," Emrys said, "but one possibility *is* Springer's Point."

I made a note to ask Burt or Glady about pine cones.

"What do we have so far?" Emrys asked.

"A child and two retirees."

"Pah." He threw himself back in the chair. "A paltry showing. Useless. I can't help but think our problem stems in part from the fact that I rarely leave the shop."

"You go to the library for the obituaries."

"That's become a loop," he said, "and because I go after hours I don't encounter anyone."

"But you do leave sometimes?"

"Allen occasionally left the island to display his wares at shell shows, taking the cameo shell with him. He hadn't done so in years, saying it was not worth his trouble. However, he did continue presenting a yearly program for the Ocracoke Shell Club."

"Do you remember anyone being especially interested in the cameo shell at any of the events?" I asked. "Burt said plenty of people wanted the shell. That some offered boatloads of money."

"My brothers ran off with boatloads of money."

"Did they ever say 'Yo-ho-ho?'"

Emrys looked blank.

"Never mind. Did you hear anyone in the shop, or at one of the shows or programs, offer Allen a boatload for the shell and then go away angry?"

"May I remind you of blipping and looping? Two of the regrettable facts of my continued existence. I can't help but notice that *you* haven't added anyone to the list."

"I don't think I know enough. About any of the people or how they interact."

"I might know less," he said.

"Maybe more than you think. Why don't I tell you the names of people I've met or heard about, and if you've encountered them or heard Allen talk about them, then you tell me what you think of them."

"Like a party game," he said. "Who's the murderer in twenty questions."

"Delightful. What about Corina's mother, Yanira Ochoa?"

"I rarely see her. I hear that she's a hard worker. The child is intelligent, so I suspect her mother is, too. What about the child's father?"

"Good question." I made notes. "Noah Horton? Glady says he's interested in animal rights."

"Allen ignored a young man named Noah who walked up and down in front of the shop carrying a sign that said 'COLLECTING IS KILLING' in uppercase letters."

"Glady didn't tell me that," I said. "But she did say I wouldn't want to get on his bad side and wondered if Allen *had*. Then she couldn't explain what she meant by it. What about Deputy Brown? Did you hear him say that Allen was nothing but an old pirate the other day? Any idea what he meant by that?"

"None. Allen was never in trouble with the law. I know nothing about Deputy Brown other than what I've seen and heard this week."

"Tracy Garber? She owns the Fig and Yau—oh. You don't know. Tracy's restaurant, the Fig and Yaupon, was broken into last night. The thieves took beer but also employee records and other business documents, and they left the place in a mess. Glady and I wonder if the same person or people took the shell and killed Allen."

"But whoever took the shell *only* took the shell," Emrys said. "There might be a reason that people who rob shell shops and restaurants use different methods for each crime, but I will need time to think of one. I do know that Tracy is kind. She brings samples of her wares, small pies, that smell heavenly. I do not use that word lightly."

"I like pie," I said. "What about the lawyer, Daniel Umstead?"

"My brothers never trusted lawyers. That would be enough to make me like Mr. Umstead, but I do not know him. I don't remember him coming into the shop."

"Dr. Allred?"

"Allen thought he pined for Glady," Emrys said, "but unless the doctor saw Allen as a rival for her hand, I cannot imagine why he would kill him. I cannot imagine why anyone on our list would kill Allen. Even Glady and Burt with all our clues and suspicions."

"I can't either, but the list isn't useless. It gives us a place to start."

"The other day I accused you of having a problem with assumptions."

"A problem I was aware of before you pointed it out."

"May I tell you what I read recently about assumptions without the two of us looping into another argument about them?"

"Sure."

"An astronomer, Adam Frank, says that science should 'force us to confront false assumptions we hadn't even known we'd made.' Being two scientists, as we are, might Adam Frank's words help us solve Allen's murder?"

"I like that," I said. "It might help. It'll be good to keep in mind, and it kind of fits my worry over my latest assumption—that owning the shop will be fantastic." I was having trouble feeling fantastic about it because I was feeling increasingly uneasy not knowing why the shell, the business, and the shore property were now mine.

"Feeling guilty?" Emrys asked. "I see it in your eyes as they first study nothing at all to your left and then nothing at all to your right."

"I'm not sure that's guilt."

"Oh, yes, it's guilt, all right. Guilt is a loop all unto itself. I am an expert on feeling guilty."

He may be an expert on guilt, I thought, but he was also an expert on being full of himself. "Here's my real loop," I told him. "I keep coming back to this: Why throw the shell in the water? *Why?*"

"Here's a new one for me," Emrys said. Then he sang, in his excellent tenor, "Here we go loopty loo, here we go loopty li, here we go loopty loo, who'll be the next one to die?"

Chapter 28

Glady arrived at the Moon Shell while Bonny and I ate lunch in the office. Bonny made her dry kibble sound delicious, but I told her she was welcome to eat the entire bowl. I settled for the peanut butter sandwich I'd packed. Emrys had either kindly vacated the desk chair or disappeared into a loop, and I'd locked our list in the desk drawer.

"Knock-knock," Glady called.

"We're in the office. Come on in."

"A royal we?" Glady asked from the office door.

Mouth full of peanut butter, I pointed at Bonny.

"I'm glad you girls are getting along so well." Glady settled on the spindle-back chair and held up a folded piece of paper. "I'm concerned about the incident at the Fig and Yaupon, so I've been working on my list of suspects. I'll read it to you." She unfolded the paper.

Flickering into view and reading over her shoulder, Emrys said, "This won't take long."

"Who killed Allen Withrow? List of prime suspects," Glady said. "Those are the title and subtitle of my report. I will provide commentary as I go." She cleared her throat and gave the paper an authoritative rattle, holding it so I had no chance of reading ahead. "Oh, before I forget, Tracy's having her clean-up party tomorrow. Five o'clock to whenever."

"Thanks."

"You're welcome. Now, first on the list—Maureen Nash."

"Well, that's a blow," I said.

Glady held up a hand. "Not to worry. Your name is crossed off."

"Good. That makes me feel better." I would've felt even better if my name hadn't been on her list at all, but I *had* spent quite a bit of time with Emrys going over our questions about Glady and Burt.

"Burt crossed it off," Glady said.

"Nice of him. Thank him for me, will you?"

"Of course."

"Do you think he'd share his reasoning with Deputy Brown and Captain Tate?" I asked.

"When I asked him why he crossed you off, he said because it's rude to accuse a friend."

"That's it?" Emrys gave Glady an annoyed look. "Not a ringing endorsement of your innocence, is it."

"Looking on the bright side," I said, "I'm glad to know he thinks of me as a friend. But aren't the rest of your suspects friends, too?"

"Friends are a dime a dozen," Glady said. "We're all more or less friends or friendly on Ocracoke. That's why so many people will be betting on you, the stranger, being the killer."

"Makes sense," I said. Sadly, it did.

"The next name is Noah Horton," Glady said.

"The Ocracat enthusiast who's a vegan and sweet on Yanira," I said. "Also a picketer?"

"Yes." Glady looked at me over the top of her paper. "How did you know that?"

"I must have heard it from someone." The someone in question now chortling behind Glady. "What did Allen think of Noah?"

"He called Noah annoying as shell."

"Allen had a wonderful way with words," Emrys said.

"Then we have Tracy," Glady said. "She likes hearing people say she has her fingers in a lot of pies."

"That's a fact of life on Ocracoke, isn't it?"

"But not everyone makes and sells pies."

"What was her relationship like with Allen?" I asked. "For instance, does she take sample pies around to other businesses?"

"She does." Glady looked over the paper at me again, then went back to reading. "The break-in might be an excellent example of misdirection—stage a break-in at your own business to throw off the authorities. Next, Dr. Allred." She held the paper to her chest. "There isn't paper, ink, or time enough in the universe to list all the reasons why he should be on this list."

"I'm happy to have him listed," I said, "but I'd also like to hear at least one reason."

"Drumming up business for his sideline," Glady said. "Fulfilling his own prophesies. Creating his own proof that it and he are the real thing. Tokens of death, my foot. If he wanted to kill Allen, all he had to do was claim he saw a token of death and then make sure it came true."

"That's . . . creepily diabolical. Glady, you like the island's ghost stories. Do you believe there *are* ghosts?" I looked at the one now leaning against the doorjamb and studying his nails. "Imagine how annoying it would be to die with a broken fingernail, end up a ghost, and spend eternity not being able to file it."

"Please don't worry yourself along those lines on my account," Emrys said, with a note of priss in his voice. "I was the fastidious brother as well as the reluctantly piratical."

"I would *love* to see a ghost," Glady said. "Absolutely love it. Burt would, too. We've wanted to since we were children. Sadly, even though we crept from our beds in the dark of night and trailed down Howard Street past all the cemeteries, we never did. But—" She thumped her fist on the desk. "That doesn't mean Dr. Irving "Irritating" Allred isn't full of baloney. On to the next name on the list. Yanira Ochoa."

"I hate to think that," I said.

"But we can't afford to be the kind of amateur detectives who don't bother to investigate the sweet and innocent people they like, only to be shown up later for the chumps they are. It's not happening on my watch."

"But Burt crossed *my* name off the list."

"I know, I know," Glady said. "Call him an inconsistent old so-and-so."

"Or not," Emrys said. "Your name isn't really crossed off. That's why she isn't letting you see the list."

I let my jaw drop. He shrugged. I turned my aggrieved jaw to Glady, where it was wasted. Eyes on her list, she moved on.

"You'll like this one. Daniel Umstead. Some years ago, he made claims that Allen cheated him out of that piece of shoreline property."

"While he was acting as Allen's lawyer?"

"We're a small, close-knit community," Glady said.

"More or less friendly," Emrys added.

"But if Allen cheated him years ago, why kill him now?" I asked.

"Maybe Allen was a serial cheater," Glady said.

"A scam artist." I nodded. "This is a good list. Back to Noah. Wouldn't it be out of character for an animal rights activist to kill a fellow human?"

"But can't you see an activist taking the shop's crowning jewel and hurling it into the ocean, back from whence it came?" Glady demonstrated the hurl with gusto, saying, "Swim, be free."

"But the shell is dead," I said. "There's nothing to set free."

"That's why *you* wouldn't fling shells. Or kill Allen, probably. You're kind. You're moral. You're a people pleaser."

"Somehow those don't sound like compliments."

"I'm just saying you need to get more inside the villain's head. Try to feel murder in your hands." She dropped the paper to her lap and demonstrated feeling murder—with a vicious twist to her lips and her hands around an imaginary throat.

"I believe Glady is playacting," Emrys said. "You can breathe again."

"Okay. Cool. I'll do that," I said. Faintly. "What about opportunity?"

"That's the first thing we should check for each of these people," Glady said. "Yanira, for instance, might have been home with Corina during the crucial time period."

"Any idea how we go about checking alibis?"

"Let's not worry about that yet," she said.

"Maybe we should worry a bit. We don't want to make anyone mad. Especially a killer." My phone rang, and I made a face at Glady. "Allred."

"Let it go to voicemail," she said.

But I'd already accepted the call. "Hello?"

"Ms. Nash, I'm glad I reached you. How are you feeling? Any more hallucinations? If so, I'm still quite happy to make an appoint—"

"No, I'm fine. Thanks for checking. If I need you, I'll call." I disconnected.

Glady sighed. "I did tell you, didn't I?"

"You did. I should have listened. Was he ever married or interested in anyone?"

"I wouldn't know." Glady said in a tone that made me think I'd touched a nerve.

"If he and Allen had been interested in the same person," I

said, offering Emrys's theory, "that could be a motive. We're short on those. Why would any of these people kill him?"

"I gave you motives for Dan Umstead and Irv Allred," Glady said. "I don't think I've ever said their names together like that. Did you notice that they rhyme? What if they worked together?"

"Captain Tate might not see rhyming names as a good enough reason to haul them in for questioning. And not to be nitpicky, but is making good on the appearance of a token of death the motive or the method? And why would Dr. Allred suddenly start doing that?"

Glady nodded her head with a satisfied smile. "Now you're catching on to Dr. Irv Allred."

"You're not serious. Do other people think he's *been* doing that?"

"I would not be surprised, but I haven't discussed it with anyone. Not in so many words."

"Did any of those words suggest that Dr. Allred is a serial killer? And offer the kind of evidence we can take to Captain Tate?"

"Evidence," Glady said. "Such an irritating detail. Let's look into these names, and if we come up with nada, then we'll start again."

"Keeping in mind that we need motives," I said.

"Burt and I talked about that, and we agreed that motives, like friends, are a dime a dozen and none of them are a good enough excuse to kill Allen."

"I agree," Emrys said.

"That sounds like there are a lot of motives for killing him," I said. "Was he that unlikeable?"

"I can't speak for others," Glady said. "We liked him well enough."

"I wish I'd known him." I told Glady what I'd told Emrys, that I didn't know anyone well enough to put them on a suspect list. "All I can do is ask questions. Like, what about Frank Brown? He looked friendly with Tracy this morning at the restaurant. Any chance they're in it together?"

"Why? What have you heard?"

"Nothing. Just asking questions."

"Are you?" Glady refolded her list, then folded it again, taking pains to be precise. "I think you know *more* than someone who says they don't know anyone well enough. I think you're holding out on us and not divulging your sources. And so I question *your* motives."

"But I *don't* know more, Glady. I'm *not* holding out."

"Mm-hmm," Glady said, and left.

Chapter 29

"I didn't like to say so at the time, but you made a few mistakes," Emrys said after Glady all but slammed the Moon Shell's door. "As lead detective, I might have some pointers for you."

I was sorely tempted to say I had a pointer for him. I refrained. I also thought about going after Glady but stopped with my hand on the doorknob. She was right. I had a source I hadn't told her about. Emrys was right, too. I'd said things and asked questions like someone who knew more than a casual visitor would. Rats. I trailed back to the office. The lead detective sat behind the desk. I took the spindle-back. Bonny commiserated with me by rubbing my ankles. Or she was angling for a treat. I picked her up and settled her on my lap.

"What if you appear to Glady and Burt?" I asked. "Or to one of them. Then I wouldn't have this problem of a secret source of information. And think how excited they would be."

"Which of them do you think is preferable. Less excitable. Less apt to call the tabloids?"

"I see the problem." Rats again.

"Not as clearly," Emrys said, "as I do." Elbows on the chair arms, he tented his fingertips. "At first, moving a candlestick from one end of the mantel to another or blowing out the candle amused me. But attracting attention grew boring long ago."

"That's why you don't appear in front of more people? It bores you?"

"As I told you, I am not fully in charge of appearing and disappearing. But yes, when I have been able to appear, it does not necessarily go in a way that I find enjoyable. Not in recent decades. People with cameras and various other con*trap*tions. *Trap* being the important syllable. One fellow arrived with a ghost trap."

"Could that happen?" I asked. "Could someone trap you?"

"No, thank heaven. Ghost traps don't exist."

"How do you know they don't?"

"I have faith."

And I had an idea. "What if you write a diary?"

"I wouldn't know how. Where to start."

"People don't. They just begin. Even if it's just notes about the weather every day."

"How tedious," he said.

"Most diaries probably are, but that's what will make this one more authentic. I want you to write your memories and observations of Allen. You told me about phone calls that left him swearing. Write down what you remember about them. Make your notes look like Allen's notes. His diary."

"So you have a reason for knowing what I've been telling you. Very clever."

"Thanks."

"Did your husband—do you think he would mind if I call him Jeff? I feel as though I'm beginning to know him."

"He'd be tickled pink. Do you know that phrase?"

The corner of his lip lifted. "Do I want to?"

"He'd be overjoyed to know you, even if you're often an ass. Probably *because* you are. What were you going to ask?"

"Did Jeff keep a diary?"

"No." Then I said, "Oh." I was an idiot. I'd gotten too wrapped up in being clever. "It won't work. Unless you can forge Allen's handwriting, no one will believe he wrote it."

"It won't work, anyway. I can't write diary entries because so far in my two hundred and seventy-four years on the spectral plain, I've not been able to manipulate a pen."

Triple rats. "What's that smirk on your face for?"

"Fond memories. Besides carving shells, I had other hobbies. I would have been good at creating Allen's diary for him."

"You're a pirate and a *forger*?"

"I prefer merchant and artist. Although I did have occasion to sign papers for friends, from time to time, that solved small problems for them."

"Was it a lucrative sideline?"

"Done as a favor and the pleasure of getting the signatures exactly right."

"You don't think that's another kind of piracy? That the reason you can't pick up a pen now is payback for those forged signatures?"

"I went to confession each time and received absolution. Although . . ."

"Although what?"

"After two or three occasions, the vicar asked me to sign his bishop's name to a document of some type. If the gates of heaven are closed to pirates and petty forgers, you might be on to something."

He flickered, and I didn't want him disappearing on that dismal note.

"If you're a petty forger, then you're also a petty pirate. There must be some other reason for your—"

"My affliction. That's what we called it the other day."

"There must be some other reason for it."

"Do you think that's news to me after two hundred seventy-odd years?"

"With the emphasis on odd, I'm sure. No, I don't. And I don't know how to help you find the reason, but you want to find Allen's killer as much as I do. Maybe solving the murder and finding the reason for that will help."

But the odd fellow across from me had blipped out, and I was speaking to no one.

Chapter 30

Saturday morning, the ginger cat was back and looking through the kitchen window. Sure enough, one ear was docked, identifying it as an Ocracat. I hadn't seen it for a few days, though, so maybe this was a different ginger Ocracat. I smiled at it and slowly closed and opened my eyes a few times, avoiding direct eye contact. I packed a bag lunch and did my few dishes. The cat was gone before I finished.

When I opened the inner door, the ginger cat stood at the screen door and meowed.

"Good morning," I said. "Do you mind if I come out?" I pushed the screen door slowly open, and the cat shimmy-danced backward. "What a graceful guy. See you later?" The cat looked at me with calculating eyes, then trotted away.

I pedaled to the Moon Shell to feed the other cat in my life. No sign of Emrys. No answer when I called, but ocean waves and the possibility of shells called to me. I headed out of town and along the highway a mile and a half to Ocracoke Beach for a day away from the shop, the ghost, thoughts of murder, and especially Glady and Burt.

There were no cars or other bikes in the beach parking lot. Maybe I'd be lucky enough to have the miles of pristine sand to myself. Shoulder pack on, following the boardwalk over dunes covered in flags of sea oats, I felt my heart quicken as the cries of gulls and the sound of the surf grew louder. At the end of the boardwalk, I scanned left and right. Not a soul as far as the eye could see.

I stepped from the walk onto the sand, becoming the first person to set foot on this undiscovered desert isle. Or, as my boys liked to say, a dessert isle made of crumbled cakes and cookies. Laughing like a gull, I went down to stand just out of reach of the curling waves. A line of pelicans skimmed the water a dozen yards from shore. The ever-present circus of sandpipers ran after waves, then turned to let the waves chase them. I spread my arms wide to the blue sky, doing a slow twirl to take in my unpopulated paradise, only to find I wasn't alone after all.

A tanned, sinewy young man appeared from behind a dune carrying a large kite. He ran with it, let it go, and paid out his string. Jeff and the boys had flown kites on this beach while I'd looked for shells. The kite flew over the dunes toward the boardwalk, and there was Patricia. I waved and went to meet her.

"Hey," she said, looking up and down the beach.

"Do you think that's the universal beach reaction?" I put a hand to my brow and looked left and right.

"Could be. Visitors are allowed back starting Monday. Do you want a ride to the ferry so you can go get your car?"

"That'd be great."

She scanned the beach again. "I was sorry to hear about Jeff. I meant to say that the other day."

"You were busy keeping us afloat and going forward."

"Always a plus."

"How do you manage to keep so calm and unruffled at a time like that?"

"It's all in the uniform. I take it off, and I become a mass of *Sturm und Drang*."

She waited. Looked expectant. "No joke? Not even a little one?"

"They come and they go. Right now, they're gone."

"You doing okay, though? Adapting to widowhood?"

Widowhood. "Sure. It is what it is. That's the best way for me to deal with it. You do what you need to do. I've had to become a realist."

"That sounds like a list you memorized."

"Nothing wrong with a good list." I'd been working hard on that list. To become a realist instead of Jeff's fabulous fabulist. "Lists are what they are. I won't get over it, but I'm working to get through it. At this point it'll take . . ."

"An electrifying change?" Patricia asked.

Oof. "Did you know Jeff died in an electrical accident?"

"I'm sorry. I did. My brains are still dealing with remnants of the storm." She pushed her sunglasses up her nose.

I shaded my eyes from the brilliant sun on this most gorgeous of days, nary a storm in sight, and watched the kite doing acrobatics. Wondered if it's possible to shade one's eyes with passive aggression. From Patricia's annoyed *tsk*, the answer was yes.

"A storm's remnants aren't just atmospheric," she said, her voice milder than the sun. "There's eroded beaches, washed-out paths, uprooted trees and boardwalks, all manner of flotsam. Some of it dangerous."

"No jetsam?" I asked.

"No reports of ships in peril. That's where jetsam comes from. Sacrificing cargo and whatnot to save a ship."

I pictured Emrys and his shell going overboard like so much jetsam, sacrificed for a rich cargo.

Patricia waved her hand in front of my face. "Are you there? I was saying thanks for keeping my name out of it and sorry to leave you on your own."

"Oh. The murder."

"We both know you're innocent. It's as simple as that."

Had anything been simple since stepping onto Patricia's boat? "Is it simple?"

"Clear cut." Patricia raised her hand, then brought it down like an axe blade. "I need this job. This is the best place I've ever been stationed. I want to finish my career here. I'm a good ranger."

She'd always been more than a decent friend, too, even if we didn't see each other often. So why was she making this difficult situation more difficult? "I tried calling you that night."

"I'm glad you didn't reach me." That sounded like her off-kilter sense of humor. She isn't totally tone deaf, though, and I expected a follow-up quip or a quick apology and explanation for why I hadn't reached her. Why she hadn't called or returned my texts. Instead, she said, "I expected you to take off up the beach. What were you doing? Your *Sound of Music* impression?" She mimicked my spread arms and slow twirl.

"Were you following me?"

"You? No. I was following Noah. Mr. Stunt Kite over there. Do you know him?"

"No."

"Noah Horton. *He* was following you."

"Why would he be following me?"

"That's what I wondered." She swatted a mosquito on her arm. "Maybe I was wrong."

And maybe I didn't know Patricia as well as I thought.

Chapter 31

Patricia left after flicking the squashed mosquito from her arm. I waited ten or fifteen minutes, during which Noah Horton flew his kite and never even surreptitiously peeked in my direction. Then I pedaled like mad for the Moon Shell. And there was Glady waiting for me on the steps when I coasted to a stop. So much for my day of getting away.

"Glady, I—"

"Walnut fig." She held out a plate with two muffins on it. "A peace offering. I'm not much of a jumper except when it comes to conclusions. Burt told me I'm a ninny. You've talked to plenty of people since you've been here."

I sat down next to her. "Wait'll you hear who I talked to this morning." While we shared the muffins, I told her about Patricia and Noah.

"What are you going to do?" Glady asked.

"It must be the steadying influence of your friendship and muffins," I said after eating my last bite. "I'm not going to jump to conclusions about either of them."

"There you go," Glady said. "And here I go. See you later."

I went inside and called hello to whoever was around. Bonny answered with a twine around my ankles. We went into the office, where I ate my peanut butter sandwich for dessert.

Then, as a sensible precaution, not a conclusion, I added Patricia's name to the list of suspects Emrys and I had made.

"Who is Patricia?" Emrys asked, appearing over my shoulder.

It took me a few seconds to get over that appearance. When I finally took my hands from my face, opened my eyes, and lowered my shoulders from around my ears, he was sitting across from me, looking contrite.

"You look as if you heard a ghost," he said.

"Nah. Ghosts are a dime a dozen. It was the pirate looking over my shoulder that scared the blue blazes out of me." I repeated the story of my morning at the beach and avoiding conclusions.

"Here is a question about conclusions." A growl crept into his voice. "Do you know how many bodies are buried in the dunes?"

"Er, no. *Why* are there bodies buried in the dunes?"

"They are the many unknown victims of shipwrecks, wrapped in sails and quilts by the villagers, buried in centuries past. I think Patricia saved your life today. It takes a great deal of good cord to fly a kite. Cord that can also be wrapped around a slender throat."

I put a hand to that throat. "Noah didn't look like a killer."

"Have you met anyone who does?"

"I'm going to change the subject now. Not because I'm ignoring what you said, but because this conversation is scarier than having a pirate ghost appear over my shoulder." I told him about going to the Fig & Yaupon that evening to help clean up the mess from the break-in. "It'll be a chance to meet people. Burt and Yanira are going. Glady's looking after Corina."

"I admire her resilience."

"For babysitting?"

"My wife and I were not blessed with children, and I was never anxious to look after anyone else's."

"Afraid of the responsibility?"

"No, I'm known for taking my responsibilities seriously. For family loyalty as well. Hence, my current predicament. Allen had amazing patience for listening to Corina's fascinations. She wanted a pony, to fly a plane, to take up journaling like her mother and Allen. Above all, she prattles on about shells in that high little voice."

"You can hardly blame her. She lives in a paradise of shells. You love them. Allen did. I do."

"Did I mention her ear-piercingly high voice?"

The Fig & Yaupon *had* been full of large, live, potted areca palms. Their remains and the remains of their pots and potting soil were spread over and around tipped chairs and tables throughout the dining room. Burt and I stopped inside the door, and he let out a soft whistle. Tracy came over when she saw us. Burt drew her into a hug.

"Thanks, Burt," Tracy said. "I'd wipe a tear but I've run dry." She held out a hand to me. "Are you Maureen? Thank you for coming to help. I swan, before this party is over I might find more tears after all."

"Where do we start?" Burt asked.

"Brooms are standing in the garbage can in the corner. More garbage cans for trash around the room. Vacuums against the far wall. Clean cloths where the register should be." She stopped and gave what was probably a healthy and oft-repeated snarl. "And the beer they didn't take, or shake and spray, is in coolers in the kitchen. Cheese and crackers, too. Have at it, help yourselves, and bless good neighbors."

"A lot of folks here," Burt said. "Keep your eyes and ears open for useful information."

"Aye, aye." We chose brooms and split up.

Most of the chatter I heard and exchanged with others was outrage over the vandalism, and understandably so. I gave a try at changing that with the next person I met over a trash can.

"Hi, I'm Maureen Nash, the surprise beneficiary of Allen Withrow's will," I said to a woman dumping pieces of broken ceramic plant pot.

"It's so good of you to come along here and help," she said.

I thought she was going to turn away and my experiment wasn't going to work, but she leaned across the trash can and said quietly, "Allen will be missed. By some." She stood back up and at regular volume said, "Welcome to Ocracoke."

"Thanks."

I introduced myself to another couple of people, and soon people came to introduce themselves to me. They told me what a character Allen was, how clever, what a source for stories—stories he told and stories told about him. I saw Noah trailing around behind Yanira. He eyed me from the other side of the dining room at one point. I waved. He came no closer. Patricia arrived, though, in jeans and T-shirt, and when she saw me, she came directly over.

"Hey, thanks for following Noah this morning," I said.

She wasn't interested in my thanks. She maneuvered so she had her back to the wall and with a smile said quietly, "You broke our agreement. You ratted me out about the boat ride." The smile was clearly not for me.

"I didn't."

"The police questioned you."

"And I said I got a lift in a boat and I didn't get a name. Captain Tate didn't press the issue. It didn't feel very good *not* telling him, but I didn't."

Patricia's smile sank beneath a roiling sea of unpleasant thoughts, then reappeared. Still not for me. "After I came back for you, to save you a soaking in the rain, and dropped you off at the rental, I drove to the point. *I* didn't tell anyone."

"Neither did I. Did you stop at the point?"

"Of course not. No parking."

"Even for rangers?"

She didn't answer. Because she didn't want to? Or because

it was a stupid question and not worth answering? And was it my imagination, or did there seem to be a lot of questions Patricia didn't answer?

"Who told you they know about the ride?"

She didn't answer that question, either. Didn't look at me. "Someone must have seen you arrive."

"Saw us get off your boat? We didn't see another vehicle at the dock." But had I looked around? "What if someone saw you drop me off in the truck and guessed? Did the person tell you they *know* you brought me, or did you jump to that conclusion?"

She jumped all right, straight down my throat with a hiss to let me know she wouldn't fall for something like that. Then she snapped her mouth shut and left.

Wow. If Glady *jumped* to conclusions, Patricia leapt like an Olympic long-jumper. I went to the kitchen and found the coolers of beer. Sipping a bottle back in the dining room, I saw Frank Brown. I nodded and he sashayed my way, holding a beer bottle by its neck.

"I saw you ingratiating yourself left and right," he said.

"Nice to see you, too." I stepped away. He blocked me.

"Know what I think?" he asked, voice low. "I'm gonna solve two murders for the price of one recent widow. The sizzled and the sliced."

I stared at him, wishing my eyes could inflict even a fraction of the pain Jeff and Allen must have felt when they'd died. The pain I still felt at Jeff's death.

"Oh, r-i-g-h-t." From his exaggerated pronunciation, he was drunk as well as cruel. Also disgusting. He pointed the neck of his bottle at me like it was a gun and belched.

"You're a jerk." The word I wanted to use had tried to force its way past my better judgment. It struggled mightily, but I'd kept it in.

"If you didn't kill him, I bet he dumped you."

"Shut it, Frank." Burt stepped between us. Total eclipse. I couldn't see Brown. He couldn't see me. I felt better already.

Yanira came and hooked her arm through mine. "Frank looked up to Allen like a grandfather. This has been hard for him. He's had too much to drink. Try not to mind his words. I'm so sorry about your husband."

"Convenient," Brown shouted, stepping sideways to look at me around Burt. "Deaths happen all the time. Convenient ones not so much."

"Frank, honey," Tracy said, "you need a cup of coffee." She presented a cup. "Voilà. Do me a favor and cool it, okay?" She further calmed the disorderly deputy with a hand in the small of his back.

I left my unfinished beer on a table and thought I might leave but Tracy came over, shaking her head. "Don't mind Frank. He's drunk as a skunk. I'm so glad you came along here tonight, Maureen. If there's anything I can do for you in the way of real estate, let me know. Where are you staying?"

"A tiny rental."

"Will you move into Allen's place?" She wrinkled her nose. "The look on your face says it all, and I don't blame you. He didn't die in the apartment, but it might take time, and in the meantime, I can take you around to look at other rentals. I keep my ear to the sand. I might know about an opening before it's official. Give the word and I'll be there."

"Thank you, Tracy. I will." Kelly had said he and O'Connor would be here if I said the word, too. There might be drunken deputies in the world, but there were more good people.

The drunken deputy was still on my mind when everyone left the Fig & Yaupon, though. On our way back to Howard Street, I asked Burt what he and Glady had against Brown personally.

"He's crass," Burt said. "When he's stressed, he resorts to particularly crass gallows humor. He got a broken nose to show for it. He apologizes a lot for it. He should see a therapist for it."

I didn't think what Brown said was an example of his gallows humor, but that Burt recognized Brown could use a therapist helped. So did his broken nose, but only as long as I was under Burt's calming spell.

Wishing I knew what Allen had thought of Brown, wondering if Allen had something *on* Brown, I stopped back at the Moon Shell.

"Emrys?" I called. "What did you say about Allen journaling?"

No answer.

Chapter 32

In the way of Glady and early mornings, she called me the next day before I'd rolled out of bed. "The ferries are running tomorrow," she said. "That means visitors. And that means a community-wide, post-hurricane spruce up. If you can be here in five, you can hitch a ride with us. We're heading down the highway to pick up any flotsam still loitering."

"Can you make it fifteen?"

"Ten and we'll come get you. I packed a picnic."

She disconnected without waiting for an answer. "Kind of bossy," I said to the dead ether and rushed to dress and bolt a bowl of cereal. I ate it over the sink, making kind eyes at the ginger cat. When I put the bowl in the sink, he turned around, raised his tail in the salute of a happy feline, and hopped down.

The cat met me at the door, doing his backward dance when I opened it. Glady and Burt weren't there yet and weren't in sight. The cat had only moved a short way off, so I crouched down low. He came closer, tail raised. He heard the golf cart before I did and turned to face the monster, giving me a clear view of his rear end. *Her* rear end. She'd been spayed recently enough that she'd obviously never had male parts, and now I saw that her belly fur, while growing in nicely, was shorter from being shaved.

"You're remarkable," I told her. "Gingers are almost never female."

She blinked at me and galloped away when Burt tooted Minerva's horn.

"Do we need to be careful of snakes?" I asked, climbing into the back seat.

"They won't be slavering after you, but keep an eye out," Glady said.

"For the slithering kind as well as the two-legged variety," Burt added.

We waved to others out picking up trash, raking strewn vegetation, arranging or rearranging outdoor furniture, and washing down or hauling whatever needed those attentions.

"Two-legger sighted," Glady said as we pulled into the beach lot where I'd parked the bike the day before. "Frank's at the boardwalk talking to Patricia."

Possibly *two* two-legged snakes, I thought guiltily. I really was keeping information from Glady and Burt. I waved at Patricia, hoping at least for a tepid nod. She adjusted her sunglasses. No wave, no nod. I told myself not to read anything into it. Her conversation with Brown was no doubt official business requiring her full attention.

Armed with long-handled grabbers and garbage bags, we set to work. Glady and Burt stayed on the ocean side of Highway 12, and I crossed to the sound side. Any work requiring machines or heavy lifting was finished for the most part. Hurricane Electra had battered and tossed, but she hadn't tried to sink the whole island like Dorian in 2019.

I grabbed all manner of plastic debris, wondering if someday I'd take hurricanes in stride like Glady and Burt. Be as unruffled in a wallowing boat as Patricia. She'd been right about the uniform. Not wearing it at the Fig & Yaupon, she'd been plenty ruffled. Before this trip, I wouldn't have questioned her integrity. I would have trusted her with my life. I *had* on the

boat trip over. But I'd kept quiet about the lift, kept that secret, and now I had to wonder if she had more secrets. And if
and when I should break my promise. Something pale at the
base of a low, windswept cedar, several yards away, caught
my eye.

A skull.

I took a step closer. A deer?

Another step. The breeze billowed it. A white plastic bag.

Laughing, I traipsed through the scrub and snatched it up.
Then, as Burt had said after seeing Allen's body in the woods,
once seen, I could not unsee the "skull." It and all its brethren.
Every misshapen bit of flotsam and garbage along the road became the skull of some unfortunate animal.

I trudged along. Haunted by skulls. Haunted by a ghost.
Dogged by this murder. Did I want to dump this garbage—lit-
eral and metaphorical—and flee back across the mountains to
Tennessee? Not yet. My storyteller's heart wanted to know
what would happen next.

Besides, something niggled at me. Something else I was sure
I'd seen, *shouldn't* unsee, that meant more than I'd realized
and now couldn't remember. A bit of Swiss cheese still took up
valuable space in my memory bank. Then again, maybe my
imagination was getting the better of me. Or Dr. Allred's
paramnesia. If the skulls started talking to me, then I'd worry.

Breezes continued to blow, keeping us cool and mosquito
free. One of them blew a scrap of news our way as we ate
Glady's picnic lunch. A storm-tossed kayak had been found.

Burt summed it up. "Happens."

"Should they worry about a missing paddler?" I asked.

"No one's been reported," Glady pointed out.

"Anyway, it'll have a registration number so it can be returned," I said, wiping that worry from my mind.

"Not required," Burt said.

"Too bad," I said. "Could it be a clue?"

Neither of them laughed, but Glady did say, "I think we've all been out in the sun too long. Let's call it a day."

When Burt tossed our garbage, he picked up a much bigger scrap of news. A real clue. "Down a sandy track, not exactly hidden," he said. "Allen's golf cart with the key still in it."

"We're lucky it was found today, then," Glady said. "With the ferries running tomorrow, day-trippers could've found it and taken it back with them."

"Maybe that was the hope," Burt said.

"Was there a knife in it?" I asked.

"Not so far," Burt said. "The sheriff's department will be taking that thing apart for any kind of clue it'll give up."

I pulled my notebook out of my shoulder pack, and on the way back, we started a list of clues. Allen's golf cart came first.

"I wish we'd found it," Glady said.

"We wouldn't have learned much," Burt said. "We couldn't have touched it, and the rain would've washed away any footprints if there'd even been any."

"We have the footprints on the porch," I said.

"And the cameo shell," Glady said. "What do we know about it? Its history? Beyond the minimal information on the card in the display case, nothing."

"I'll see what I can find out," I said. "Allen's letters to Jeff might be a clue. And the envelope Deputy Brown found in Allen's pocket."

"The weapons," Burt said.

"The break-in at the Fig and Yaupon," Glady added. "Maureen's arrival on Ocracoke." Turning to look at me, she said, "That might be a catalyst instead of a clue."

"Catalysts count," I said and wrote it down. "What about Allen's jeans and ring?"

"Add them," Burt said.

"And what Deputy Brown muttered to Allen's body.

'You've always been more trouble than you're worth.' That gives me chills. Anything else?"

They didn't answer, maybe nursing their own chills, and then we were back on Howard Street.

I took a picture of the list, sent it to their phones, and thanked them for the interesting day. "I'll stop in across the street, feed Bonny, and give her a few cuddles." Also to make my own private list of clues. And to see if Emrys was free to talk about what he'd meant when he said Allen journaled.

Bonny greeted me. Emrys didn't. I fed Bonny and wrote down my first clue: Emrys. What I meant by that, I didn't know. But he was here, he was an anomaly, and anomalies might be clues.

Glady and Burt's possession of a spare key to the Moon Shell came next. Then their knowledge of where Allen kept the two keys to the display case. And their suspicions of other people. Were they real, or were those suspicions meant to throw me off? Distract me from looking more closely at them?

Making this list was not fun. I continued, anyway.

Glady's doodled spirals—what did they represent? Spiraling debt? She'd said they could use the money if they sold the Moon Shell building. Or was their relationship with Allen spiraling out of control? Had Burt wanted an end to Allen's pressure to sell him the Moon Shell building? Glady said she'd been harassing him to get more help for years. Was she really? Or was she harassing him about something else and they'd finally had enough?

Then there was Patricia. Why hadn't she answered her phone texts when I found the body?

Was anything on my list really a clue? Or was I messing with my head and messing up the chance to keep friends?

I stayed at the Moon Shell longer than I meant to, losing myself in the displays of shells and in what-ifs. What if Allen hadn't been killed? What if we stumbled too close to the killer and he, she, or they felt cornered? What if I wanted to stay here? What if I decided I couldn't?

Stayed too long waiting for a ghost who never showed up, probably because he was lost in his own shell.

I gave up and finally rode the bike home.

The clamshells lining the gravel path to the rental looked like the teeth of a long-jawed, long-dead creature. I walked gingerly between those gnashing rows to the door of my mousehole and crept inside.

Chapter 33

Monday morning—had I arrived only a week ago? I watched the ginger cat dance backward when I opened the screen door, told it I'd be back later, then pedaled off to feed the cat living in my shop. Odd to think of it as mine. And to find the irritating pirate in residence. He and Bonny met me at the door, both smiling.

"What shall we do today?" Emrys asked as Bonny meowed. "She has the same question."

"Breakfast and bones." While I fed Bonny, I told Emrys about seeing bones and teeth the day before. "And that put a question in my head. Do you know where your bones are?"

"That's a rather personal question, don't you think?"

"It's a curious question," I said. "You're a curious person."

"Thank you for that. For calling me a person."

"I wonder if your body washed ashore somewhere. If you were buried. Maybe in a sand dune?"

"Not that I know of." He sat in the desk chair and clasped his hands. "*Would* I know?

"No idea. Would you like to . . . rest?"

"I would like to know why I'm *not* resting. But I've grown used to my lot. Allen, however, was keen on the idea of finding a way for me to at last rest in peace."

"How?"

"Research, is what he said. Not that I stood over his shoulder ever after that, to check his progress, but I was never aware of him doing any research along those lines. Here is a greater mystery than where my bones might be. Why am I not wet, and why do I have my hat? Surely it floated off when I went in the drink."

I opened my mouth. Closed it. "Any answers?"

"None so far," he said. "I waited up the night Allen died to see if he might come back, and if he did, would he also be whole? Or at least not covered in mud."

"You might get used to the mud," I said.

"We'll never know. He didn't come back."

"Don't give up on him. This house didn't exist when you died, but here you are. Maybe he's somewhere else on the island."

He shrugged, and it occurred to me that no one shrugs quite like a two-hundred-forty-seven-year-old ghost who's never met another ghost. Even sadder, I couldn't put my arm around him to make him feel better.

"Here's a more down-to-earth question," I said. "What did you mean when you said Allen journaled?"

"Absolute agony. Do you remember my complaint of Corina's high-pitched voice? Allen's whistling was worse. He whistled tirelessly, tunelessly, and off-key."

"What does that have to do with his journaling?"

"The whistling? It was enough to make me wish I'd been sent straight to Hades."

"Is this obsession with his whistling a new loop?" I asked.

"No, I'm trying to explain," Emrys said. "As soon as Allen pursed his lips, I removed myself from his company so as not to lose my mind. It is because of his whistling that I don't know anything about his journaling. Only that he did it and nearly drove me mad. Why is this suddenly so important to you?"

"Not suddenly. I asked you if Allen kept a diary, and you said no. A journal is a diary."

"A journal is, yes, but *journaling*, as I heard Corina describe it, is more of an art project for one's mementos. She mentioned stamps, which sounds wasteful and not particularly interesting.

"She probably meant decorations made with reusable stamping tools and ink pads, not postage stamps."

"Bits and bobs of ribbon and lace might also be involved," he said, "and something called grunge."

"Journaling is also the act of keeping a journal."

"Forgive me for being ancient history, but that wasn't true in my lifetime."

"Don't worry about it. You do pretty well for a fossil. But you don't know what kind of journaling Allen did because he whistled while he worked. I bet it wasn't the ribbons and lace kind." I spun around on my heel, taking in the small office. I'd never seen anything like a journal in here. "Do you know where he kept it?"

"I'm afraid not. I'm sure you find me foolish, but you have no idea how ghastly the whistling was. It put me in mind of banshees coming for my soul."

"I would run from banshees, too," I said. My phone buzzed. A text from O'Connor.

"**Where are you right now?**" he asked.

"**In the shop.**"

"**Open the front door.**"

Without thinking I sent back "**What?**" Then I ran to the door and threw it open and there stood my grinning boy. There is nothing in the world half so nice as the hug of a grown-up child. I hugged him right through the door into the shop.

"I drove down yesterday so I could be at the ferry dock early," he said while I mopped my eyes and blew my nose. "My gear's in the car. I'll camp on the property. So show me around the shop. Oh—" He jabbed his thumb over his shoulder. "There's a guy picketing out front. The place isn't open, is it?"

"Nope." I looked out the window. Noah.

"So, if an activist pickets where no one hears him," O'Connor said, "does he make a point?"

I hugged him again. "It's so good to have you here. Come meet—"

We both glanced around at the general lack of anyone. Bonny trotted from the office to my rescue.

"Meet Bonny." I scooped her up, and she and O'Connor politely touched noses. "Glady and Burt live across the street. You can meet them later," I said. "Want to see the mousehole?"

We locked the shop behind us and had the kind of day I'd longed for. O'Connor laughed at the mousehole's tiny outside but marveled at the compact arrangement inside. We ate lunch at the reopened Fig & Yaupon. Tracy welcomed us, told O'Connor what a good friend I'd been to help in the aftermath of the break-in, and refused to let us pay the bill. We walked around the village, took pictures of each other at the lighthouse and more of a green heron in the shrubs nearby. It hunched in a tangle of branches, like an old man with a preposterously long and pointy nose, trying to hide. O'Connor bought a Blackbeard T-shirt, and we sipped cold beer at a harborside café while watching boats, seagulls, and people. I hadn't heard from Patricia since she'd stormed out of the Fig & Yaupon, so O'Connor and I made plans to pick up my car in the morning. We didn't say a thing about murder the entire day.

"You're sure you want to camp?" I asked.

"Are you kidding? Kelly's already ticked he couldn't come with me. Camping's the extra touch to really rub it in. The Blackbeard shirt's to placate him."

"Come for breakfast, though," I said. "And if you get spooked out there, you know where to find me." *Spooked*. If he only knew.

* * *

The ginger cat arrived shortly after O'Connor did the next morning. O'Connor enthused over his night in the wilds and over the cat.

"She's a rarity," I said. "Ginger cats are usually male. I named her Rogers."

"Roger, Mom? For a girl?"

"Rogers, with an *s*, after Ginger. She dances backward when I open the door."

I watched him slowly sink to the floor near the screen door but out of the cat's view. Slowly, slowly he leaned forward until he could peek around the corner. They came face-to-face as Rogers peeked in at O'Connor. The care he took not to scare Rogers away was how he got the reputation as the family cat whisperer.

We lazed around, called Kelly. I took O'Connor to meet Glady and Burt, who plied him with muffins and questions. When O'Connor asked if anyone had ever found buried pirate treasure on the island, Burt laughed and said if they did, he'd never heard it. Then we left his car at the landing on the Ocracoke side and took the ferry to Hatteras to get my car.

"And soft-shell crab sandwiches for lunch," O'Connor said as we rode the ferry with the wind and sun in our faces. "I saw a place in Hatteras, and I haven't had one in years."

Soft-shell crab sandwiches aren't an acquired taste so much as an acquired look. They're delicious, but because it's the entire, recently molted crab, breaded and fried, on a bun, legs sticking out, the sandwiches look a bit spidery. We sat in a booth, not saying much but moaning indecently over the sandwiches and a mound of onion rings. Then O'Connor's eyes sharpened. He took out a pen, wrote on his napkin, and pushed it across to me.

"*Just sat down in the booth behind you. The guy picketing the shop yesterday.*"

I raised my eyebrows.

O'Connor nodded and whispered. "Same guy, same shirt."

We heard the waitress take his order—a soft-shell crab sandwich. For a vegan? It couldn't be Noah.

But it was. We passed his booth on our way out, and he was enjoying his sandwich every bit as much as we'd enjoyed ours.

"He's vegan," I said when we were outside. "Claims to be, anyway. Was he on the ferry with us this morning?"

"I didn't notice. If we see him on the way back, we can ask."

"Nah."

But after I drove my car onboard, I told O'Connor I was going to stretch my legs. I made a tour of the ferry and didn't see Noah. Feeling silly, I joined O'Connor where he stood at the front of the boat. He was talking to a squatty man who had a thick head of gray hair and a heron's hunch, who gestured expansively with a sandwich in one hand.

"Ms. Nash?" the heron said.

I knew that voice.

"I'm Irv Allred. So pleased to finally catch you." He held out the non-sandwich hand, looking as if he'd won the lottery and I was the prize.

A seagull, having spotted its own prize, swooped down and grabbed the sandwich, making Allred duck. I took a step back and jammed my hands in my back pockets. Handshake averted. Saved by the gull.

"I'm going to make a guess about you," he said to O'Connor. "*Two* guesses." He looked O'Connor over, from running shoes to shiny brown hair. "First, you are Ms. Maureen Nash's son. Second, you arrived at Ocracoke yesterday, one week to the day after your mother. I know because you have the look of a Monday traveler."

"There's a look for that?" O'Connor asked.

"Oh, yes, because if you start a journey or vacation on a Monday, you drag bad luck along with you."

Chapter 34

"How long can you stay?" I asked O'Connor over breakfast in the mousehole

"I'll need to leave Saturday. I wish I could stay longer. How about you?"

"I took the mousehole for three weeks, through the next Sunday night, and can't extend the lease. I might stay longer. I don't know. There's a lot to think about. A lot of details to work out. It might be better to think about them back home."

"Away from island magic?" he asked.

"Something like that. I can stay in the apartment above the shop. I'm getting used to the idea, but—" I smiled, shrugged, sighed.

"You don't need to make any decisions right now. Not for weeks or months. You can keep the shop for good or for a while. Allen left enough money that you can run the shop as a hobby and not worry about profits."

We made our plans for the day. O'Conner wanted to tramp around the property so we knew what we had and could make decisions about keeping or selling it. I wanted to know the details of the lease for the Moon Shell building so I could start making decisions about the business. That meant stopping at Glady and Burt's because I hadn't found a copy of the lease agreement.

"I'll pick up something for supper," O'Connor said.

"Great. Text me. I might be at the shop."

He exchanged meows with Rogers on his way out.

"Kitchen's a mess," Burt said when I knocked on their door. "We'll meet you at the shop."

"Okey-doke," I said to the door he closed in my face. That gave me time to feed Bonny and brief Emrys. I didn't see him, but I told the ether the Weavers were coming over in case he was lurking instead of looping.

"We might as well be comfortable," Glady said when they arrived, and she led the way upstairs to the apartment.

"Comfortable and well-fed." Burt put a plate of muffins studded with toasted almonds on the coffee table. "And who knows, maybe we'll be in touch with Allen's spirit up here and he'll tell us whodunnit."

"Anything's possible." I glanced around the living room. It was cozy, like the mousehole, but on a more livable scale. Emrys flickered into view on the window seat. "I haven't found Allen's copy of a lease for the building."

"There isn't one to find," Glady said. "Oral agreement has always been good enough."

"Would a written one be okay?" I asked. "Burt, these are great. Do you make muffins every morning?"

"My morning ritual," he said. "I took up baking during the pandemic."

"I took up eating them," Glady said. "We'll talk about leases later. For now, we're happy to know you're thinking about keeping the shop. We're also happy you aren't opening immediately."

"I need time for things to settle," I said. "Time to ease into it."

"And we don't want anything interfering with our investigation," Glady said.

"We'll use the shop for our base of operations," Burt added, "and I won't feel pressured to immediately clean up after my morning muffin meditation."

"We could leave the investigation to the police," I said.

"To Frank Brown?" Glady made a rude noise. "Forget that. We're on the murder trail."

"Let's maybe not call it that," I said, then told them about Noah in the café in Hatteras.

"What a fraud," Glady said.

"He must have been following you again," said Burt. "How did he explain himself?"

"He would've denied it if I'd asked."

"You *didn't*?" Glady said. "We need to teach you nosier ways. You pussyfoot around like an Ocracat."

I was scouring the place, looking for Allen's diary, when Daniel Umstead knocked on the door. He greeted me warmly and Bonny like an old friend. He picked her up, and she purred when he rubbed her between her ears.

"If you're looking for a home for her, I'll be happy to have her," he said. "I haven't had a cat since my wife passed away."

"I'll keep you in mind. Thanks."

"I could take her off your hands now . . ."

"I'm not ready for that yet. She's a sweetie, isn't she?"

He nodded and looked around with what looked like appraising eyes.

"Is there something else I can do for you?" I asked. "Are you interested in shells?"

"I've never paid much attention to the shell at the center of all this. When I saw the lights on, I thought I'd come take a gander."

"Gander away. It's the one preening on the blue velvet in the upright case."

Umstead let Bonny jump down and stooped to peer at the shell. "Astounding. Is there more carving on the back?"

"Just the front."

"Do you take it out for special customers?"

"I've heard that Allen did. I'm more comfortable acting in a custodial role for now."

"I'm disappointed," he said straightening. "But you're wise. You know, I might also be interested in the shoreline property Allen left. Have you been to see it?"

"Not yet." I didn't like the idea of telling him O'Connor was camping there. Hadn't liked that he wanted to take Bonny with him, for that matter.

"It isn't suitable for much really," he said.

"That's too bad. What would you do with it?"

"Fishing. Duck hunting."

"Well, I'll keep that in mind, too."

He looked around again and didn't say goodbye to Bonny or me when he left. I locked the door and looked for the diary with renewed effort.

Captain Tate called that afternoon to say he had the autopsy results. "I thought you'd be interested. They show that Allen died well before you say you found the body. It also says the blow to the back of the head was delivered by someone taller than you. Lividity suggests he spent more time on his back than facedown. He might have survived either the stab wound or the blow if he'd received aid in time. Given where he died, either wound on its own could have been fatal. With both, he didn't have a chance."

"That's so awful," I said. "Thank you for letting me know. I almost hate to ask, but does it clear me?"

"You could have arrived earlier than you claim," Tate said, "but—"

"But I didn't."

"Let me finish."

"Okay."

"It's good news. We know what time you bought gas in

Manns Harbor, and we've spoken to the motel in Hatteras where you left your car. As far as I'm concerned, you're in the clear. There's one more detail. They were able to remove his ring. It was his, all right."

"I didn't know there was a question."

"There are always questions." He sounded tired. "But the inscription proves it's his. 'GLADY & ALLEN, MARRIED NOW & FOREVER, JUNE 3, 1963.'"

O'Connor brought goat cheese, Gruyère, and fig pizza for supper. We ate it in the office, and it was fabulous.

"Here's to good police work," he said when I told him Tate no longer considered me a suspect. "We might want to call on them again. Someone's been digging holes on the shore lot."

"Recently?"

"Since the last rain," he said. "There are footprints, too, and they don't look like they weathered a hurricane."

"Interesting. After we found the body and Deputy Brown searched here, someone found muddy footprints on the porch and covered them until Brown came back in the morning. He took pictures. I did, too."

"Cool." O'Connor pulled out his phone. "Wanna see if they match?"

I found the clearest picture I'd taken and held my phone next to his. "Okay, we need to send these to Captain Tate. I have an uneducated shoe eye, but it looks like the same tread pattern and wear at the edges of the heels."

We sent the pictures to each other, then I sent both to Tate. O'Connor, taking precautions, suggested we email them to ourselves, too.

"Should we send them to Glady and Burt?" O'Connor asked.

"Done."

"Good thinking, on their part, for covering the porch prints," he said.

"They didn't." Then, as carefully as O'Connor talks to cats, I took a chance and told him about Emrys.

"This is one of your stories, right? It's great, Mom."

I shook my head.

"But you don't really believe all that," he said.

"I wondered at first, but now I know it's true."

And I saw the same immeasurable pain in his eyes that I'd seen when I told him his dad had died. "Sweetie?"

"I'm going to—" He nodded to the door. "To the campsite. Sleep on it." He looked in my eyes and kissed my forehead. "See you in the morning."

I went to the door and watched him go, wondering what I'd done, saw him texting on the way to his car. Probably telling Kelly they were losing their mom, too.

Emrys shimmered into view as I sat at the desk, staring at nothing. "I'm sorry," he said.

I couldn't even shrug.

"I've remembered one of Allen's shouted phone conversations," he said. "It was about a shoe. A nasty, smelly shoe. And bribery. That sounds as though it ought to be helpful, although I cannot imagine how."

"Maybe."

"Other than the oaths, I'm afraid I remember nothing more about it. I tried to give him his privacy, but with the shouting that was difficult. Where's a good loop when one needs one? Your discussion of the footprints sparked that memory. Would you like to know my ambition?"

"Sure."

"I have read Sherlock Holmes. He may be a character in stories, but I admire his intellect and focus. I would like to use my own intellect and focus to become an expert on shoe tracks. As much of an expert as someone can be who almost never ventures outside and who learns everything from newspapers, books, and the World Wide Web. Does that amuse you?"

"No. It delights me. Why such a specific interest?"

"My father wanted me to learn his trade. Follow in his footsteps, so to speak."

"Why didn't you?"

"If I had, I'd be alive today."

"Not really."

"Fair point. I chose to follow my brothers to the colonies."

"How do I say I'm sorry you're dead but glad you're still here without sounding—"

"Ghoulish? Sentimental? Ghoulishly sentimental?"

"I was thinking nuts. For want of an interest in shoes, you followed your brothers to your doom. You hear about first-world problems and third-world problems, but I've never thought about netherworld problems. Speaking of them, though, who rescued your shell from the water when you fell overboard?"

"It was more memorable than merely falling overboard. Being shot is highly memorable. But I did get hold of the shell, there at the bottom of the sea, and I managed to hold on to it through whatever else happened to me. Perhaps that's how my essence became attached to it."

"But you used me to get it this time."

"It's a large shell, and heavy. Larger than many a mutton joint. Certainly heavier than a piece of paper or a newspaper page. And if I remember correctly, you were eager enough to retrieve it."

"If *I* remember correctly, I wondered why I should risk my life to get it."

"I knew you were bluffing," he said pompously, but looked at me out of the corner of his eye, as if checking my reaction.

"You had no way of knowing that. Plus you're afraid of water."

"A healthy fear," he huffed. "Considering what it did to my health."

"It *is* a healthy fear. Like mine of sharks."

"But you've never died at the teeth of one."

"Nope. You win again."

"Win what?"

"Never mind. See you later." I stopped at the door. Spoke to the doorknob. "You always have to be right."

"In this instance, I am. I dare say you've never even been nipped by a shark, whereas I—" He cut himself off. Came to stand by the door, brow furrowed and arms crossed over his chest. "I don't understand why being right is wrong. And why it makes you study the doorknob."

At times like that, like the bike ride back to my mousehole, feeling small, I missed Jeff. He liked to say, "Snits are fits of pique. Let's kick sand in this one's face and move on." He was right. He was easy to live with. I'm not sure I am.

Glady called as I was getting ready for bed. "Rob Tate had an anonymous tip that told him to look under the trapdoor in Yanira's living room. They found a bloody kayak paddle."

Chapter 35

Emrys the Accidental Pirate Ghost battled with gusto and pratfalls from one glorious, hilarious defeat to another, ineptly wielding a kayak paddle in place of a cutlass and forever getting his toes or fingers (and one time his nose) slammed in an enormous trapdoor throughout my dreams that night. It would have been so easy to entertain O'Connor with the tales over breakfast and tell him he'd been right. I'd made the whole ghost thing up. To lie. I couldn't.

But I did take the Ocracat pussyfooter's way out by ignoring the ghost thing. Over quick bowls of cereal, we talked about the property, which he remained enthusiastic about, the kayak paddle found under Yanira's trapdoor, and our plans for the day. Mine included dashing to the apartment to meet Glady and Burt.

"Mind if I come with you?" O'Connor asked.

"I'd love that." Maybe he'd be reassured I was the same old Mom.

"Baking frees my brain cells," Burt said, passing chocolate chip muffins.

"When have they ever been corralled?" Glady smiled and passed the plate to O'Connor, who was in the window seat with Bonny. "*Your* gray cells are a welcome addition, O'Connor."

"Unless Yanira put the paddle under the trapdoor herself," Burt said, "the only time it could've been put there is during the cleanup party at the Fig and Yaupon."

"I called her this morning," Glady said. "She hasn't been away from the house long enough, except for the party."

"Also in her favor—she isn't tall enough," I said. "That goes for you and me, too, Glady." I told them about the autopsy results.

"We're getting somewhere." Burt rubbed his hands. "Where's the list of suspects? Let's see who *is* tall enough."

"What if Allen was on his knees when he was hit?" O'Connor asked. He took another muffin while we stared at him. "At least Mom's still in the clear because of the timing."

"Right," Glady said. "Yanira picked up Corina right after Burt got home. Did she leave at any time during the party? Did any of the other suspects? I typed the list and made copies. You take one, too, O'Connor. I have the original."

"Patricia Crowley left early," I said. "Allred and Umstead weren't there."

"Patricia's not on the list," Burt said. "Should she be?"

"I . . . think so." I told them about seeing her taillights heading toward the point after dropping me off when I arrived. "That on top of not answering her phone or texts that night? And now leaving the party early."

Glady patted my knee. "We felt bad putting your name on the list, too."

"Frank might have slipped away," Burt said. "He was there when we finished, but I don't recall seeing him after he cornered Maureen. I did see Noah leave."

"Frank is Deputy Brown?" O'Connor asked. "And he's a suspect?"

"It's hard to say what his motive would be," Burt said.

"It's more like he's trying to find a way to pin the murder on your mom."

"And Dr. Allred is the guy on the ferry who told us we'd dragged bad luck with us?" O'Connor asked.

"Hard to believe that man graduated medical school," Glady said.

"Daniel Umstead stopped by yesterday." I told O'Connor who Umstead was and all of them how he wanted Bonny and the shore property. "He wanted to see the shell, too. He said it's at the center of all this."

"As good a theory as any," Burt said. "I thought we were getting somewhere. Now I'm not so sure."

"Thank goodness we're only amateurs." Glady put the lid on the muffin tin.

"At the autopsy, they got the ring off Allen's finger," I said.

"We'll be on our way," Glady said. "Come on, Burt."

"It's inscribed with the names Glady and Allen," I said.

"That's our Glady," said Burt as Glady tried to shush him.

"All right," Glady said. "All right. I admit it. We were married."

"Why didn't you say so when you saw the ring?" I asked.

"Why bother?" Burt said. "Everyone knows they were married, and everyone knows he didn't deserve Glady."

"That's a bit harsh." Glady picked up her coffee cup. Took a sip. "I married him in my wild-child, off-island youth that lasted for only slightly longer than the marriage or my nursing career. I saw the error of my ways and came home to Ocracoke. Neither of us ever wore our rings again, so that night I couldn't be sure that's what he had on his finger. Why would he suddenly start wearing it? His legs sure looked good in jeans, though. And out of them."

"But you said you were never married," I pointed out.

"When did I say that?"

"The night we met. I thought you and Burt were married, and you said—"

"I said *maybe* I hadn't married." She looked at me over the rim of her coffee cup. "And there, my friends, is a lesson in how tricky words are."

Captain Tate phoned midmorning. "At your convenience, can you and your son come by the station? I'd like to return Allen's laptop and discuss the footprints."

The station is across the highway from Howard's Pub, and O'Connor and I agreed to eat lunch there after talking to Tate.

"Does Tate know that you and the Weavers are playing detective?" O'Connor asked as we pulled into the station's parking lot.

"I bet he knows that most people who knew Allen are trying to figure out what happened."

Tate welcomed us into his office and offered coffee. O'Connor introduced himself and accepted. I'd reached my limit for the day.

"Another person has stepped forward to say she saw you arrive on the island *after* the time of death and that she gave you a lift to your rental."

"Patricia Crowley," I said.

"You didn't tell us about her before."

"There was a lot that disappeared from my memory for a few days," I reminded him.

"Didn't you tell me you wondered about taillights you saw after she dropped you off?" O'Connor had his father's theatrical gift and did a credible imitation of someone dragging his mind for details.

Conflicted, I told Tate about the taillights. Then told him I was conflicted.

"Completely understandable," he said. "Put your mind at ease, though. Ranger Crowley was on Hatteras, assisting with hurricane response, until not long before she gave you that lift."

"That's—" I shook my head. "Thank you. You've lightened my worries. So what about the footprints?"

"They might belong to someone who knew Allen and local legends about buried treasure," Tate said. "Rumors fly every few years."

"They didn't match any footprints around the body?" I asked.

"Inconclusive. What concerns me is the man you say waved. Tell me about him again."

"I'd like to hear about him, too," O'Connor said, now sounding like a stern parent. I couldn't be sure, but I thought Tate suppressed a smile.

"I was ready to leave the beach," I said. "A man appeared at the edge of the woods and waved. That's how I found the path again."

"What did he look like?" Tate asked.

"I really only saw a silhouette. Dark clothes, nothing light."

"You're sure it was a man?"

"Deputy Brown asked that, too."

"We like to repeat ourselves. We're boring that way."

"Like a crossword puzzle clue you can't get the first time. Look at it again the next day, and the answer's obvious."

"Thanks, that sounds more intelligent than being boring. So what's your answer?"

"The person looked like a man. It was getting dark, and he stood just within the trees. If he hadn't waved, I might not have seen him at all. When I was on the path, I didn't hear anyone ahead. Should I worry about this guy?"

"If he waved," O'Connor said, "that sounds friendly. Otherwise, why draw attention to himself?"

Tate agreed. "I was hoping you'd remembered something that would help identify him. He might have seen something useful. But waving and turning Allen over only to club him are two different kinds of behavior. If the same man did both, then he could have come after you that night. He didn't. And if he's also the person who left footprints, again he's had plenty of time and opportunity to harm you since then. Have you heard or seen anyone around your rental or the shop? Anything suspicious other than digging activity at the property?"

"No."

"You don't look convinced."

"I've never been in a situation like this before. I thought Noah Horton was following me. Twice. Patricia Crowley's the one who saw him the first time. But really, either time could have been a coincidence."

"Fear is your friend," he said. "Keep your eyes open and be aware of your surroundings. Feel free to call anytime. I'll have a chat with Noah. Don't be overly worried. Our killer is lying low if he's even still on the island."

"I like 'The Man at the Edge of the Woods' as a title better than 'The Man Who Waved,'" O'Connor said over lunch. "I'm going to think he was a good guy."

"Me, too."

"If he hadn't waved, would you have seen him at all?"

"I doubt it." And now I had another question. Legally speaking, is a ghost a man?

Chapter 36

Then we had an interesting situation. As if my entire life wasn't already one of those lately. O'Connor and I, back at the Moon Shell, prowled Allen's bookshelves in the apartment. Emrys, back from a loop, watched from the window seat next to Bonny.

"Someone on the porch," Emrys said. He flickered out for a moment, then flickered back in. "Deputy Brown."

"Someone's at the door, Con. Be right back."

Brown was looking in a porch window, nose pressed to it, hands cupped around his eyes.

I crept to the front door and did something childish. And fun. I swung open the door and said, "Boo!"

Emrys would have died laughing if he weren't already dead.

"Funny," Brown said. "Got a minute?"

"You're not in uniform."

"Day off. I know something you'll be interested in. Let's say it will be to your advantage if you listen."

He sounded like a mobster. He also sounded like Allen's letters. He came in, and I closed the door behind him. Debated taking him upstairs, but would he talk in front of O'Connor? Tate said fear was my friend. Did I fear Brown? No, but I'd fear him less with O'Connor beside me.

"My son's upstairs. Come on up." I walked up the stairs. He could leave if he wanted to. He didn't. He came up the stairs behind me. "O'Connor, this is Deputy Frank Brown. Deputy Brown, my son O'Connor." They shook hands.

"Sit down," Brown said.

"After you, Deputy."

He sat on the edge of the recliner he'd commandeered from Burt the first morning we came upstairs. O'Connor and I sat across from him on the green settee. Emrys appeared in the window seat.

"Couple of years ago, after Allen had a few too many, he told me about a job he and a buddy pulled. A long time ago, far away but not too far. He wouldn't tell me the details, but he said he planned to make restitution."

"Did you tell Captain Tate?" I asked.

"No. The statute of limitations was long, long gone. This would've happened midsixties."

"Ancient history," O'Connor said.

"Allen kept a journal." Brown pulled a black leather book, the size of a slim paperback, from his back pocket.

"How did you get it?" I asked. "Did you take it the night you searched here?"

"No."

"He must have," Emrys said. "I might not have known that was a diary, but it belonged to Allen."

I remembered Glady's lesson about tricky words and took a chance. "You're right, Deputy Brown. You didn't take it from here. But you did take it. You took it from Allen's body."

"Can you prove that?" Brown asked.

"Call his bluff," Emrys said.

"Do you want to take the chance that I can?" I asked. "Because I will, and it will ruin your career. That's a promise." I took out my phone, glanced at O'Connor. He had his out, too.

"Don't do that," Brown said.

"I will take no pleasure in helping *you* do that. I'm not the one who took the diary." I put my hand out, and Brown put the diary in it.

"I came here to give it back," Brown said. "You know that, right?"

"And you did. Thanks," O'Connor said. "So what's the deal with it?"

"It's the connection between Allen and your dad. It's why Allen left everything to him. Allen's buddy was your dad's father. They pulled this job, Allen took the loot, and your grand-dad took the rap."

"Jeff's father was never in prison," I said. I handed the diary to O'Connor. "He wasn't, was he?"

"We'll get to that. Allen felt remorse late in life," Brown said. "When it was too late to make amends to Jeff's father. But he reached out to Jeff to atone by leaving the Moon Shell and the property to him."

"Jeff didn't know anything about this. His father never told anyone any of this."

"It's all in the book," Brown said.

"There aren't any names in here," O'Connor said. He flipped through the pages, with Emrys reading over his shoulder. "There are initials, but how do you know Allen was talking about Grandpa? What did they steal?"

"What do people steal that they can hide away?" Brown asked. "Money. Jewels. All we have to do is find the loot."

"Ah. There we are," I said. "If any of this is true, you're like Allen. You want the loot. But why do you think any of it is left?"

"Allen made it sound like he never touched any of it. And I think you know more than you're letting on. You might not know where the bodies are buried, but I think you know where *something* is."

"What's the heck is that supposed to mean?" I asked.

"Allen was a pirate. Pirates bury things. Clever people find treasure maps."

"You're delusional."

"Read that, and let me know if you still think so," Brown said. "I'll see myself out."

"I'll see you out," Emrys said and flickered after him.

"We'll need to read this more carefully," O'Connor said, "but Brown's capsule summary matches what I've skimmed. A burglary, worth a lot. I think Allen liked drama. He used initials, saying, 'It isn't for me to divulge names.' But there are only three initials—single letters only. Two burglars and one victim. *W*, *N*, and *E*. *W* for Withrow. *N* for Nash. I wonder who *E* was or is?"

"He never did tell us if Grandpa was in jail or prison," I said.

"And I don't believe it," O'Connor said. "Grandpa wasn't good at keeping secrets. Remember when he bought that classic Mustang for their anniversary? He swore us to secrecy, then told Granny himself. And it should be easy enough to find out. Can I use Allen's laptop?"

"If you can get in."

"The password is 637163," Emrys said.

I looked from Emrys to O'Connor. "Maybe the password's in the desk." I ran downstairs, wrote 637163 on a piece of notepaper, folded it, and stuck it in the top drawer. Ran back upstairs. "Try 637163."

"Cool. Got it."

"While you're in there, look for any files about burglary," I said.

"You mean this one called 'My Crimes'?"

"You're kidding."

"Mom."

We settled into a jolly afternoon, me with the diary and O'Connor on the laptop, searching for our family's criminal past. In the end, we both came up empty.

"Allen didn't write anything except about himself," I said when O'Connor closed the laptop's lid. "I had great hopes for this diary. That he'd dish on people who had it in for him or people he'd crossed. I wanted a smoking gun and a pointed finger."

"You knew he kept a diary?"

"It's an idea I heard floating around."

"No news is good news about Grandpa," he said. "And no personal files about the burglary or other crimes makes sense. The one burglary might have scared Allen straight. After writing it in the diary, why put it in a computer file, too?"

"Unless there was a file with more details and Brown copied and deleted it," I said.

"You think he'd do that?"

"Glady and Burt told me not to trust him. They've been right more often than not. I think we have a new suspect, too."

"Who?"

"Person or persons unknown—someone else Allen cheated or stole from."

Chapter 37

"You look comfortable in that desk chair," O'Connor said. "Do you remember when you and Dad took me to college for the first time and you said it felt like releasing me into my natural environment?"

"I do. It was."

"That's how you look in this office. In the Moon Shell. In Ocracoke."

"I don't know yet. I haven't gotten used to the idea of being here long-term or running a shop."

Emrys flickered into view. "Pie proprietor approaching."

I hadn't quite gotten used to his sudden appearances, either. I waited until Tracy knocked on the door and asked her in.

"Hey, Maureen, how's it going?" She came in with a cloth-covered basket on her arm and an aroma of freshly baked pie. O'Connor came to the office door and gave an appreciative sniff. "Oh, hey, O'Connor. It's nice you can be here for your mom. How long do you get to stay?"

"Leaving reluctantly on Saturday."

"But you're here today, and I'm on my pie rounds. I try to get around to businesses once a week to offer hand pies as samples to customers. Allen never minded."

"I won't either," I said.

She beamed. "When are you reopening?"

"I have so much up in the air I need juggling lessons," I said. "But I'll let you know. I'll have to go back to Tennessee at least for a while."

"In the meantime," she said with a wicked smile, "let's each have one."

"Ooh, my wish came true," O'Connor said.

"And if you have a minute?" Tracy cocked her head. "I'd like to bounce an idea off you. You, too, O'Connor."

"Let's go upstairs," I said.

"I—" Tracy darted an uncomfortable look toward the stairs.

"Come on in the office."

Tracy settled in the spindle-back. O'Connor brought another he found in the stockroom. Tracy handed us each a pie and a napkin. O'Connor and I dug in. She held hers but didn't eat.

"I saw a car passing the Fig and Yaupon the day Allen died," she said. "Just before dark."

"Do you know whose car?" I asked.

"I think it was Yanira's. I've seen her car often enough. I didn't think anything of it then. But now? After they found the paddle?"

I put my pie down. "Was Corina with her?"

"No, but I figured Yanira left her with a relative or neighbor. But that also made me think it wasn't Yanira, because she said she couldn't come to a post-hurricane wingding that evening. She didn't have anyone to leave Corina with, and leaving her alone isn't like Yanira."

"Neither is murder," I said. "Have you told the police?"

"No, because I'm not sure, and I feel guilty about wanting to tell and guilty about *not* telling."

I knew the feeling. "So why are you telling me?"

"I heard that you're asking questions."

So much for doing that quietly. Although, due to my pussy-footing ways, I hadn't asked many.

She picked at the edge of her pie. "And you're a stranger, so that makes it easier. But also, and you'll think this is superstitious, when you go back to Tennessee, maybe the guilt and bad karma will go, too. Not *with* you. But away."

I wanted to tell her that the person she really needed to talk to was Dr. Allred. Then I wondered if she already had. "I can't tell you what to do, but I think you should tell Captain Tate."

"Not Frank Brown?"

"Whoever you feel most comfortable with."

She stared at the pile of broken pastry on her napkin. "I destroyed my pie."

"Leave it on the desk. I'll clean it up."

"You want to know another reason I don't want to say anything? Because Yanira's a great teacher and a *really* great long-term, part-time employee. Do you know how hard it is to find someone so responsible and capable who'll stick with the restaurant business? Isn't that ridiculous? So now I have to remind myself that the act of murder is ridiculous. There's no good reason for it."

After I locked the door behind her, I composed a text telling Glady and Burt what Tracy had said and the questions it sparked. "**Did Yanira go to Springer's Point? Why? Allen was already dead by evening. If she turned him over and hit him with the paddle, why didn't she get rid of it in a better place? No opportunity to do that? Who is the anonymous tipster?**"

"Do you want to send it to me, too?" O'Connor asked.

"Do you want it?"

"I want to help if I can."

That sounded awfully grown-up. But he was. "I know people and places change and that I fall into the trap of freezing them in time. I wanted to find Ocracoke the way it was the last time your dad and I were here."

"That's normal," O'Connor said. "That's why you still see Kelly and me as nine and eleven."

"But did I miss seeing that Dad changed? That he kept secrets from us? From me?"

"I don't think he did, Mom."

"Will you ask Kelly for me?"

"I did last night, and he doesn't think so, either."

"Good." I swept Tracy's dismantled pie into a trash can along with that worry.

"But we're both concerned about what's happening," he said.

"Because of the murder? No kidding. So am I."

"*And* that you're being detectives with Glady and Burt. Mom, you're engaging in dangerous behavior. And you almost got electrocuted, too." O'Connor put his arms around me, hugging like he didn't want to or couldn't let go. For a son half a foot taller than me, I could still imagine I was cuddling my knee-high boy.

"Oh, sweetie. But I'm here. I'm fine." I tapped the back of my head, gently. "Bruise almost gone."

"But you're not behaving the way we're used to. And yes, people change, but you've held things together so well since Dad died, and maybe you're having a well-deserved breakdown. Neither of us wants you to, but we're here for you if you do. I can get away more easily than Kelly. If you need me to stay or to come back, let me know. Kelly says he'll make time, too. We're here for you. You aren't alone."

He was so earnest. How not to upset him more? "What makes you think breakdown, sweetie?"

"Everything. But do you really want to know? Come on, Mom. A *ghost*?"

Chapter 38

Over another breakfast of cold cereal, I snarled about Allen Withrow to O'Connor. "He has a lot to answer for. Sending cryptic letters to people he didn't know. Getting himself killed and leaving me with suspicions, questions, and suspected by police and who knows who else. Giving my boys doubts and worries no sons should have. Not to mention saddling me with a shop. Thanks a lot, Allen." I kindly didn't upset O'Connor's digestion by mentioning the pirate ghost.

"Got that out of your system?" O'Connor asked. "Good. Let's go."

We said good morning to Rogers and went to meet Burt for a sortie to the shoreline property. Glady had declined our invitation, saying she wasn't into mosquitoes. Burt took us in Minerva.

"There's a tiny bit of sand beach," O'Connor told us on the way, "and lots of salt marsh. But there's a rise, too, with firm ground and pine woods. I've found five holes so far."

"Let's look at the holes first," Burt said. "Any new digging since you've been camping?"

"I can't tell. None of it looks old, though."

Burt parked Minerva at the edge of a gravel road. We slathered on bug repellant and followed O'Connor along a narrow path into the wilds of sound-side Ocracoke. Gulls cried, feet occasionally squelched, grasses rattled their spikelets like sabers, and the sun shone down on the intrepid explorers traveling in single file from their golf cart.

"I found the first hole that first night when I got up to pee," O'Connor said. "Here's my camp. The hole's beside the tree, there, where the crows are. How many crows do you need before you can call it a flock?"

"Any group of crows is a murder," Burt said.

As we approached, the crows left the tree, cawing.

First," Burt said, "this rise, as you called it, is what we call a hammock." He looked at the hole. Slapped a mosquito and crossed his arms. "And then," he said, nodding sagely, "you're right. This is a hole."

The hole was at least two feet deep. I was appalled. "O'Connor! You could have broken a leg or your neck if you'd stepped in it."

He showed us the other four holes, each with evidence of whoever had walked to and from it.

"But nothing to really tell us who, when, or why," Burt said.

"And why in these spots," O'Connor said. "They're so random."

"Everything is random these days," I said.

"Ain't that the truth," said Burt. "Where's your beach?"

We trekked to the narrow beach and gazed across the beautiful waters of Pamlico Sound, which is really a lagoon. An eighty-mile-long lagoon upward of thirty miles at its widest point.

While the guys looked inland and Burt and O'Connor talked geology and trees and storm surges, I beachcombed and found a handful of olive shells. Cylindrical, oblong, and sometimes shiny, they're among my favorites. Lettered olives look like they're covered in ancient messages we no longer know how to read. I rinsed them in the sound and put them in my pocket.

* * *

"Do we dare ask Yanira about driving to the Point?" I asked Glady when we returned to their kitchen and Burt's muffins. "Talk about an awkward conversation."

"We don't *ask*," Glady said. "We commiserate over the kayak paddle, listen, and watch. Do you remember when Corina came in the shop the day after the murder? She said she was checking to see if her mom was right about Allen being gone. Does that look suspicious now?"

"Doesn't everything?" I asked. "Do you want to go now, before I chicken out? Uh-oh. What's that face mean?"

"I'm sorry," she said. "I'm covered up today. Meetings I can't get out of."

My inner chicken felt better immediately.

"But you'll go, won't you, O'Connor?" Glady said.

"I'm sure not letting her go alone," O'Connor said.

We decided we couldn't just show up to commiserate. I and my inner chicken decided. So I took a nice little bag of shells, including one of my lettered olives, for Corina as a cover story. So many cover stories, I thought. Was this what the boys meant by me not behaving the way they were used to?

We pulled into Yanira's drive as Noah came from around the back of the house. We hopped out of the car, and I trotted toward him. "Hi! Are Yanira and Corina out back?"

"I was knocking at the back door. Island custom."

"Thanks." I shrugged at O'Connor and knocked on the front door, anyway. No answer.

"Did I imagine it," O'Connor said as we got back in the car, "or did Noah practically run off after you spoke to him?"

"You might think I'm behaving oddly," I said, "but odd times call for odd behavior. Let's go back to the mousehole."

"You think he's going to take a chance on snooping?"

"He shows up in the most amazing places."

"Then let's cover two of them," O'Connor said. "Noah's on foot. You can drop me at the mousehole before he gets there. If he's feeling snoopy, he won't know I'm there. You go on to check the shop."

"Be careful," I said. "If he shows up, call Captain Tate. If Rogers is around, she'll let you know if Noah shows up. She's a good silent intruder alert."

"You be careful, too. I'll text Burt. Tell him to keep an eye out before you get to the shop and while you're there."

We texted back and forth while we waited for Noah. He never showed. Did I feel silly? A bit. But I also felt very warm inside because O'Connor took it all seriously and in stride.

I treated him to a meal at the Fig & Yaupon for his last night on the island. We had an ulterior motive—to look for Yanira and maybe have a chance to talk.

"Hey, you two," Tracy said, stopping by the table. "Taking off tomorrow, O'Connor?"

"Yeah, and I hate to go. Say, is Yanira here this evening? We have a bag of shells for Corina."

Tracy shook her head, looking worried. I liked that about her, but I didn't like this disappearing business. No Yanira and then no Noah. No Emrys, come to think of it. And after tomorrow, no O'Connor.

A note, taped to the mousehole's door, fluttered in the breeze when we got back. Printed in red marker, it said, *SHARK BAIT.*

Chapter 39

We called Captain Tate and waited in the car. I locked the doors and told O'Connor, "Fear of land sharks." It wasn't a joke.

Brown came. He took a picture of the note on the door, bagged it, prowled one circuit around the outside of the mousehole, and spent a few minutes inside.

"Any idea who left it?" he asked when he came out.

"No." I couldn't believe Patricia had, and she was the only one who knew about my shark phobia.

"I won't find your fingerprints on this?" he asked O'Connor. "Practical joke on your mom?"

"No. It looks like a threat."

Brown lifted his hat and scratched his head. "If you're worried, Ms. Nash, you've been cleared of murder, so you're free to leave the island any time."

"Am I also free to stay?"

"Of course," Brown said. "In my opinion, the note's malicious mischief. There's no sign anyone tried to get in. Call if anything else happens," he threw over his shoulder on the way to his truck.

We went back to the property, with flashlights, and packed up O'Connor's camp. He spent the night on the floor of the mousehole.

*   *   *

"Easy solution for uneasy minds," Glady said. "Stay in the apartment. I'd ask you to stay with us but—" We were talking on their porch because Burt had gone into high mess-making mode.

"Don't worry about it," I said. "I'm not sure Brown aimed to make me feel better by calling it malicious mischief, but I do feel better in the light of day. I have the rental for another eight days, and I like it."

"Mom, you don't have to prove anything."

"If I were trying to prove something, I'd sleep in the murdered man's bed that now belongs to me. Still not keen on that." Also not sure about cohabiting with a there-again, gone-again ghost of an accidental pirate.

"Are you taking off now?" Glady asked O'Connor.

"This afternoon. Library first."

"Crossword competition with his brother," I told Glady and went across to the Moon Shell.

O'Connor and Kelly had a long-running rivalry over who could finish the Saturday *New York Times* crossword puzzle fastest. I'd told him he'd find the paper at the library. He planned to copy the puzzle and come back for a morning of cutthroat crossword solving.

I fed Bonny, then entertained her and Emrys by trailing a string around for her. I was about to ask him if he'd tried holding a string, thinking it would entertain me to see a string twirling in midair for the cat, when O'Connor came in.

"They don't get the *Times*," he said.

"Then how—" How did Emrys read the obituaries?

"How what?"

"Sorry, a friend told me they did. Or I misheard. You can't find it online?"

"No subscription." O'Connor gave me his "assessing Mom's mental health" look. "Was this friend your pal with the yo-ho-ho?"

I gave O'Connor my best "Mom is all here and not at all loony" look. And I did something very brave. Or loony. I nodded. "Emrys goes to the library to read obituaries in the papers."

"Dad used to read obituaries."

"I didn't realize you'd noticed that. He loved them for the stories they tell. He loved the nuances and occasional humor."

"He got sappy and sentimental over some of them, too," O'Connor said. "That's how I found out. I caught him getting weepy, one morning, over a woman named Floella Oliphant. You miss Dad a whole lot."

"A whole lot and every day."

"So . . . you don't think you might be imagining this ghost as a way to—"

"Replace your Dad? Not only no, but hel—" I held up a hand. "One of your Dad's favorite expressions. But no. I might be hallucinating, that *is* a possibility, due to concussion, but there is no way in hel—" I held up my hand again. "I wish you could see Emrys. Meet him."

"I started reading the obituaries with the idea I might find others in my situation. Friends, as it were." Emrys flickered into view beside the locked display case, six or seven feet in front of O'Connor.

"That makes it sound like a ghost dating app," O'Connor said.

I laughed. Stopped. O'Connor was suddenly acting in the same careful way he does with a skittish cat.

"O'Connor. You heard that?" Judging from his wide eyes, he saw, too.

"Sorry about the dating app crack," O'Connor said with a quiet and uncharacteristic stammer. "It wasn't really funny." He hadn't blinked since Emrys appeared, hadn't looked directly at him. "On the other hand," he said, voice a bit steadier, "has it ever worked? Have you found other ghosts?"

"Since my own tragic demise, I have come across very few people in my state of being. And, quite frankly, those I do meet are all dead ghastly."

A smile slowly spread across O'Connor's face. Eventually, he did blink, and then tried several times to speak again. Finally he blurted, "I am so happy to meet you, Mr. Lloyd."

"You said you read obituaries in the *Times*," I said. "How?"

"Allen has an online subscription. I know his username and password." Emrys disappeared.

"That happens a lot," I said. "The appearing and disappearing, but *not* appearing to other people. Allen saw him, but he says no one else does."

"I feel honored, and now I really don't want to go."

"I know."

"How long are you going to stay?"

"That I *don't* know. You said I look comfortable here. I am. Being a young widow—youngish—is lonely. Friends your dad and I used to do things with don't call so much anymore. It makes me feel invisible. I don't feel that way here."

We heard a snort, and Emrys said, "You don't know what invisible is."

"There are other kinds of invisible," I said.

"The killer's invisible," O'Connor said. "Or thinks they are."

"Or is it a motive?" I asked. "For someone unbalanced who feels that way?"

Chapter 40

"I like your son," Emrys said, as we stood on the porch until O'Connor's car disappeared around the corner.

I half-expected the car to hit a tree because O'Connor kept looking back at the ghost waving goodbye. How to explain *that* kind of distracted driving?

"Are your sons interested in conchology or your ology?"

"My ology is malacology."

"I will try to remember. I don't have a firm grasp of modern scientific terms."

"You called yourself a conchologist, though. The first known use of the terms *conchology* and *conchologist* was in 1776."

"Perhaps *I* used those terms first and they died with me. I might have all manner of inventions still in my head. Sandwiches, which came along only twelve years after my demise. Electricity, which Franklin claimed to discover on June 10, 1752, a mere two years after I perished." He put the back of his hand to his forehead and sighed. "All for want of a ballpoint pen. Tragic."

"There's a bit of the fabulist about you."

"I do know that *conchologist* is a modern word. A scientific fellow by the name of Poe says the word comes from the

Greek. I forget what the Greek is, but he says the word embraces both the animal and its shell."

"Poe, huh. What's Poe's first name?"

"Edgar."

"Are you confusing the names of two authors? Edgar Allan Poe was famous for his short stories and poetry, not science. He's considered the father of horror and mystery stories."

"I like a good ghost story but not horror. I've seen enough tragedy for several lifetimes. About the book by Poe, however, I'm not confused and I can prove it. Take that seascape off the wall."

I did and behind the painting was a good-sized wall safe. "You didn't think to show this to anyone? Like the police?"

"Not easy for one in my position. The combination is the same as for the computer. 637163."

On a shelf inside, I saw a stack of five books. A wooden box sat on the safe's bottom.

"Top book," Emrys said.

The book I gingerly lifted out had the amazing and cumbersome title of *The Conchologist's First Book: A System of Testaceous Malacology, Arranged Expressly for the Use of Schools, in Which the Animals, According to Cuvier, Are Given with the Shells, A Great Number of New Species Added, and the Whole Brought Up, as Accurately as Possible, to the Present Condition of the Science* by Edgar A. Poe.

I was in complete awe. I felt like I'd missed part of my education by never hearing about the book before. Green leather spine. Marvelous illustrations. Published in 1839. First edition in fine condition. I laid the book on the desk and did a quick search on the laptop.

"This is the only book of Poe's to go into a second printing in his lifetime," I said. "He took some grief over it, too. He was accused of plagiarism, which he completely denied. He wrote it because he needed the money. Wow. This was Allen's?"

"So one would assume. If not, why is it in his safe?"

"Wow."

"He rarely opened the safe," Emrys said. "He brought this book out one night and showed it to me. It was after one of the Pirate Jamborees. I think he'd had one too many pints of Ye Olde Pirate Grog. When I asked him why he kept it in the safe, he snatched it back and locked it away again."

"So you haven't seen the rest of the books?"

"No."

"Then let's see if we have more 'wow.'" I laid each book on the desk, then took out the wooden box.

We had *so* much "wow."

The books were more mid-nineteenth century scientific treatises and monographs on mollusks and conchology—beautifully illustrated. The box held two pieces of Victorian shell art—glass apothecary jars, about a foot tall, filled with seashells arranged in fanciful, intricate patterns.

"These are gorgeous, in a frou-frou Victorian way," I said. "Have you ever seen them?"

"Not that I remember, and I do think I would remember." Emrys stared at the jars, a hand on his cheek, one eyebrow raised. "Are they as old as the books?"

"In the ballpark."

"How do you know?"

"The shells tell me. Some of them are rarely found these days. Some are all but extinct."

"Are these frou-frous worth a lot of money?" he asked.

"My qualified guess is quite a bit."

"If they were Allen's, that makes them yours."

"*If* they were his." If they *weren't*, what did that mean? And whether they were his or not, should I tell anyone else about them?

But then I did. I invited Glady and Burt over to see the treasures from the safe and Allen's diary.

And then the three of us hatched a plan.

Chapter 41

"Isn't this exciting?" Glady said.

After letting them *ooh* and *aah* over the contents of the safe and the diary, I locked all of it back in the safe. We devised our plan upstairs in the apartment.

"And, Maureen," Glady said, "may I give you a piece of advice? Don't tell O'Connor what we're up to."

"No point in making him turn right around and come back," Burt said. "Children never think their parents should have harebrained ideas. Glady and I never did, and our mama had some doozies."

"Cockamamie," Glady said. "She died last year at 103. What a gal."

"Ask them to tell us more about their cockamamie mama," Emrys said.

"When the case is solved," I said, "will you tell me about some of your mama's doozies?"

"That might not be wise. Now—" Glady rubbed her hands. "We'll split the suspects between us. Who wants to inveigle whom?"

"I'll be gallant and leave the inveigling to you charmers," Burt said. "I'll use all the skill and art of the retired librarian I am to search for that burglary."

"Tracy offered to show me rentals," I said. "Why don't I

take her up on that and practice the art of a pussyfooting invei-
gler on her? I'll take Patricia, too. I'm *not* taking Dr. Allred."

"Let's skip him for now," Glady said. "We're amateurs. We
can do anything we want. I'll take Yanira and Noah if I can
find them. That leaves Daniel Umstead and Frank."

"If this works right, we won't need to talk to each of the suspects," I said. "When we tell the first few the 'secret information' about the diary, the burglary, and the booty, it won't stay
secret for long. It's a great story. Too juicy not to spill."

"Then we sit back," Burt said, "and watch the fun."

Tracy picked me up at the mousehole Sunday afternoon.
"OMG," she said. "I've been past this dollhouse a million times,
and I've never seen the inside. Do you mind?" The house tour
took all of four or five minutes instead of thirty seconds because, as she said, "Curiosity is an occupational hazard. This
place is capital-A adorable."

Tracy's SUV had bells and whistles on top of bells and whistles. Leather seats, sunroof, mellow jazz playing softly in the
background. She gave me a tour of Ocracoke's neighborhoods
with a running commentary about who lived where.

"You know where *I'd* like to live?" She gave me a rueful
look. "I've tried and tried to buy the house the Moon Shell's in,
but I think it's not meant to be. You know how some things are
like that? You have to pick up your dreams and move on."

"Allen wanted to buy it, too," I said.

"Did he? Well." She rolled to a stop. "That bungalow with
the screen porch is a rental. Minimum of three days, otherwise
by the week. How long are you staying?"

"Not sure yet."

"Take something that rents by the week, then. I'll show you
some more over on the sound side. I'm so glad you told me
Allen couldn't get Glady and Burt to sell the house to him. If
he couldn't convince them, I don't think anyone can. What's

funny is he never told me he tried to get it, and there I was wooing him with a home-cooked meal, hoping he'd talk Glady and Burt into selling to me. I went all Julia Child on him."

"How'd that go?"

"Who knew he was a purebred meat and potatoes man? And bacon! He waxed poetic about bacon with anything while I served up a medley of roasted vegetables and quinoa with a balsamic reduction." She laughed again. "At least he was polite about it. Even kept some of the leftovers."

"Let me guess. Brussels sprouts with chestnuts?"

"That was three weeks ago. How did you—oh *no*. Still in the fridge?"

"Not anymore."

Tracy hooted. "What a sneaky devil. Not to speak ill."

That was a segue made to order. "I think he was sneakier than a lot of people knew."

"Do tell," she said.

So I did. Told her about the rumor of his criminal youth, a hidden safe holding suspiciously valuable antiques, and his diary.

Tracy rolled to a stop and listened with a suitably dropped jaw. When I finished, she shook her head. "Sneaky devil."

"With bacon," I said, and she snorted.

Driving again, she said, "I talked to Frank Brown about Yanira," then pointed at one of the old one-story clapboard houses on short brick piers. "That place is haunted. A lot of people like it because of that. Not me."

"What did Frank say?"

"He laughed. Said they checked Yanira's story when they found the paddle. Every minute of her time is accounted for. If I did see her car, she was on her way to pick up Corina from another one of the teachers. She'd been checking damage at the school and hadn't take Corina in case there was anything dangerous."

"You did the right thing to mention it," I said.

"Did I? I feel like a fool and like I betrayed a friend."

"I know. I'm sorry."

She looked at me out of the corners of her eyes. "With bacon."

It was a fun jaunt and didn't take long because there wasn't much available. People had booked places months or a year in advance, she said, and I'd been lucky to get my miniscule place on short notice.

She slowed again and pointed to another house on short piers. "I sold that place to Rob Tate. One of the old fishermen lived there. See the porch? It goes all the way around."

A crow on the chimney cawed and flew off. Frank Brown's truck was in the drive. I wondered if they were meeting away from the office. Had Brown told him about the diary? He should have told him immediately. He shouldn't have taken it from the body.

Now *I* had the diary. Was he in there setting me up?

Chapter 42

"I think I might be paranoid."

"It's easy to be paranoid when you're being followed," Burt said.

"Who's following her now?" Glady called from the kitchen.

Burt and I were in his study the next morning—his wreck of a study according to Glady—waiting for her so he could show us the fruits of his library skills. We heard a crash from the kitchen—the ruins of a kitchen according to Burt.

"It's all right. I'm all right," Glady called. "Can't say the same for the aspidistra." She came into the study with three mugs of coffee in one hand and a plate of muffins in the other.

"No one new is following me that I know of," I said, grabbing the plate as it tipped to a dangerous angle. "But I hope I *am* paranoid. The alternative is believing Deputy Brown set me up when he gave me the diary." I reported on my afternoon with Tracy.

"That's excellent," Glady said. "I saw Yanira after church and told her our juicy information."

"And we can cross her off the suspect list," Burt said.

"Rookie mistake." Glady set her mug on a pile of magazines less like a stack than a sinuous upward growth. "What if Tracy was lying? Or Frank when he told her Yanira's in the clear? Either of them might be playing our game of pass the juicy info. What did you find, Burt?"

"Juicy, juicy info. I started out by looking for information about missing or stolen copies of the books in your safe. The International League of Antiquarian Booksellers maintains a database of missing books. Yours don't show up."

"That's good news," I said.

"Or they were stolen too long ago or not reported missing. But—" Burt wiggled his fingers over his keyboard. "After many dead ends and frequent snacks and—"

"Rude language," Glady said.

"Those were incantations, and after many hours and a few more incantations, they worked. The tabs across the top of the screen are articles from the *Raleigh News and Observer* in late winter and early spring of 1961."

"I don't think I want to know what Stub was doing in 1961," I said.

"Who's Stub?" Glady asked.

"Jeff's dad. He never liked his first name."

"It's okay," Burt said. "Stub, aka Cornelius, isn't mentioned in these articles. He's listed as a survivor in his father's obituary. His father being Edward. Edward features prominently in the articles about the burglary. Allen does, too. He testified against his pal."

"That's not in the diary," I said.

"Hence, Allen's guilty conscience late in life," Glady said. "What a rat. What was he doing working with someone so much older?" She clutched my arm, sloshing my coffee. "Don't tell us Edward died in prison."

Burt opened one of the tabs. "I'll send the URLs for the articles to you, Maureen. Your boys might like to have them, too." He looked at me. "Ready for the juicy information?"

"No, but yes."

"Allen and his pal didn't steal money. They stole a valuable collection of seashells and antique shell art. Edward, Jeff's grandfather, wasn't one of the burglars. He was the victim. Incarcerated for the crime was Neil Jackson."

"The initials," I said.

"William, Neil, and Edward," Glady said. "First names. Allen never went by William, and he used it in the diary to throw off anyone who found it and read it."

"I told you he never deserved you," Burt said. "Jeff never mentioned the collection or the burglary?"

I shook my head. "Lost in the fog of family stories, I guess."

A crow cawed in the kitchen.

"My phone," Glady said. She trotted off to answer it. She wasn't gone long but came back slowly and dazed. "Frank's dead." She dropped into her chair. "Drowned. Not an accident."

"Who was on the phone?" I asked.

"Yanira."

"Where and when?" Burt asked. "How?"

"She didn't know anything else, except that Dr. Allred is claiming he saw another token of death. Then Corina came into the room, so she hung up."

"I wonder if Frank verified that Irv Allred wasn't on the island when Allen died," Burt said.

I remembered the crow on Tate's chimney the day before and Patricia's macabre rhyme—"If a crow is on the thatch, death soon lifts the latch." Maybe I was getting as weird as Allred. "Could it be suicide?"

"A week ago, I would have said no. Now?" Glady shook herself. "We didn't like Frank much, and I'm sorry for that. Does his death tell us anything new?"

"If it's murder and not suicide," Burt said, "do you think it clears him of Allen's murder?"

"Not necessarily." I felt sick. "Do you think our game of juicy info killed him?" My phone rang. Captain Tate.

Chapter 43

"Drowning is easy once you get started," Emrys said.

We were sitting on the top step outside the Moon Shell waiting for Captain Tate. He'd said he wanted to come see the cameo shell. I wasn't sure I believed him. I wasn't sure I believed Emrys about drowning, either. When Tate arrived, I brushed the seat of my jeans and the three of us went inside.

"I was across at Glady and Burt's when you called. We heard about Deputy Brown. I'm so sorry."

He closed his eyes for a brief moment, his lips moving soundlessly. A prayer, I thought. "Thank you. I want to see this cameo shell. It must have something to do with Allen's murder. Now maybe Frank's, too. But why? And why drop the shell back in the ocean?"

While he let his frustration show with a vigorous scalp rub, I unlocked the case.

"It's a conch, isn't it? No." He peered at the small label in the display case. "Clench's helmet. Never heard of them."

"It's a variety of queen helmet." I took the shell from the case. I'd warned Emrys that Tate might want to take it with him.

"May I?" Tate took the shell from me, turning it over the way I had when I'd first held it. "I'm suitably impressed by the carving, and a critter living in one of these must be good eating. This thing's massive."

"That's one way to tell it isn't a conch, because it looks inflated, like a football."

Tate held it like he was about to throw a pass. I flashed on an image of Emrys's brother Owen pulling his arm back and letting the shell fly. Owen hadn't. When I'd "seen" him he'd merely dropped the shell over the side of the ship. Considering the tragic results, though, he might as well have let the shell fly.

"Sorry," Tate said. "That was uncalled for. You've gone as white as a sheet." Holding the shell in both hands, he set it carefully back on its pedestal. "What can you tell me about the carving?"

"The carving is early to mid-eighteenth century. Crews of sailing ships had time on their hands. Think of scrimshaw. Shells are another carving medium. People do still carve shells. Artists like helmets, like this, because they're thick, with lots of layers to carve through. Each layer is a slightly different color. They cut through the layers, using the colors to create the picture or pattern."

"You mention the eighteenth century and sailing ships, and I immediately think of pirates. You know that Ocracoke was a pirate haven, right? What's the chance this is a valuable pirate artifact?"

"It's possible."

"Only accidentally," Emrys said.

"Other people carved shells, too," I said. "I don't know this shell's provenance—where Allen or his mother got it. With documentation that names the artist or traces ownership over the years, it would be much more valuable. I'd love to know it's full story."

"Is there anyone who *would* know more about?" Tate asked. "At the preservation society?"

"Maybe. Glady and Burt say they don't know, and you'd think Allen or his mother would have tracked down every bit of information they could. I haven't found anything in his files. Did you know Allen kept a diary?"

"Tell me about it." He looked puzzled when I didn't say anything. "Ms. Nash?"

"Will you tell me, first, if you know about the diary? Did Frank Brown tell you about it?"

"Until you mentioned it, I didn't know it existed."

"I didn't either, until Frank showed it to me. Come on in the office. There's a lot to tell."

"Where did Frank get it?"

"From Allen's body."

Emrys stayed with the shell. Tate sat in the spindle-back and listened intently to the story.

"Have you told anyone else about the diary?" he asked when I finished.

"Glady and Burt know about it. It's a good story, though, so we didn't keep it secret. We didn't know the details of the burglary until Burt did his research. I'm pretty sure Frank thought Allen had money from the burglary hidden somewhere and wanted to find it."

Tate said nothing more, stared at nothing.

"So did coming here to see the shell really help?" I asked. "Or is everything murkier because of the diary?"

He stood up. "I'd like to take the shell with me."

"You won't find helpful fingerprints on it. It's been washed and dried and then handled by several people."

"I want it for safekeeping," he said. "For you as well as the shell. If people know it's in our evidence locker, then the person who took it won't come looking for it again."

"That person threw it in the water and hasn't been back since."

"We don't know either of those things, and we don't know the motive for taking it from here in the first place."

He made good points. "Can I offer an alternative?" I took the picture off the wall behind me and showed him the safe. "What if you say you took the shell, but we put it in the safe? The diary's in there. Would you like to see it?"

"I'd like to take the diary with me, too, and if you insist on keeping the shell, I'll wonder if that's because you don't trust me to take good care of it or if you have another reason for holding on to it."

"I do trust you, but will you trust me that I have a good reason to keep the shell here?" I opened the safe and took out the diary. "Or am I still a suspect?"

"No."

"Deputy Brown seemed to think I was."

"I don't agree with him."

"It felt that way. Like you two had a good cop, bad cop routine."

"He liked to say, 'I'm from the school of making it as hard on perps as you can.' It was usually a couple of beers talking."

"It makes him sound like a villain."

Tate stood to go. "If he was, he was a small one."

I handed him the diary. He thanked me and left without asking for the shell again. I moved the shell to the safe and wondered if being a small villain was like being an accidental pirate.

Chapter 44

With Deputy Brown's murder, Glady, Burt, and I decided to shelve our campaign of spreading juicy info. I spent the next day and a half reassuring the boys after telling them of Brown's death and then clearing the apartment bedroom and bathroom of Allen's clothes, linens, and toiletries. Clearing proved easier than reassuring. Glady gave me the number of a woman who was happy to do it for me. She took what she wanted to keep, sell, or donate, and bagged the rest for the garbage tote.

Wednesday morning, Burt had an adventure. He and Glady came across the street to tell me about it (Burt), and to complain about how he handled it (Glady). The commotion drew Emrys's attention.

"I like to get out in the dawn light and take pictures," Burt said.

"He saw Noah going through your trash, and all Burt did was snap a picture of him." Glady looked like an angry chicken.

"Not all I did. I asked him what he was doing, and he said he saw something relevant to the murders. Relevant and significant. Then he said he'd said too much and refused to say anything else. I said I'd send the picture to Captain Tate to prove he'd been trespassing and pilfering."

"Go on," Glady said. "Tell her the rest."

"He scoffed and said anything thrown in the garbage is no longer private property."

"And then Burt watched him saunter down the street, look back with a grin, and scamper off around the corner."

"When did Noah see this thing?" I asked.

Glady tsked. "He didn't ask."

"Did he have anything in his hand?" I asked. "Or did he have a bag or backpack?"

"No and no," Burt said. "He could have had it in his pocket. He could have taken pictures of it."

"But maybe he found this thing another day," I said, "and was trying his luck again. Did he give any indication he'd told Brown or Tate?"

"I don't know any more than what I've told you," Burt said. "Short of stuffing him in the garbage tote, there wasn't anything else I could do."

"You could have stuffed him in the tote and wheeled him to our place," Glady said. "*I* would've made him tell us what he found and what he's up to *and* what he knows."

"What he thinks he knows," I said. "Or pretends to."

"Sorry," Burt said. "I muffed it. We should find a way to tackle him all together."

"Tackle him. Good plan," Glady said. "I've always wanted to be part of a rugby scrum."

"Brown didn't tell Tate about Allen's diary," I said. "What if Noah found something before Brown's murder and told him about it. And Brown kept *that* from Tate, too, but not someone else, and got himself killed?"

"Then Noah could be playing a dangerous game," Burt said.

"Unless he knows it isn't dangerous," Glady said, "because he's the killer."

"Rather than find a clue, I daresay he planted one," Emrys fumed. "A contrived bit of evidence, for I doubt that beetle-headed knave would know a significant or relevant clue unless it pinched his nose like a crab or stung his pasty white thighs like a jellyfish. You say he lies about what he eats, and I am certain he robbed Allen by pocketing merchandise from the shop without paying."

"How do you know he has pasty white thighs?" I asked.

"When he pickets, he wears short trousers cut well above the knee."

"You didn't mention his stealing before."

"I am only reminded of his petty thievery by hearing of his deceitful interest in our garbage." He was in a foul mood because Burt hadn't detained Noah. "He's a knave and guilty of these murders. And I'll wager that *he* does not know much about *anything*. 'Ignorance is the curse of God; knowledge is the wing wherewith we fly to heaven.' *Henry VI, Part Two*. The second half of that quotation is proof the Bard did not know everything."

That evening, as Rogers sat on the bird feeder platform cleaning her toes and I complimented her fastidious toilette from several feet away, Daniel Umstead rode a bicycle slowly past the mousehole. He made a wide U-turn, came back, and planted his feet.

"I'm a lifelong birdwatcher," he said, "and I've never seen a bigger catbird." He stood smiling, then said, "I've recently remembered a story Allen told me about his wild youth. No details, but with the implication that something valuable changed hands and was hidden away. Interesting, isn't it?" He waved and started away, then stopped and called over his shoulder, "At the time, I thought he might be bragging." He waved again and continued his ride. A friendly encounter that left me feeling like the bird being watched.

Chapter 45

"Say hi to Glady and Burt for me," O'Connor said at the end of my reassurance call Thursday morning. "Patricia, too. I didn't get to see her when I was there."

"I'll tell her you'll see her next time."

"I like the sound of 'next time.' Thanks for checking in, Mom. Bye."

Oops. I hadn't thanked Patricia for letting Tate know she'd seen me arrive and given me a ride to the rental. I sent her a text inviting her to lunch at the Fig & Yaupon.

"You're lucky I saw your text," Patricia said as we took seats at a window table. "I don't usually pay attention to my phone when I'm off duty." She was wearing cotton drawstring pants and a floaty kind of top. The top wasn't ruffled, and she didn't appear to be, either.

"That doesn't interfere with the job?" I asked.

"No. It interferes with my social life, but that's kind of the point."

"Is that why you didn't answer my call or texts the night Allen died? Off duty?"

"Yeah. Sorry. It's a sorry business about Brown, too, isn't it?"

"Rough times."

We both ordered grilled portobello sandwiches with sweet potato fries. Glady and Burt and I had decided not to spread our juicy info, but Tate had said Patricia was in the clear. She wasn't the kind to run right out and repeat things, anyway, so I told her about the diary and the burglary. It's not often I've had the chance to amaze her.

"The loot's still around somewhere?" she asked when I finished.

"No idea."

"But Brown knew about it."

"Yup. There's someone else who might. Noah." I told her about Burt finding him going through the Moon Shell's trash. "His explanation for it explained nothing. What do you know about him?"

"I've been investigating disturbed shorebird nesting sites. Someone reported seeing him near the sites. That's what I was doing when I saw you at the beach. You were perfect cover. He saw us talking and didn't catch on that I was following him."

"O'Connor took me to get my car, and we ate lunch in Hatteras. Noah sat in a booth behind us."

"Following you?"

"You thought he might be that day at the beach, but I don't know. I do know he claims to be a vegan, but in Hatteras he had a soft-shell crab sandwich. O'Connor says hi, by the way."

"Hi back." Patricia ate her last fry and took a swig of sweet tea. "You know he pickets the Moon Shell?"

"He was at it Monday, even though it's closed."

"Closed for good?" She asked.

"Closed for now."

"Are you thinking about keeping it?"

"Seriously considering," I said. "Leaning toward yes."

"Good. Noah's got a sign you might like. It says THOU SHELL NOT KILL."

"Cute, but it doesn't really get the point across."

"No," she said, "but he likes making statements. Maybe he made a couple of really big ones named Allen and Frank. Watch out he doesn't make another named Maureen."

Chapter 46

Noah returned to the scene of his villainy the next morning. I spied him at the Moon Shell's garbage tote. He hadn't seen me, so I texted Glady and Burt. Glady was getting her hair done but wanted Burt and me to jump Noah. Burt and I opted for tailing him. Noah made it easy. On foot and obviously on a mission, he never looked behind him. He turned a couple of corners, then sidled around the back of a house.

"Allred's," Burt whispered.

Noah, engrossed in sneaking to a window near the back door, didn't hear us sneaking, too.

"Turn around and sit down," Burt whispered in Noah's ear. "On your hands."

Noah froze, then obeyed. Thank goodness he wasn't a screamer. When he faced us, back to Allred's house, we crouched in front of him and held up our phones.

"Video of window peeping," Burt said.

"One tap and Captain Tate is on the line," I said. "Tell us why I shouldn't tap it."

Noah, looking younger than my boys, glanced up over his shoulder to the window we sat under. "I'm trying to figure out why he's been snooping in the Moon Shell's garbage."

"How often have you seen him there?" I asked.

"Three times. Weird, huh?"

"Why didn't you tell me that yesterday?" Burt asked.

"I like doing things for myself. I can't figure Dr. Allred out, though."

"That should be easy enough," I said, and I did something I'd told myself I never would. I knocked on Allred's back door.

Allred came to the door barefoot, in flannel pajama bottoms, a T-shirt, and an apron, holding a large knife. He looked from our faces to the knife. "Sorry. Should've put this down first. I'm in the middle of getting stew ready for the crockpot. But what a pleasant surprise. Come in."

We trooped after him into a kitchen full of good smells and culinary gadgets. He set the knife on a cutting board and started layering vegetables in the crockpot.

"Irv," Burt said, "why have you been snooping in the Moon Shell's garbage?"

"Caught in the act, eh? I'll tell you, but don't spread it around. I'm looking for evidence of a ghost."

"In the garbage?" I asked.

"Various places," he said airily. "Allen confided in me, over a marvelous Beaujolais, that the shop is haunted. That's why I wanted to see you for an appointment, Ms. Nash. To know if you were hallucinating after your concussion, or if you'd seen the ghost."

"My head is feeling much better," I said. "Have *you* seen a ghost in the shop?"

"I've not been so privileged."

Noah, silent, stared at Allred.

I stared at Allred's bare feet. Bigger than mine but not by much. "Dr. Allred, in your search for evidence, were you on the Moon Shell's porch the night Allen died?"

"I'd evacuated."

"Deputy Brown said you were here."

"As of early the next morning. I caught a lift from a fisherman."

I wondered how many people had landed on the island, one way or another, in those days before the ferry service resumed. And how many slipped away after Allen was killed?

Distracted by those thoughts, I hadn't noticed Allred moving closer to me. Too close, searching my face. I stepped back. If he believed in tokens of death, maybe he believed he could see signs of spectral activity, too—like shreds of silvery cobwebs caught in my hair or trailing from my sleeves. Poor Emrys if Allred ever got hold of him.

"Time I was off," I said. "Please don't snoop around the Moon Shell anymore."

Burt and Noah followed me out.

"Be seeing you," Dr. Allred called.

As soon as we'd left Allred's yard, Noah's mouth thawed. "Do you think that was the murder knife he had in there?" He took a small book and fancy pen from a pocket, stopped walking, and started writing. "And ghosts! Holy cow."

Burt grabbed the book. Noah tried and couldn't get it back. I've always hated that game. When Burt held the book behind his head, I snatched it and handed it back to Noah.

"Nice pen," I said. "Don't you take notes on your phone?"

"Not since I read an article that said writing by hand engages the creative side of your brain in a different way. I like trying new things. Gathering experiences."

"Writing by hand isn't a new thing," Burt sputtered. "But Allred's definitely an experience. What other experiences are you gathering?"

"Veganism. Advocating for animals and the environment. Waiting tables. Studying shorebird nesting patterns. I'm catching up because I missed out on so much being raised the way I was."

"How were you raised?" I asked.

"Too much money," he said with a shudder. "Private school. Summer camps, sailboats, ski vacations."

"A terrible hardship," Burt said.

"For a serious writer it is. What can you write about if all you know is feather beds and made-to-order meals from the family's private chef?"

Glady put mugs of coffee in front of us at their kitchen table and listened to a rundown of our encounters with Noah and Allred. Burt's part of the rundown mostly ran down Noah, winding up with "Noah is a—"

"Forget Noah for a minute," Glady interrupted. "Has Irv Allred gone stark staring mad? Looking for ghosts? In the *garbage*?"

"Irv's eccentricity is nothing new," Burt said.

"I think Noah's growing on me," I said. "For a kid who hasn't grown up yet."

"A kid in his midtwenties," Burt groused. "At least."

"But if he wants to be a writer, then more power to him." Glady brought the coffeepot to the table. "*Except*—"

"Except he's a jackass." Burt poured more coffee for himself, offered some to me, then slopped half in my cup and half on the table.

"It takes one to know one," Glady said.

I grabbed the dishcloth from the edge of the sink, glancing out the window.

Noah looked back at me.

Chapter 47

I sprinted out the front door. Noah, running down Howard Street, vaulted a picket fence, stumbled, regained his footing, and tripped over a footstone in the cemetery where he'd ended up. He sat up, hugging a bloody shin.

"Are you okay?" I opened the cemetery gate and went in.

Glady and Burt were coming now. I asked them to bring their first aid kit. Burt went back for it and brought his mug of coffee, too.

"I'll clean that and let you know if you need stitches," Glady said. "If you do, we'll take you back to Dr. Allred's."

The look on his face, at that thought, was priceless. Then Burt got right in that face.

"Noah, son, stop peeping in windows. It isn't nice. It isn't safe. Cutting your leg is one experience. Getting beaten up, or worse, is another. While you're playing peekaboo, there's a murderer on the loose."

"Here's a theory." Glady looked up from cleaning what turned out to be nothing more than a long, nasty scratch. "You aren't worried about the murderer because you've been experiencing something else firsthand. Committing murder."

"I think you're right," I said. "Three *kinds* of murder. Bash, slash, and splash. What's method's next, Noah?"

"No, no, no, no, no, no, no." Noah tried to crab walk backward. Burt blocked him. "I wouldn't. I didn't. I evacuated. Like Dr. Allred."

"Easy to lie about," Burt said. "We should call Captain Tate."

"Don't call. I'm not lying. I heard about a watch party on Hatteras, and I'd never been in a hurricane, so I went, and I stood on the beach as Electra crashed around me, and it was *awesome*. Then I had to be rescued."

"Was that awesome, too?" Burt asked.

"I thought I was going to die."

"What's your alibi for Deputy Brown's murder?" Glady asked.

"Competing in a stunt kite competition in Nags Head."

"Can you prove it?" I asked.

"A videographer liked my kite. He followed me the whole time. The video's awesome. It's on his YouTube channel."

Burt patted Noah on the head. "Be a good boy. Behave yourself."

Allred knocked on the Moon Shell's door that afternoon. Glady and I were looking at the newly emptied bedroom and bathroom upstairs. I clattered down the stairs, saw him, and stepped out onto the porch rather than invite him in. Glady joined us, then Burt because Glady sent a text. Then Emrys.

"Doing your ghost hunting out in the open now?" Glady asked.

"Might as well," Allred said.

Emrys waved a hand in front of Allred's face. Allred didn't even blink.

"It occurred to me, after you left, that the young man with you, and perhaps you, as well, suspected me of Allen's murder. Correct?"

"No hard feelings, I hope," Burt said.

"What evidence did you have?" Allred asked.

"It hardly matters now. Evidence, clues, questions—" I bit my lip; Emrys stood nose to nose with Allred. "They were all red herrings."

"*All red* herrings. Delightful! Ms. Nash, I still want to hear about your hallucinations. Please come for supper, all of you."

"I'd rather die," Emrys said.

Glady, Burt, and I declined, too.

"How are you so sure Noah is innocent?" Emrys asked when we were alone in the shop. "We built an ironclad case against him."

"Not ironclad. I thought *you* might be the villain to begin with because I thought you could do more that turn a deadbolt or flip a newspaper page. But if you can't pick up a pen or the shell, how could you drive a knife into Allen's chest?"

"I was a poor excuse for a pirate, and now I can't even be a murderer."

"And thank goodness for that. Emrys, it's the problem of assumptions your astronomer talked about. We're being forced to confront a false assumption we didn't know we'd made about Noah. We had evidence, but we read it wrong."

"It's humiliating. I shall give up detecting."

"Don't be so hard on yourself."

"You will not hear from me, and it will not be because of a loop."

"For how long? Emrys, don't go. Please don't be like that."

"Like what?"

Like a prima donna ghost, I wanted to say. A diva phantasm. A poor loser. "Can I tell you how I try to face the world?"

"I can't stop you talking."

"True, and you don't have to listen, but I'll tell you, anyway. I like to prepare for the best, be aware of the worst, and if the worst happens, I say, with conviction and optimism, "On to Plan B.""

He was quiet for a moment.

"What do you think?"

"I think the problem is deeper than conviction or optimism can dig themselves out of."

"Does that even make sense?"

"The real problem is that you arrived in this shop as a liar, so how can I trust you?"

"Where did *that* come from?"

"Truth."

"You want truth? Okay, I came here and I wasn't going to tell anyone who I was or why I came. Then I let everyone *think* they knew why I came."

"Right," he said, the roll of his *R* and the flash in his eyes mocking me. "You are an imposter."

"*Was.* I admitted my lies. But why should I trust *you*, Mr. Lloyd? You're a pirate." I willed my eyes to one-up his, to not merely flash but also to split the night with bolts of lightning and peals of thunder.

Maybe they did. The next thing I knew, he was gone.

Chapter 48

"Who's left on our list?" Burt asked. Then he stage-whispered to Glady, "Maureen looks like she's giving up."

I wasn't, but I kept stumbling over the worry that I'd lost Emrys. Presumably, he couldn't make the decision to disappear on his own or he could have done that decades or a century ago. But there I was making assumptions again. I glanced around the apartment again. No ghost. "We have Daniel Umstead and Tracy," I said, "with lame evidence and clues."

"That hasn't stopped us so far," Glady said.

"If they have alibis, they might be lame, too," I said.

"Do we know that?" Burt asked.

"If we knew all the answers, then we'd be drinking mimosas at the beach," Glady said. "Is all of this finally getting to you, Maureen? If so, pull yourself together."

More or less what I'd told Emrys. "You're right. Sorry." I listened for the sound of a ghost admitting his own mistake with a slap to the forehead. Silence. "Umstead's tall enough to hit Allen with the paddle."

"That isn't lame at all," Burt said.

"He and Allen had that feud over the shoreline property, too," Glady said. "He hasn't killed you for it, Maureen, but maybe he killed Allen, banking on your husband being more reasonable."

I told them about Umstead's creepy ride-by. "The burglary and the booty—*they* seem to be at the center of this, whether or not the shell is." And he wanted Bonny. "When I go back to Tennessee, will you take care of Bonny?"

"Please say that won't be soon." Glady put her hands to her heart.

"Today's already Saturday. Before all this happened, I planned to leave Monday morning. We'll see, though. Nothing firm."

Burt rested his chin on his fist. "We've just been through Electra. The weather's fair, seas are calm. So why do I feel like we're waiting for a real blow to hit?

Chapter 49

I packed up my things, said goodbye to Rogers, and moved to the apartment that afternoon. I hated to leave the mousehole, but Glady and Burt said they'd feel better knowing I was across the street. Kelly and O'Connor did, too, when I called them. None of us used the word safer, but I'm sure it's what we felt.

I didn't sleep well. New place, I told myself. New sounds and smells to get used to. Glady had loaned me sheets. Even so, it was a murdered man's bed.

And still no Emrys.

Glady called at Glady time—too early. The morning felt fall-ish. I threw on one of Jeff's old flannel shirts over my T-shirt and crossed the street. Burt was on his morning photo ramble. Over coffee and muffins, Glady and I wrote down what we knew and what we surmised about Umstead. Not much.

"I don't think we dare nose around Dan Umstead," Glady said. "That might be what got Frank killed."

"Where did he drown?" I asked.

"Some fishermen found him floating in the sound."

Glady told Burt how thin our information was when he ambled into the kitchen. He grunted and put a muffin on a plate. The muffin slid off. In picking it up, he dropped his phone.

"What's got you rattled?" Glady asked.

"I saw a danger token. Like Allred's tokens of death but not so final."

"Don't be absurd," Glady said.

"Now I'm worried about myself for thinking I saw such a thing *and* worried something's going to happen."

"What was it?" I asked.

"Crows," Burt said. "They're a sign of change and transformation. I can feel it. There's change in the offing. Not the good kind."

"Now you're *sounding* like Allred," Glady said. "In the *offing*."

"I'm going to watch Daniel's house," Burt said. "Tail him if he goes out."

"You're serious." Glady appraised him with her bird eyes. "Go ahead. It can't hurt."

"Yes, it can," I said. "If we're right about him, then this is more dangerous than Noah's 'I spy' game. And how will you watch his house without being completely obvious?"

"Shave my beard off, use your car, wear Glady's sunhat. If he sees me at all, he'll see any old tourist. I'll check in with you regularly."

"Desperate times," Glady said. "He grew that beard in 1978."

I handed him my car keys.

I'd planned to spend the morning in the Moon Shell trying to lure Emrys back. Instead, Glady and I spent a couple of nail-biting hours jumping every time Burt sent a text to say nothing was happening. Then we got one with a terse "**on the move**," and we sat staring at the phones cradled in our hands like they were the orbs of mystic seers.

Ten minutes later, he sent "**in line for the ferry**."

"**You?**" Glady sent back.

"**Him.**"

Then, "**Heard him say he'll be back tomorrow afternoon. Should I continue the tail?**"

"**No**," Glady sent. "**Come home and start re-growing your**

beard. Your chin's fish-belly white." She put her phone down. "If I were a whiskey drinker, I'd down a double right now."

Burt was back and whistling before we came up with an appropriate substitute for whiskey. "I know it'll only last until tomorrow afternoon, but I feel my spirits getting lighter. Think I'll go chuck pine cones at a few crows."

"Leave the crows alone and put away your sharp tools," Glady said. "Yanira's dropping Corina here at four."

I left them squabbling amiably, packed a sandwich, and spent the afternoon beachcombing. Bliss without a soupçon of a scintilla of murder. I found unbroken scallops, a turkey wing, part of a horseshoe crab, and a handful of mermaid's purses, and I left them all behind for the next beachcomber.

Back at the Moon Shell, I tried again. "Emrys? I miss you."

Silence.

I hummed the drunken sailor song, then sang it, then changed the words to "What do you do with a depressed phantasm."

Still nothing.

I took a sheet of Moon Shell letterhead and a pen from a desk drawer. Maybe if I wrote him a letter. But what to say? Before I figured that out, someone knocked on the door—Tracy, with a smile and a basket of pies. A wonderful aroma trailed the pies. An interesting entourage trailed Tracy.

"I have a great big favor to ask," she said. "This is Marcel. He's all the way from Montreal in Canada."

A dapper, elderly man beamed beside her. Corina peeked out from behind him.

"Marcel's leaving tomorrow," Tracy said, "and he desperately wants to take home a necklace he saw here a couple or three weeks ago for his granddaughter's tenth birthday."

"Not completely desperate," Marcel said with a charming accent and equally charming shrug."

"Oh, you," Tracy said. "Fess up. You're desperate."

"Come on in," I said.

"You are so kind," Marcel said. "Her name is Michou. I call her *ma petite choux*, my little cabbage."

"I know where all the necklaces are," Corina said. "I'll help you find it."

"Okay with you, Maureen?" Tracy asked.

"Sure. Great. I'll be in the office." Did I sound like I'd choked on a cabbage? My mind raced through connections. *Choux*, which sounds like *shoe* and means "little cabbage." The angry phone call Emrys overheard about a nasty, smelly shoe and bribery. What had Tracy said about fixing dinner for Allen? *I went all Julia Child.*

A rapid online search brought up a Julia Child recipe called Choux de Bruxelles aux Marrons—Brussels sprouts with chestnuts. Like Tracy's leftovers in Allen's fridge. Like his angry, oath-filled phone call about a nasty, smelly shoe and bribery.

I went back out when I heard Marcel thanking Corina and Tracy with rapturous *mercies*. Tracy told him to put his money away, the necklace was her treat. He kissed our cheeks left, right, and left again, and took his rapturous leave.

"Where's your mama, Corina?" Tracy asked.

"Miss Glady is watching me."

"Then you better scamper on back to Glady's house so she can." Tracy watched her go. "She's a cute little rascal. Come on in the office. I've got something for you."

"Pie?"

She didn't look any different. Relaxed, happy, not murderous. She set the basket on the desk.

"What kind of pie is it today?" I asked.

She reached into the basket to take one out. "Glock," she said, and just like that I had a gun pointed at my heart. "You're going to show me where the money is buried on that shoreline property."

If it had been me, I would've held that gun like it was an

electric eel. Tracy, with her smile, made it look as delightful as holding a bouquet of sweet-smelling roses.

"What money?"

"I know you're not stupid," she said, "so don't play like you are. I found a letter to you in Allen's pocket."

"You've read it, but I haven't, so I don't know about any money."

"Again, don't play stupid."

A ghost with a karate chop to her wrist would've been great right then. "If there is money, what makes you think I know where it is?"

"Something I heard."

"You heard wrong."

"No, see, I have inside information. I heard it from Frank. It's buried on that property. Frank liked the idea of a treasure hunt, but he was wasting time pecking around for it with his shovel. So you're going to stop wasting mine and take me to it."

"Tracy, I don't know where any treasure is buried. If I did, don't you think I would have dug it up by now?"

"Are we going on a treasure hunt?" Corina stood in the office doorway.

Tracy turned a sunbeam smile on Corina. "Come on in, honey. Do you like treasure hunts? I know you like my cute pies." She moved behind Corina and put her left hand on the girl's shoulder. Her right held the gun behind Corina's head. Corina, smiling, had no idea.

"We should let Corina run back across the street before Glady misses her."

Tracy didn't take the gun off Corina or her eyes off me.

Corina had eyes for nothing but the pie basket on the desk. "What kind of pies did you bring?"

"If Tracy gives you a pie, will you go back to Glady?" I asked. "We're having a business meeting."

Tracy gave a little flourish with the gun and slipped her

hand and the gun into the kangaroo pocket of her hoodie. The barest outline of the tip of barrel remained pointed at Corina.

"Are you making a deal?" Corina turned to gaze up at Tracy.

"We are," Tracy said. "A super-duper deal." She put a finger to her lips. "Don't tell anyone. It's a secret."

"I can do deals. Want me to show you?" Corina folded her hands at her waist. "If you give me *two* pies I'll keep it secret and go back to Miss Glady. Deal?"

"Fee fie foe feena," called Glady's voice. "I hear the voice of Miss Corina." She stuck her head around the office door. "There you are. No secret deals for pies, missy, unless you give one of them to me. Hello, Tracy. Don't let me or this little sea urchin bully you out of pies."

"Not a problem," Tracy said, maneuvering so Glady couldn't see the gun but Corina remained the target. "Take two, Corina. One for each hand."

"It's a deal! Can I look for the two biggest ones?"

"Knock yourself out." While Corina compared pies, Tracy caught Glady's eye and motioned her closer. "Not a word," Tracy whispered when Glady was close enough and showed her the gun. "I will shoot. Stand beside Maureen. It's trickier now, but I guess all four of us are going on a treasure hunt."

Glady inched behind the desk and stood next to me.

"With Corina, it'll be like herding cats," I said.

"Not. A. Word. Give me your phones." We did. "Tell you what, Corina, honey. Will you take the basket of pies upstairs for me?"

"Then can I have three?"

"Of course. And close the door behind you so the cat doesn't follow you." When we heard the door close, Tracy hissed, "Lock it. Lock it or I'll shoot Glady."

I locked it, then threw my storytelling skills into a drastic ploy. "Tracy, I don't know where the money is, but the carving on the shell holds the key."

"There's no map on it, and Tate has it."

"He said that, but I've got it in the safe. There's no map, but there are clues. I knew Frank wouldn't be able to find the money on his own, but I didn't want to dig it up and then have him get it from me somehow."

"Poor you, now I'll get it from you."

Forgive me, Emrys. I took the shell from the safe. "Have either of you heard of a shell carver named Emrys Lloyd?" I said his name loudly.

Tracy looked ready to snap. Or shoot. Glady looked too frightened to speak.

If he was here, I was sure he'd help us.

If he wasn't so pigheaded.

If he could.

If.

Chapter 50

Tracy took us to the property in a skiff, motoring out of Silver Lake through the inlet called the Ditch. "This was Frank's fishing boat," she said. "And that's his shovel there. Gives one heck of a wallop."

At the property, we had to get out and wade to the small beach. Tracy held the gun on us as we pulled the boat up. Glady fell and cut her leg on a clamshell. She insisted it wasn't bad, but she limped and it didn't look like an act.

I put on one heck of an act, though. Like a soothsayer, with the dark blue velvet wrapped around my shoulders, I "consulted" the shell. I counted paces, gauged angles, examined tree bark, then counted more paces. I almost had fun, but I didn't want to get carried away and make Glady, in flip-flops and limping, do too much hard walking. Also, Tracy had the gun. Her patience lasted for about fifteen minutes of trailing around the property.

"This is bullcrap." She jammed the shovel in the ground. "You don't have the faintest idea where the money's buried."

"I don't know if there's any money at all."

"Give me the shell."

"No."

"I will shoot you and take it."

"Tracy," I said. "Listen to me. There are no clues on the shell. As far as I know, there's never been money or anything else buried here. And now it's almost too dark to see."

"What's your plan?" Glady asked gently. "How do you see this ending for you? We can promise to say nothing, but things are falling apart for you. Think about that."

Tracy had the kind of eyes that wheels whir behind. "You're right. Time for me to vamoose. But tell you what. I'll drop you off first and no hard feelings, okay? You win some, you lose some. Come on."

We pushed the boat off the beach, climbed back in. But Tracy didn't point the prow back toward the Ditch and Silver Lake. She headed down below—the term islanders use for the area between the village and Hatteras Inlet.

"Did you know that Frank and I were kind of a thing?" she asked. "A thing about as sure as an oceanside beach house on stilts. Still. A thing's a thing and all part of the game. The gamble. The chase."

"You killed him with the shovel?" I asked.

"Aw, Frank. I miss him," she said. "You know what comes after the chase, if you're successful? It's the kill. Do you think maybe I wasn't supposed to take that literally? Too late now. When you and I looked at rentals that day, Maureen—and I did notice you never called back about any of the places, way to hurt a girl's feelings—we passed by Rob Tate's house and I saw Frank's truck there."

I'd seen it, too. And the crow on the chimney.

"I think Frank was collecting evidence, and he was at Tate's making his case against me. I asked him, and he said he wasn't, that they were watching a game. But I know he was adding nails to my coffin. So I put him in a coffin first. Getting ahead in life is about being first. Glady, honey, I don't mean to be rude and leave you out of this conversation. My mama raised me better than that. I almost left the bloody knife at your house, along with the keys I took from the restaurant during the faux break-in. Frank would've liked that touch."

"Oh, yeah," Glady said. "Perfect touch."

"I am nothing if not a perfectionist."

Tracy took us farther out into Pamlico Sound. It all looked like water to me, but she knew where she was going. "Here we are, gals. Legged Lump Reef."

"I don't see a reef," I said.

"You can't, silly. It's covered in water. Not much. A foot or two. Get out and you'll see for yourself."

Glady and I looked at each other.

"Get out," Tracy said. "Do you need to hear the magic word? Here it is. Gun."

I scrambled over the side of the boat and helped Glady out.

Tracy laughed. "You'll never win a prize for grace. Do you think that's because you're like a couple of cows or because you'll be dead? It's kind of a trick question because it could be both. If you want, you can stay here until a boat comes by. That's not what I'd recommend, though. You might get run over in the dark. Your best bet is to walk back to Ocracoke. It's only about a mile and a half, and the water's between a foot and four most of the way. That's not so bad, is it? There *are* those pesky deep holes between here and there, so it's not a straight shot. And just your luck, I *am* a straight shot." She laughed again and waved the gun between us.

"Now, when you reach Ocracoke, good luck finding your way through the salt marsh without getting snake bit or sinking in the mud. Oh! And have you heard about the juvenile great whites spotted in the sound recently? Isn't *that* a hoot? Shark bait! Did you like my note on your door, Maureen?"

I ignored that question. "What about Corina?"

"She's a smartie," Tracy said. "If she's smart enough, she'll find a way to get herself rescued."

"She's a child," Glady said.

"One with a tummy ache if she eats all those pies. Don't bother to call for help, ladies. Sound travels over open water, and if I hear you, Ms. Glock and I will be back. Bye, ya'll."

We watched the skiff putt-putting away.

"Heading across the sound?" I asked Glady.

"Looks like it—oh, dear."

The skiff turned and came back. Too slowly to run over us. We instinctively held on to each other.

"Maureen," Tracy said, drawing alongside us. "I almost forgot. I texted Burt from your phone confessing to all three murders. Then your phones went overboard."

"Three?" Glady said.

"Allen and Frank." Tracy held up a finger for each of them, then pointed a third finger at Glady. "And you."

I closed my eyes. Glady screamed.

Chapter 51

Glady stopped screaming before I opened my eyes. When I did, we stared at each other. Listened. Heard the skiff's motor growing fainter.

"She tried to kill me by heart attack," Glady said.

"How is your heart?" I asked. "Will it make it to shore?"

"Let's find out."

"In a sec." I swaddled the shell in the length of blue velvet still around my shoulders, then handed the bundle to Glady.

"Oh, no," she said. "I don't want to be responsible for getting this back to dry land."

"You won't. Hang on." I took off Jeff's flannel shirt and rolled the velvet bundle in it. Then I tied the flannel bundle snugly around my waist with the sleeves. "Ready."

"One foot forward at a time," Glady said. "Feel with your foot before putting your weight on it. Then take the next step."

I hooked my arm in hers, and we set off.

The silhouette of the island showed low and dark against the sky. The water was calm and not terribly cold. The air felt colder by comparison, but there wasn't much breeze. A nice enough night for a stroll in waters mostly not too deep and infested by only two teenaged sharks. It crossed my mind that I should've carried my pink life preserver with me absolutely everywhere since landing on the island. Live and learn.

As we moved off Legged Lump, the water got deeper. Midthigh, waist, rib cage, back to thigh and waist. We inched like wary sea snails.

"What's the first thing you'll do when we get home?" Glady asked.

"See if Corina is safe. Email the boys. Can't text, no phone."

"Use Burt's."

"Thanks. What about you?"

"Emotional support food. Cheese. Chocolate. Cinnamon toast."

"No ice cream?"

"In a pinch. Ow." Glady stumbled and hopped.

We were in water that almost reached her armpits. With every hop, she floated a bit. I pulled her closer to me.

"Crab pinch?" I asked.

"Stepped on something."

"Did it go through your flip-flop?"

"They're long gone. I didn't want to worry you. We'll keep going."

"We have to."

A slow while later, we reached a place where the water was only up to our knees. I made her sit down, and I worked at getting my wet shoelaces untied.

"You need them," she said.

"It'll be easier for me if you can walk."

She put them on. Not a bad fit.

"Think they'll stay on?" I asked.

She pretended to kick up her heels.

"No more of that or you'll have all the sailors whistling at us." I got us moving again. Glady was shivering. I worried about her cut leg, cut foot, blood trails, sharks. "What about your writing?" I asked. "Working on anything new?"

"Always. But not sending it to my agent. My editor probably thinks I died of old age ten years ago."

"Can I ask a nosy question?"

"I can't think of a better time."

"How old are you and Burt?"

"Pffft. That's not nosy. Age is a badge of honor. We're not all that old, anyway. I'm eighty-one. Burt's seventy-nine.

"I wonder how much farther to shore."

"That's all you have to say?" she asked.

"The rest was silent. A prayer that I don't let you drown or become shark bait before you're eighty-two."

"Thank you."

"Or succumb to hypothermia."

"I wondered why you left that out. I'm thinking about starting a new series. Always thinking about a new series. This one's set in Scotland. I went there once. Loved it. Don't know enough to set a series there, so I told Burt I'm going back."

"Will he go with you?"

"He says he will." She laughed. "The truth is, neither of us like to travel and rarely leave the island."

"Well, you did today."

"So I did. God, how I love getting one up on that brother of mine. And now I know what else I'll do besides overdo the emotional support food. I'll tell myself to quit whining, sit down, and write."

"Excellent. Do it," I said, and I promptly stepped off into a deep hole, pulling Glady with me. We sank, rose, floundered—probably with flounders—sank, gulped water, coughed, paddled, and blessedly found our footing again until the sand shifted under us and we did it all over again. We were gasping when we reached water only up to our waists.

"Are we turned around?" I tried not to sound panicked.

"No." Glady pointed.

"I wish it looked a whole lot closer."

"It's the classic nightmare. Trying to run in water." She was shivering again.

"Glady, if we can't hear Tracy's boat, she can't hear us yelling for help."

"But I'm afraid to yell. Afraid she will."

"Then we won't."

Silent, exhausted, one step in front of the other, we plodded on. And on.

"I want to do a picture book about an accidental pirate," I said.

"Not want to. You will. And now I'm jealous. I love that idea. But when I'm jealous, I get mad. Do you know what that means?"

"You'll raise the Moon Shell's rent?"

"No. I'll have a snit."

"Oh, snit," I said. "We're in a pickle because Tracy's a pickle snit."

"Snit." Glady giggled. "My mama used to say snits are fits of pique."

"Glady!" I grabbed her arm tighter, and she yelped. "Jeff used to say that. My husband. He said *his* mother used to say it, but I've never heard anyone else say it ever. What if your mother knew his mother? What if they met sometime? Or what if she knew Jeff?"

"Whoa, calm down. I can't move that fast."

I stopped moving, stopped tugging her along. "That could've happened, couldn't it?"

Glady wiped at the tears running down my face with her soaking wet sleeve. "Sweetheart, you're babbling. We're both drunk with exhaustion. We need to take deep breaths and keep moving."

In that moment, I smelled wet wool again and remembered how she'd held me to her on the floor in the Moon Shell, where it all began. "You're right. One foot forward at a time—"

"Crows!" Glady let go of me, cupped her hands around her mouth, and cawed.

Two crows flew toward us, then back to the dark shoreline. Then to us again, but on a zigzag path. They repeated the path back to shore.

"Do you think they're—"

"Crows are brilliant," Glady said. "Follow them."

We did, and finally, finally, like primordial creatures, we crawled out of the water, onto a narrow strip of seaweed-covered mud that smelled of muck. Helpless, we lay there, exposed to the elements, insects, and predators.

"I'm waiting for David Attenborough's voiceover," Glady said, and we dissolved into hysterical laughter.

A bright beam of light stopped us.

"Got them!" a voice shouted. "I must be losing my touch. They're still alive." It was Allred.

"Allred, you wouldn't know a token of death from a hole in the ground," Burt shouted.

"The tokens of death I see *are* holes in the ground," Allred said. "But not always accurate."

"You loon, get out of the way. Glady, old girl!" Burt said. "Maureen! Are you still with us?"

Chapter 52

Burt had a thermos of coffee for us. Allred had blankets and insisted we not be peppered with questions. We were grateful, but *we* had a question. Glady asked it.

"How did you find us?"

"Found the note," Burt said.

We must have looked confused. Burt pulled a piece of Moon Shell letterhead from a pocket and showed us. In shaky printing, the note said, "Tracy is armed and dangerous. She took Maureen and Glady to Allen's property at gunpoint. Corina is locked in the apartment. Follow the crows."

I looked up at Burt and saw fireflies. Emrys, almost indiscernible, appeared next to Burt. I mimicked writing. Looking depleted, Emrys nodded, flickered, disappeared.

The dark blue velvet was a goner, but I washed the shell, dried it, and put it back on its pedestal in the display case. It didn't need the added luster of velvet to shine like a gem. I hung Jeff's flannel shirt to dry in the bathroom and climbed into bed. Bonny joined me. Nothing disturbed our sleep. No ghost flickered or hummed that night or in the morning.

Captain Tate sat at Glady and Burt's kitchen table with us the next morning. Burt put a plate of poppyseed muffins on the table. We each nursed a mug of coffee. Tracy was having her breakfast in the Hyde County Jail in Swan Quarter. Burt had called Tate as soon as he'd found the note Emrys had managed to write.

"I put out an all-points bulletin," Tate said. "Included a picture of Tracy I grabbed from her website. And it's amazing the power four little words have to rally every available officer."

"What words?" Burt asked.

"*Suspect in deputy's death*," Tate said. "I took a leap with that, but all the puzzle pieces seemed to fall into place when Burt called. A deputy out of Swan Quarter happened to be gassing up his boat for some night fishing when he got the APB. And wouldn't you know it, here came a woman in a skiff who tied up at the next pump. He recognized her from the APB but also because he'd seen her with Frank at a picnic last summer. In his words, 'She came quietly after she stopped kicking and screaming.'" Tate yawned. "I spent most of the night there. She's real proud of herself. When she opened her mouth again she talked for hours."

Burt gave him more coffee, and Tate gave us what he called "the highly condensed" version of what she'd told them.

"Frank had told Tracy Allen's burglary story and his plan to find the money. Tracy decided she'd have a better chance of sweet-talking the location of the money out of Allen and that the money would be better in her pocket. Sweet-talk didn't work, so she hatched another plan.

"She lured Allen to Springer's Point with a love note from Glady. Love for Allen, love for the cameo shell. It told him to bring the shell for their happily ever after."

"*That's* why he was wearing blue jeans and his wedding ring," Glady said. "But he should've known when he read 'happily ever after' in the note that it wasn't from me."

"Tracy threatened Allen with the knife. But she says the threat she's most proud of involved the shell. She took it from him and threatened to beat it to dust with the paddle if he didn't tell her where to find the money. She said that infuriated him, he came at her, and he fell against the knife. Fell to the ground. Stubborn as ever, got to his knees. So she claims she did what she had to do, what she always does. Finished the job. She saw he was in agony and hit him on the back of his head with the paddle. A mercy killing, she said."

"A mercy for her," said Burt. "He could have identified her."

"But if she hit him on the back of his head, he would have fallen forward," I said. "I found him on his back."

"She said he turned over onto his back himself. Dr. Allred says people with mortal head wounds can walk or even run, so turning over isn't surprising."

"But we found him on his face," Burt said.

"We'll get there," said Tate. "Tracy threw the shell in the water to make it look like the store was robbed. She also liked the idea of blowing a beachcomber's mind. She waited until dark to stage a break-in at the Moon Shell, but Maureen was there. Then Glady and Burt showed up. She went back to the Point to make sure Allen was dead. He was. She didn't like seeing his accusing eyes staring up at her. She removed the knife, turned him over, ditched the golf cart, and went home. When she went back to the shop, much later, Brown was there. She went one more time but decided to leave well enough alone."

"The muddy footprints," I said. "She told us she staged the restaurant break-in. She was awfully busy."

"She stayed busy. Planting clues here and there. She wanted Frank to pin the murder on Glady. Then Maureen. Then Yanira. She said he was too stupid."

"Not stupid," I said. "Better."

"I think he started to suspect Tracy after the restaurant break-in," Tate said. "But I also think he was doing his best to clear her."

"Rob," Glady said. "Some hard questions. The night we found Allen, don't you think Frank already suspected Tracy?

That he searched the Moon Shell for evidence that night, to take it, or clear it away? Did he let us loose in there the next morning to mess up anything he missed?"

Looking beaten down, Tate said he didn't know.

I couldn't stay indefinitely. Friends, obligations, and a house waited back in Tennessee. Huge decisions, too. But the most important thing to go back for was happening the third weekend in October. The university theater department was staging a special performance of *Brigadoon* in Jeff's memory. He'd loved that musical. There was no way in the world I would miss it. I stayed on the island for only a few more days, decompressing and tying up loose ends.

Glady and I wondered how Corina was doing after her ordeal, so we went to see. Yanira laughed when we asked.

"She ate so many of the little pies she fell asleep."

"Then Mr. Burt ran up the stairs shouting 'Coquina! Coquina!'" Corina said. "Mami, I could have been scared when he shouted. Instead, I was brave."

"You are the bravest girl I know," Yanira said.

"That's because I am facing the world as I am—a tiny, colorful, beautiful girl named Coquina, a name I gave myself, because that's the kind of brave girl I am."

"You're exactly right, my Coquina."

I felt bad about our suspicions of Umstead. How easy it had been to read menace into ordinary conversations. One afternoon, I rode the bike to his office to let him know that Bonny was going to stay with Glady and Burt until I knew what I was doing.

"Kind of you to let me know," he said. "To tell you the truth, I'm relieved. I attribute my request to being suddenly overwhelmed by how much I'll genuinely miss Allen."

"Did he cheat you out of the shoreline property?"

"He did and he didn't," Umstead said. "He knew I had my eye on the land. He knew I was going to make an offer. He got his in first. That's fair. I'm ashamed to say that I did call it cheating. Loudly. Angrily. Memorably. That cheated us out of quite a few years of friendship. I asked you about that the other day, too. I used to be an avid sportsman—fishing, sailing, crabbing. I dreamed of designing and building my own house with water access. I still like to dream."

"What changed?"

"I'm eighty-seven. When on earth did that happen?"

Patricia called to say she'd heard I was leaving and that she'd known all along everything would turn out fine.

"That's one of the things I like about you," I said. "You're confident, like the beach you love so much."

"What do you mean?"

"You're both one hundred percent shore."

Glady and Burt and I had a lovely dinner in the apartment. I made a cheese omelet and a green salad. Then I packed up what was left in the fridge for them. They were trying hard to pretend I wasn't leaving in the morning.

"Glady, Burt, I need to know a few things," I said during a lull.

They were immediately attentive.

"The wheelbarrow that Burt didn't want to fall for again. When did he fall for it before? What does that mean? And why were people going to wonder what you were up to? Are the people who wonder really nosy parkers, or do you two get up to things? *What* things?"

"Those are cockamamie Mama stories, and we're not going there," Burt said. Neither of them would elaborate.

"Okay. One more. When you texted Deputy Brown to meet us at the Point, what exactly did you say?"

"That's all," Burt said. "Well, that and I told him not to act like the hind end of Ikey D."

Burt had a going-away present for me. He'd framed two of his photographs. One showing the front of the Moon Shell. The other was the picture he took that morning I sat on the Moon Shell's steps in the sun with the dappled shade behind me—Emrys.

When I climbed the stairs, after locking the door behind them, Emrys stood looking at that picture where I'd propped it in the window seat.

"You saved our lives, Emrys. Thank you."

"Returning the favor."

"Are you feeling better?"

"Still dead, but it could be worse."

"It's nice to see your smile again. How did you . . . how were you able to write that note?"

He shook his head and I realized I'd never seen a ghost look more bewildered. That wasn't saying much because I'd only seen one ghost and hadn't known him for even a month. Then again, knowing a ghost at all was saying a whole lot more than I'd ever imagined.

"I think," he finally said, "that my ability was born from the urgency of the situation."

"I like that theory. Have you tried writing again?"

"I've been somewhat afraid to." A sly smile crept across his face. "However I'm working up the courage."

"I am so happy to hear that. Best of luck. You know I'm leaving in the morning?"

"So I heard, and I am loath to see you go."

"I'll miss you, and I'll come back. You're a good friend, Emrys. Pirate or not."

Chapter 53

But back home in Tennessee, surrounded by green mountains and memories of Jeff still green with grief, I had trouble settling in. I rattled around in the house. Familiar smells triggered tears. I felt like a hermit crab living in a shell far too big.

Then the university theater department put on its splendid memorial performance of *Brigadoon*. The boys came for a long weekend. The Friday night performance was joyful, with tributes to Jeff that had the audience laughing and crying and laughing again. Then the play—a wonderful farewell to a part of our lives that we couldn't have faced any sooner.

We all slept in the next morning. I made French toast for a late breakfast. Kelly heard the mail delivered and brought in an envelope from the Moon Shell.

"Glady and Burt do you think?" O'Connor asked.

"Oh, fun," I said. "Go ahead and open it. I need to flip these."

Kelly slit the envelope. "It's on Moon Shell letterhead. There's a quote written under the shop's name. *'Words are easy, like the wind; Faithful friends are hard to find. William Shakespeare.'*"

"Emrys." I forgot the French toast and dropped into a chair. Startled, Kelly held the letter out to me. I took it, looked at it, looked at O'Connor, handed it back to Kelly, and asked him to read it.

"Who's Emrys?" Kelly asked.

O'Connor, who'd jumped up to rescue the breakfast, widened his eyes, made his mouth into an *O*, and said, "Boo."

"No." Kelly stared at us. "You can't expect me to believe the ghost is real and he's your pen pal."

"It turns out there's a first time for everything," I said.

"You believe this?" Kelly asked O'Connor.

"It turns out he's very convincing."

Kelly, his eyebrows meeting over his nose, read, "Dear Mrs. Nash, You may assume that I am writing because the situation is urgent. I assure you it is. You must return to the island and soon.

"Glady is a good-hearted soul but she feeds Bonny far too much. Worse, Coquina is learning to whistle. She practices incessantly—on the Moon Shell's porch. She must have absorbed Allen's 'talent' for the art. Which brings me to the reason I am writing and why I say that you must return.

"I have found a haven where the girl's noise cannot reach me. It is Heaven, or as close to heaven as I apparently will get, if you will forgive my poor joke. It is not, however, a haven suitable for anyone who would worry about cramped quarters or adequate headroom. The place I speak of is the area above the ceiling of the Moon Shell's half-story and below the rooftree—a sealed-off attic of triangular shape and mean proportions.

"Although there is no ready access to this space (except for those of us corporeally unencumbered), there appears to have been a trapdoor, at one time, in the ceiling of Allen's bedchamber closet. The opening is still visible in the attic, but plastered over in the closet, possibly by Allen. At a guess, he did this decades ago after storing a number of boxes in the attic.

"At this point I should tell you how lucky you are that I ignored my better judgment concerning small, dusty spaces."

I laughed.

"Inside joke, Mom?" O'Connor asked.

"*Inside* joke? More than you know." I laughed until Kelly made me drink a glass of water. "It's one of the theories Emrys has for why he's a ghost. He doesn't like confined spaces, and he's allergic to dust. He says that he wouldn't have been able to stand being in a coffin, but if he's exposed to too much dust, it has him coughin', and then he's back to square one."

Kelly rubbed his hands over his face.

"He takes some getting used to, Kel. Read the rest."

Kelly took a breath and plunged ahead. "There are boxes in the attic that don't appear to have been opened since being squirreled away. I, however, being able to pass through cardboard as well as lath and plaster, have had a look at the contents and received one shell of a surprise.

"Mrs. Nash, our conjectures were all wrong. Allen did not bury the spoils of his plunder beneath our feet. Rather, he sealed what he stole from your husband's family in the attic over our heads. The treasure the varlets carried off is far better than coins and jewels. In short, it is time for Plan B. You really must return to the island.

"Yours in all sincerity, Emrys Lloyd, Accidental Pirate, Doughty and Ever Loyal.

"P.S. There is also the small matter of the gentleman who arrived this morning and whom I overheard say that Allen is expecting him.

The boys helped me pack the car, and the next morning, I crossed the mountains heading east into the rising sun.

Recipes

Burt Weaver took up daily muffin baking during the pandemic. He's continued the practice, calling it his morning muffin meditation. Here are three of his recipes.

Toasted Almond Muffins

Yield: 12

Ingredients
2 cups unbleached all-purpose flour
⅔ cup sugar
2 teaspoons baking powder
½ teaspoon salt
1 cup milk
½ cup unsalted butter
1 large egg
1 teaspoon vanilla extract
½ teaspoon almond extract
1 cup sliced, toasted almonds, divided

Directions
Preheat oven to 400° F.

Butter 12 muffin cups or line with muffin papers.

In large bowl, combine flour, baking powder, salt, and ½ cup of the almonds.

In medium bowl, melt the butter, then whisk in the sugar. Continue whisking and add milk, egg, and the vanilla and almond extracts. Add mixture to the large bowl and stir until just combined.

Divide batter evenly between muffin cups. Sprinkle the tops with remaining almonds.

Bake until tops are golden and toothpick or tester comes out clean, 15–20 minutes.

Cool on a wire rack before removing from pan.

Banana Chocolate Chip Walnut Muffins

Yield: 12

Ingredients
2 cups unbleached all-purpose flour
2 teaspoons baking powder
1 teaspoon baking soda
1 teaspoon salt
1 teaspoon cinnamon
½ cup chocolate chips
1½ cups mashed ripe banana (two or three bananas, depending on their size)
⅔ cup brown sugar
⅔ cup unsalted butter
1 large egg
1 teaspoon vanilla
½ cup coarsely chopped walnuts

Directions
Preheat oven to 400° F.
Butter 12 muffin cups or line with muffin papers.
In a large bowl, combine the flour, baking powder, baking soda, cinnamon, and salt. Stir in chocolate chips.
In a medium bowl, melt the butter, then whisk in the mashed banana, sugar, egg, and vanilla until well combined. Add to the large bowl and fold until combined but not over-mixed.
Divide batter evenly between muffin cups. Sprinkle tops with the chopped walnuts.
Bake until tops are golden brown or a toothpick or tester comes out clean, 15–20 minutes.
Cool on a wire rack before removing from pan.

Fig Walnut Spice Muffins

Yield: 18 (or 17)

Burt Weaver here. This is the first muffin recipe I've come up with on my own. It makes eighteen muffins. Sometimes seventeen if I'm heavy-handed in filling the muffin cups. When Glady asked if I was ever going to fix the recipe so that it makes a standard dozen, I asked who she was kidding. Seventeen or eighteen muffins is better than a dozen or a baker's dozen any day. This recipe makes a *Burt's* dozen.

Ingredients for Large Bowl
2 cups unbleached all-purpose flour
2 teaspoons baking powder
1 teaspoon baking soda
¾ teaspoon salt
1 teaspoon cinnamon
½ teaspoon nutmeg
¼ teaspoon ginger
¼ teaspoon cardamom
1 cup dried figs, stems removed, chopped into raisin-size pieces
(or a little bigger)
1 cup walnuts, chopped

Ingredients for Medium Bowl
6 tablespoons unsalted butter
1¼ cup brown sugar
2 large eggs
1 cup plain Greek yogurt
1 teaspoon vanilla extract

Directions
Preheat oven to 400° F.

If you have two muffin pans (for a total of 24 muffins), butter 18 of the muffin cups or line them with muffin papers. Otherwise, bake 12 muffins and, after the pan cools, prepare 6 of the cups again to bake the final 6 muffins.

In the large mixing bowl, stir together all the ingredients but the figs and walnuts. Now stir in the figs and walnuts.

In the medium bowl, melt the butter, then whisk in the brown sugar, yogurt, vanilla, and the eggs. Pour into the large bowl and stir until just combined. Batter will be thick.

Fill muffin cups about ¾ full.

Bake until toothpick or tester comes out clean, 15–20 minutes.

Remove from oven and turn muffins out of pan to cool on a wire rack.

Bake the rest of the muffins if you're working with only one 12-muffin pan.